THE BLOODY RUIN ASYLUM & TAPROOM

SEANA KELLY

The Bloody Ruin Asylum & Taproom

Copyright © 2024 by Seana Kelly

Ebook ISBN: 9781641972727

POD ISBN: 9781641973069

NYLA Publishing

121 W. 27th St., Suite 1201, NY 10001, New York.

http://www.nyliterary.com

Titles by Seana Kelly

The Sam Quinn Series

The Slaughtered Lamb Bookstore & Bar
The Dead Don't Drink at Lafitte's
The Wicche Glass Tavern
All I Want for Christmas is a Dragon (short story)
The Hob & Hound Pub
Biergarten of the Damned
The Banshee & the Blade (short story)
The Viper's Nest Roadhouse & Café
The Nocturne's Gatekeeper (short story)
The Bloody Ruin Asylum & Taproom
The Mermaid's Bubble Lounge

The Sea Wicche Series: Bewicched: The Sea Wicche Chronicles

Bewicched: The Sea Wicche Chronicles
Wicche Hunt: The Sea Wicche Chronicles
Wicching Hour: The Sea Wicche Chronicles

For Greg,
who wears all my merch
and hypes me up to strangers on the golf course.
Thanks, honey!

ONE

I Could Get Used to This

F lying private was the shit. Don't let anyone tell you differently. As I'd never flown commercial, my opinion might not mean much, but I'd seen movies and video clips. I knew how tight and uncomfortable normal planes were.

Maybe I shouldn't say *I knew*. The first time I'd ever flown on a plane was in this one last year when Clive and I went to New Orleans. Much of my childhood had been spent in a car with my mother, driving from one cheap, short-term rental to another, trying to escape my homicidal sorcerer of an aunt.

At seventeen, with both parents gone, my body covered in scars and more trauma than I thought I'd ever be able to recover from, I was dumped in San Francisco where I hid from the world in my bookstore and bar.

So I was certainly no expert on air travel, but Clive—my husband and vampire (that part's important)—had a private jet. When you're a vampire, you have very specific no-sun needs when you travel. It was just the two of us in the posh cabin, which meant I could do whatever I wanted.

"Darling, do sit down. We often experience turbulence over the Rockies." Clive was mostly on his phone, but it didn't keep him from watching me pace around the cabin and stretch.

My leg was finally out of its cast. Clive's maker Garyn had broken my femur in a fight. Werewolf genes meant I healed faster than most, but I'd still been laid up for too long. Not being able to run every day had had me crawling up the walls. Fergus too.

Our Irish Wolfhound pup was my running buddy. Clive started taking him out for me, but it wasn't the same. The poor little guy—if one could call a one-hundred-pound dog little—was desperately out of breath every time Clive brought him back. When I took him running, we stopped to sniff cool things or get drinks of water. Wolfhounds weren't known for long-distance running, and I wanted him to have fun. I think Clive was more of a if-we're-going-to-run-let's-run kind of partner.

"I miss Fergus," I said, dropping back into my chair.

Clive checked his watch. "We've been in the air three hours. I'm sure he's fine."

"Says you. He could be wasting away, heartsick at my absence. You don't know." Poor little guy was probably staring out the window, waiting for me to come back.

"Fyr has him, so he's likely driving Fyr's dog crazy by stealing all her toys and lounging in her bed."

I smiled. "Yeah, that sounds right." Fyr was Fergus' original owner. He had kindly allowed us to adopt the eight-week-old pup. Fyr was also a dragon shifter and a bartender at The Slaughtered Lamb. I pulled my phone out of my pocket and considered. "I should call and check." When Clive didn't respond, I glanced over.

One eyebrow up, he gave me a look that told me exactly what he thought of that idea.

"He could miss me," I contended.

"I'm sure he does, but it's not yet five in the morning and Fyr works nights. Perhaps we could let them all sleep and you could check in later in the day."

"I guess." I pocketed my phone and sat, dejected.

Clive continued his work while I reclined my seat and looked out the window at nothing but blackness. My phone buzzed and I checked it. An image from Fyr. I pulled it up and saw Fergus snuggled in with Wolfhound big sister Alice, both fitting on her huge bed. Grinning, I glanced over and found Clive watching me.

"Better?" he asked.

I nodded. "Thank you."

The plane bounced. Here was the turbulence I'd been warned about. "Hey, are you done talking to people?"

He put his phone aside. "For a while. I didn't mean to ignore you."

I waved a hand. "Not that. I know we're late showing up for this shindig because we had to wait for the cast to come off. Hopefully my making us late isn't costing you points in the Counselor competition."

He stood, leaned over my chair, and kissed me thoroughly. "First, it's less a competition than a series of meetings and interviews." He dropped back into his seat. "And I'd wait until the end of time for you," he added, hand to his heart.

I rolled my eyes. "You're competing with other Master vamps for the North American Counselor gig. Therefore, ipso facto, it's a competition. Plus alliteration."

He relaxed into his seat across the narrow cabin from me and said, "I concede the point. Second, you were only injured in the first place due to vampire politics and posturing. And we're now headed to Budapest for more of the same. If anyone is to blame for your broken bones and being separated from Fergus, it's me."

I lifted my left hand and flashed him my blue diamond wedding ring. "Partners. You've had to deal with a lot of my crazy crap too."

"It is my honor and privilege to deal with any and all of your crazy crap, darling."

He was gorgeous—blond hair, gray eyes, chiseled features—but his outside was nothing compared to his inside. "I love you, you know."

His gaze softened. "And I love you."

I nodded once. "Good. Now, you've only told me bits and pieces. We have time and I really want to know exactly what the

Guild is. I know you said it's a governing body for vamps, but are they, like, vampire cops or more of an advisory council?" I glanced out the window again. "And is it cool now for me to get up and get some food?"

There was no air steward, as this was a hush hush flight. There was a pilot and the two of us. That was it.

Clive stood. "Let me. I have excellent balance and my leg wasn't recently broken." He went to the galley area and picked up a white card. "It's a long flight. Would you like breakfast, lunch, or dinner?"

Hmm, according to my watch it was breakfast, but I hadn't slept all night. "Dinner, I think."

He scanned the card. "Your meal is from Maxfield's and you have an ahi poke appetizer with a main of grilled chicken, sweet and spicy Brussels sprouts, and fondant potatoes."

Shaking my head at the ridiculousness of such a fancy meal on a plane, I said, "What? No dessert?"

He turned the card toward me. "And a vanilla bean crème brûlée for dessert."

My stomach rumbled. "No time for jokes. I want all of it now, please."

He loaded up a tray for me, pulling items from the refrigerator and the warming thingy. It wasn't an oven—I didn't think. Honestly, I didn't know or care. I moved to the small table opposite the one Clive had been using.

He placed a tray with silverware wrapped in a napkin and a tall glass of water in front of me, sitting on the bench seat beside me. "Sorry, darling. I hadn't realized I was being so circumspect with information. Most vampires don't even know the Guild exists." His expression turned thoughtful. "Even now, I'm finding this conversation very uncomfortable." He shook his head. "You're my mate. You've a right to everything I have, including information."

I wasn't sure if he was talking to me or himself.

"I had to explain it to Russell," he continued, "when he

ascended to Master of the City, so you'd think this would be easier."

you is your suspicious nature. It's true enough. Vampires who flout our laws disappear. Our secrecy is paramount."

I swallowed a bite of fondant potatoes and almost wept. So. Flipping. Good. "So the Guild has its own goon squad?"

He squeezed my hip. "Yes and no. They eventually created the role of Counselor, but that wasn't how they started. Darling, who in their right mind would make Vlad the Impaler a Counselor? Or Cadmael, for that matter? Vlad was chosen by the Guild because he has a reputation for killing huge swaths of people. Reveling in it, really. And that was when he was human. Cadmael is a renowned warrior with unparalleled mental skills. So, yes, early members were a kind of hit squad. The Guild was created for the protection of our kind. The first order of protection is silencing those who, through word or action, would expose us."

I put my fork down and turned in my seat. "You'll be a hit man?"

He tipped his head side to side. "If necessary, yes. Thankfully, most of the problematic ones have already been disposed of. Masters are usually good at controlling their own people. The Guild comes in when a Master can't or won't kill the rogue or if the rogue is living far outside the nocturne system."

"Ergo the need for a nocturne system." I leaned back to look at him. "I'm totally paying attention, but just so you know, I'll be ordering all my meals from this restaurant from now on."

Some of the tension in his shoulders relaxed. "I'm glad you're enjoying it."

The plane bumped, but I grabbed my glass and steadied the tray. "So, in addition to counseling Masters on problems they're having, you'll need to go out and hunt down rogue vampires whose reckless behavior is threatening the exposure of vamps to the human world? I mean, where was a Counselor when Garyn and her planeloads of vamps were invading San Francisco?"

"I believe I've mentioned that Eli was worthless. Russell informed Cadmael after that first night when Garyn captured all but yours and Audrey's minds. He explained the situation and our plan to deal with her. Cadmael waited, because Counselors don't just rush in to fix everyone's problems. He did end up coming, but it was after Alcatraz, so his help wasn't needed."

"Convenient," I grumbled.

"Be that as it may," he said, "how do you feel about my taking on this role?"

I stared at my empty plate and felt my stomach twist. "I worry about you being hurt." I sat back again and grabbed his hand. "You can take me with you when you have to fulfill your sheriff duties. I can be your deputy."

"And a more beautiful deputy I couldn't find, but—"

I pressed my finger against his lips. "None of that. I have a unique set of skills, as you know. When Garyn brought planes filled with vamps, most didn't get a chance to leave the plane because of me, so I'm going to pretend I didn't hear that *but*."

He kissed my finger and said around it, "*But* then you'd have to leave Fergus again."

My shoulders slumped. Damn, that was true. "Still," I said, sitting up straight. "I'd do it for you."

"Thank you, love. Now eat your dessert."

"Don't mind if I do," I said, scooping up a spoonful. "I don't get why all of that is super secret."

He rested his hand on my thigh. "The Guild makes the laws for all vampires and then enforces them. In its early days, Guild members were hunted down and tortured horribly. Vampires don't appreciate being told what to do. It took a show of overwhelming brutal force to silence the biggest problems and get everyone else to fall in line. The Guild has been around long enough that most just accept it as what's always been—if they're even old enough to know about it. The Guild is shrouded in secrecy so those bent on rebellion can be put down before they can identify and locate Guild members."

I thought about that a moment. "Uh. Everyone knows you live in San Francisco. You were the Master of the City for two hundred years."

"True, but our home is heavily warded. As you recall, neither Garyn, nor any of her people, could make it past our protections. My larger concern is your safety, as everyone also knows I would do anything for you."

"Sucker," I crooned, leaning in for a kiss.

"Mmm, vanilla. I wouldn't consider the position if I didn't know for a fact that you can defend yourself."

"Damn straight."

"The Guild headquarters are top secret. I had no idea where it was before I received the invitation," he said. "The other candidates had to meet in New York and were then flown blind to Budapest. I take it as a vote of confidence that Sebastian gave me the city name."

"Wait. The other candidates know where the Guild is now. When this is all decided, one will get the job and three will be bitter, right? What if one of them gets pissy and decides to spread the word?"

"Well, they'd be killed, of course, but my guess is someone in the Guild—probably Cadmael, who has those superior mental abilities—will erase the location from our memories."

I gave him a sour look.

"Yes, I know what you think him, but he's the other North American Counselor, so it makes sense for him to be present and voice his opinions. Regardless of how you two feel about each other, it would be good for you to get to know him better."

"He started it." The crème brûlée was almost gone, which added to my disgruntlement. I knew Cadmael was an extremely powerful vampire, an old Mayan warrior, but he disapproved of me. He was one of Clive's close friends who'd come to keep on eye on the nocturne while Clive and I went to New Orleans to deal with Lafitte.

Cadmael had taken an instant dislike to me, insinuating that Clive was only interested in me because I was an oddity or because of my Quinn heritage. Long story short: he's an asshole, but a ridiculously powerful one. In his mind, I'm a dog and beneath

Clive's notice. There was also the fact that I'm pretty sure he shuffled around in my head and saw what happened to me eight years ago.

"Be that as it may, I'd appreciate it if you made an effort."

I shrugged one shoulder, scraping the last of the goodness out of the corners of the ramekin.

I didn't want to think about Cadmael anymore. He gave me a stomachache. "Will Vlad be there? How cool would it be to meet Dracula?"

"I've met him, so I'll say not terribly. You'll be happy to hear, though, that The Impaler is there. He doesn't usually attend this sort of thing, so there's some question as to why now." He drummed his fingers on the table. "I suppose we'll find out soon enough."

I picked up the tray and brought it back to the galley kitchen, hoping to hide the strange fear that had been growing in me the last week. I wanted Clive to get this job. He'd been at loose ends since he'd given up control of San Francisco—for me. Mustn't forget the guilt surrounding that. This Counselor gig would be a vampy promotion and allow him to be in the thick of it again. Plus, I knew he'd be wonderful at it.

What I couldn't get past was the invitation for me. Since when did vampires invite me to anything? Clive and I had done a lot of damage in the vampire world. Did Garyn and her people attack us? Yes, but we'd still killed—with the local nocturne's help—over a hundred vampires, many of them Masters. Garyn herself was over a thousand years old and tied to very powerful vampires all over the world. Vampires held on to grudges like a dragon does his treasure.

That invitation had been keeping me awake at night. What were we walking into? Was this a legitimate opportunity for Clive or were we getting pulled away from our extraordinarily formidable friends so we could be ambushed?

TWO

The Asylum

The plane touched down about an hour before sunrise. Planning trips like this in the summer was a nightmare. The private flight to Budapest was almost seventeen hours. Hungary is nine hours ahead of California. We left at two a.m. our time and flew all through the day and night, only to arrive just before sunrise. We'd planned to leave at midnight so the timing wouldn't be so tight but had run into a fog delay.

Clive was asleep-ish during the day, of course, and I had hoped to nod off as well, but it hadn't happened. Even though I was exhausted, I was restless about the trip, more so the closer we got to Budapest. If this offer was on the up and up, I wanted to make a good impression.

I doubted Clive would ever have made the decision to step down as Master of San Francisco if the nocturne hadn't hated me. Leticia, Garyn's spy in the nocturne, had been able to turn way too many of Clive's vampires against him because of his love for me. I knew none of that was my fault, but I couldn't help feeling responsible.

I needed this visit to go well.

And if this was all an elaborate ruse to separate us from our support system, I needed to keep my guard up and be ready to fight.

When we came down the metal steps off the plane, a black car was waiting for us, a driver standing beside it. He opened the rear door and then took our luggage, placing it in the trunk. We slid into the back seat, and I did my best to stifle a yawn.

The driver got in and said something in Hungarian. Clive responded in kind before speaking to me mind-to-mind, a gift we had.

He says we'll beat the dawn, though it will be close. The Guild is about thirty minutes away.

The driver took off, driving much faster than what would normally be considered safe, but vampires had excellent eyesight and reflexes. I doubted he wanted to be burned up in the sun, so we were racing.

I found his blip in my head and dipped into his thoughts. He was annoyed he'd been chosen to go out so close to sunrise and was battling back a stupor that was beginning to take hold. We might get into a car wreck, but at least he wasn't *trying* to kill us. I withdrew from the driver's mind, still looking out the window, hoping Clive didn't pick up on my paranoia about this trip.

I couldn't see much of Budapest, but what I could was a strange mélange of Baroque masterpieces and blocky, utilitarian buildings. A few people were walking quickly to work, I'd assume, though the streets were still dark and empty at this hour.

We traveled through a downtown area, crossed a bridge over the Danube River, and then drove up green hills, past ancient monuments. The driver turned off a street with shops and cafés, onto a dirt road beside tall cyclone fencing bearing signs shouting messages in Hungarian. Mist hovered over the ground beyond the fence, hiding what lay beneath.

The driver slowed and a gate slid open. He floored it, moving toward a huge, menacing institution that looked condemned. It stood three stories high and had two long wings jutting forward, seeming to punch through the murk. Jagged glass hung in window frames, ready to bite trespassers. With stone walls blackened by time, it crouched, waiting for prey, ready to pounce.

The main entrance was recessed, the building an inverted U. Two incongruous turrets stood sentry on either side of the over-sized double doors. The fanciful architecture, rather than softening the foreboding building, added an element of *I have candy in my van, little girl*. This, I assumed, was the asylum, the headquarters of the Guild.

A chill ran down my spine, looking at it. I did *not* want to go in there. As the car came to a stop at the base of the stairs, I blew out a breath and did my best to tamp down the fear.

"The interior has been remodeled," Clive said, holding the door open for me.

The building had already shown me what it was. Adding makeup didn't conceal the predator.

Darling, are you all right?

Nodding once, I took my bag from the driver and followed Clive up the stairs. He was right, of course. Once inside the door, the entry was white marble and dark wood, with lofty ceilings and huge chandeliers. Of course.

A vampire stood in the center of the entry, giving Clive a cordial nod. Two men—human—both dressed in black suits, stood behind a long, polished counter and inclined their heads to Clive in respectful greeting. Another vampire stood off to the side, all but disappearing in the shadow of a high archway leading into a dark hall.

The main vamp, in a black suit of a far superior quality than the humans', moved forward. "Clive, it's good to see you again. I'm glad you were both able to make it." He didn't shake Clive's hand. In general, vamps didn't do that unless they were dealing with outsiders.

"Sebastian, it's been a very long time. Thank you for your patience. Please allow me to introduce my mate Samantha. Sam, this is Sebastian, the Guild Master and one of the European Counselors."

Sebastian held out his hand and I shook it. He was pale with light brown hair and blue eyes. Both men were angled toward me, so they didn't see the looks of disgust the humans behind the counter wore. And so it began.

Sebastian glanced over his shoulder. "József, come take our guests' bags to their room."

The shorter of the two came out from behind the carved wooden desk and bowed to an oblivious Sebastian before picking up the bags. He silently sniffed, pulling a face while the men discussed a gathering at ten that evening.

It hit me why the entry felt so odd. There were rows of broken windows outside, but inside there were no windows at all. I spun to study the walls. Smooth plaster. "What happened to the windows?" I hadn't meant to interrupt them, but it was strangely claustrophobic for such a huge, airy entry.

"We want the outside to look as derelict as possible," Sebastian explained.

"Mission accomplished," I muttered.

"Yes, exactly," he said. "Were anyone to trespass, to look in, all they'd see is rotting wood planking. We plastered over the windows on the inside, though, as windows can be dangerous to our kind. We have trip wires and security cameras set up, so we're not blind to attack." He glanced between Clive and me. "I wish you both a good rest. We'll have more time to get acquainted this evening."

Nodding, I said, "Until tonight."

He extended his arm toward the darkened hall. "József will show you to your room." He waited a moment for us to follow the shitty little Renfield—Dracula's deranged human assistant in the novel—and then walked in the opposite direction.

The vampire who had been lurking under the arch was gone. This close to sunrise, everyone was probably safe in their rooms, other than the human servants, of course.

Clive took my hand as we walked down the main hall and then turned right, down a narrow, musty-smelling passage.

We can always get a hotel room. We don't need to stay here, darling.

I'm okay. Really. It's going to take me a minute to get used to no windows. That's all.

All right. If you change your mind, we'll leave.

I squeezed his hand. Renfield opened the door and placed our bags just inside before giving Clive a shallow bow and returning the way we'd come.

It was pitch-black. I tried the light switch and nothing.

"Do they turn off the lights during the day, since you guys are going to be dead to the world?" I pulled out my phone and hit the flashlight. "Or are there candles in here?" I glanced around the filthy, barren room. A single stained mattress lay on the floor. Cobwebs gathered in the corners under a ceiling blackened with mold. "They're really embracing the creepy asylum vibes, aren't they?"

I don't know if this is an insult or an ambush.

I'd been braced for an attack as soon as I'd seen the room. Directing us here hadn't been an accident.

Clive strode across the room and opened the only door. I could see part of a broken sink. He glanced to the left and his face went rigid.

"Be right back," he said. "Why don't you wait in the hall." And he flew out the door.

I looked through the bathroom door and found a litter box over a hole in the floor where a toilet would be. Right. Hilarious. Grabbing our bags, I rolled them back toward the main hall. When I heard Clive's deep voice raging in Hungarian, I ran.

By the time I made it to the entry, Clive had the human by the neck, dangling him off the floor. Sebastian, no longer wearing his jacket and tie, stood beside them. Clive said something to Sebastian.

"May I?" Sebastian inquired.

Clive slammed the glorified bellhop against the wall, releasing him. Sebastian caught the young man and twisted his neck. The loud crack echoed in the quiet entry. Throwing the body toward the other human, Sebastian said, "Sándor, get rid of that and clean this floor."

He bowed to me. "Please accept my apologies." Glancing at Clive, he asked, "Were you given your keys?"

Still furious, Clive took a moment and then said, "No."

Sebastian checked József's pocket and came up with two keys. "I'll take you there myself."

Clive took the bags from me and we followed Sebastian down the long main hall again, but where József had turned right there was now a large scrollwork screen blocking the passage entirely. That hadn't been there a minute ago. József had an accomplice.

This screen must have been placed in front of the hall on the left, where Sebastian now led us, when we'd come here earlier. I would have noticed and questioned why we were turning into the dingy passage instead of the clean, well-lit one. This hall had white marble floors, creamy plaster walls, and, of course, crystal chandeliers glowing overhead.

There were tall black doors at intervals on both sides of the hall, but Sebastian led us past them all, stopping in front of the last door at the end. Pulling out a key, he opened the door and flicked on the lights. It was sumptuous, the white marble continuing, fanciful Baroque furniture in white with gold leaf. The sofa and chairs by the fireplace were upholstered in a watery blue silk. The tall headboard was tufted in the same material, the bedding a cloud-soft white.

Sebastian handed Clive the two keys and left, his movements sluggish. The sun had risen but he was trying to make up for his servant's offense.

"Better?" Clive asked, closing the door.

"A public restroom would have been better than the last one," I said, pulling the suitcases to the closet.

He nodded grimly. "Yes. There's that." He held out his arms and I walked into them. "I'm sorry. I should have let you stay home. I miss you when you're not around and I worry. Too many powerful being have been after you lately. I couldn't bring myself to leave you alone." He kissed me. "We'll move to a hotel tomorrow."

"No way." I gestured at our surroundings. "This place is gorgeous. And we already know vampires hate me. It's fine. I'm not going to get my feeling hurt." I squeezed him tight. "I want this for you. You'll make a fantastic Counselor. I'm so proud of you."

His expression finally softened. "Thank you, darling." When he kissed me this time, we both lost track of where and when we were.

When his arms dropped from around me, I remembered we were long past sunrise, so I helped him undress and get into bed.

He was almost out when he suddenly grabbed my wrist. "You can leave during daylight hours. Take the main hall all the way to the end. You'll take steps down and then back up. There are a series of doors. They'll lock behind you. You'll exit into The Bloody Ruin Asylum and Taproom...and...It's a ruin bar... There's a commercial street back along the edge of the Guild property..."

I patted his chest. "It's okay. Sleep now. I'm going to sleep today too."

He made a quiet sound and was out.

First, though, I was going to unpack and get cleaned up. I started to calculate how long I'd been awake but then butted up against a time change and stopped. I was too tired for math, especially as I was pretty sure it had been more than thirty hours.

After I'd hung up the fancy clothes, Clive's suits included, I took my toiletry bag to the bathroom. More white marble and ornate decorations. It was elegant but cold. Temperature-wise cold. I supposed if everyone was snoozing, they didn't need to fork out for heat during the day.

I put my things on the gray-veined marble counter, turned on the hot water in the walk-in shower, lined up my travel-sized bottles, and stepped under the rain head. The water started off strong, filling the room with steam, but then went cold not long afterward. Caught with soap on my body and conditioner in my hair, I darted in and out of the frigid water, trying to rinse off.

Once reasonably sure the water was running clear, I turned it off and stood a moment, shivering. Squeezing the excess out of my hair, I put it up in a towel and then grabbed a bath sheet off a warming bar, quickly wrapping it around myself. I brought a corner up to my face and breathed into it, trying to warm my frozen head.

"I thought this town was sitting on thermal pools," I mumbled to myself. Why the frick was the water arctic?

The overhead lights flickered, and I jumped. Fearing the power would go out as quickly as the hot water had, I dried off and dove into my pajamas. Returning to the bedroom, I grabbed a hoodie and slid it on. It was summer. Why was it so cold? I slipped on a pair of running socks too, as my feet were freezing on the cold floor.

One of the perks of having a vampire husband was not having to tiptoe around in the dark, afraid of waking him up. I could have had all the lights on while playing music and he wouldn't have cared. Some of it might slip past what he says is death and I contend is deep, restorative sleep because it wasn't unusual for him to ask me about something he heard while he was out, which proved my it's-not-death point.

I went back in the bathroom and pulled out a hairbrush and comb, unwrapping my hair and using the towel to wipe the fog from the mirror. My arm went back and forth, clearing the glass for far too long. The steam in the room had all but cleared, yet the mirror reflected nothing by gray smoke. Was it the mirror itself that was the problem? I had seen my own reflection earlier, hadn't I?

Wait. Did the Guild use two-way mirrors to spy on people? I leaned in close, trying to see myself in the glass.

A swollen, bloodshot eye stared back. My body recoiled in horror. The mirror now reflected a woman who wasn't me.

Long, matted hair obscured parts of her battered face. Dark

circles seemed to weigh under her wild eyes. I stared into a gaunt face with a bruised jaw and a split lip. A damp, stained slip hung from boney shoulders. My initial fear disappeared, pity taking its place.

Trembling, I remembered the attack that had almost ended me eight years ago, remembered how horrified I'd been at seeing my own battered reflection in the mirror.

But this wasn't me. I reached out a hand, wanting to help, knowing what it was to be the one on the other side of the glass, brutalized and in shock.

Baring her stained teeth, she screamed, the sound echoing off the tile, piercing my heart. As I stared into her black eyes, a chill ran down my spine.

Who was she? Was I seeing into a room beyond our own? Was I looking into the past, into the asylum?

On a last wail, she reached through the glass, her clawlike fingers scrabbling over the frame. I had a moment to panic, remembering a horror movie much like this. I jumped back as she dove out of the mirror, her cold fingers brushing against my throat.

THREE

I Should Have Learned Some Key Hungarian Curse Words Before I Came Here

I threw my arms up, but no one was there. Instead of a battered woman screaming, there was only terrified me in the mirror. I looked in the bedroom. Nothing. Clive was resting in the bed. No traumatized woman was wandering around, which was a huge relief.

I'm a necromancer. Seeing ghosts is not unusual for me, but this was something different. She felt like a live wire. Normally, ghosts can't hurt me, but there had been those two in New Orleans who'd pretty successfully attacked me. They'd been supernaturals in life. Perhaps I was dealing with the same here. The one in the mirror, though, had felt human to me.

The crazy chill in the bathroom left with the woman in the mirror. Hopefully that meant she'd used up her strength to scare me and would now be quiet. I supposed I should have been prepared for ghosts when I saw the building. I'd been so worried about vampires plotting against us, I hadn't considered ghosts.

Deciding it was safe to proceed, I blew dry my hair, turned on the gas fireplace, grabbed my e-reader, and curled up on the couch. There was no way I was telling Clive about the poor lady in the mirror. I knew him. He'd worry and want to move me out of the

Guild, but I didn't want anything to get in the way of him becoming a Counselor. Besides, I could deal with ghosts.

Right now, I needed to relax if I had any hope of sleeping. I was reading the latest in a mystery series I enjoyed, but I couldn't concentrate. I had to keep stopping myself and going back, realizing I hadn't been paying attention to the words my eyes were skating over.

Had the young woman in the mirror been a patient in the asylum? She'd been bruised. Had she done that to herself or had someone else hurt her? I'd read such horrible things about asylums...

A shadow passed over me. Flinching, I sat up, looking around. I'd become accustomed to light and shadow flickering with the fire. This was different, though. I'd seen something tall and dark pass in my peripheral vision, seen the shadow momentarily block the fire.

I put aside the e-reader that had gone into standby mode while I'd been zoned out and stood, studying the darkened corners. I searched my mind for supernatural blips, finding lots of vamps, but none in the room with me besides Clive.

Lighter, almost indistinct in my mind, were hazy forms surrounding me. I couldn't see them, but ghosts were hovering all around me. The floor creaked near the door and something crashed in the bathroom.

Jeez, was I a necromancer or what?

I sat back down, closed my eyes, and gathered up the spirits crowding me. I'd done this outside The Wicche Glass Tavern when I was still learning about my powers. I could certainly do it now. I let out a breath and then realized I had a problem. I didn't speak Hungarian. How was I supposed to tell them to go?

Pulling out my phone, I tried to find a translation program, but I didn't have a signal. *Shit*. The flames in the fireplace shot up, making me jump. Rude, stupid-ass ghosts. I went to Clive and tapped his chest.

"Sorry. I really need your help."

His eyes blinked open but they were unfocused.

"I'm fine. It's not an emergency. I just need the Hungarian word for *go*. Can you tell me what that is?"

His speech was slow, but he said a lot of words. A lot.

"All of that to just say *go*?" What the hell kind of weird language was this?

He spoke again in what I assumed was Hungarian. I could have gone out and asked one of the human Renfield assholes, but I just knew if they spoke English, they'd probably lie to me.

"Clive, I need you to tell me in English how to say *go* in Hungarian."

He opened his mouth and I said, "In English, please."

He paused and then said, "Go."

I thunked my head down on his chest. "Yes. The word is *go* in English. What is that word in Hungarian?"

"Megy."

Oh, thank goodness. One word. I said it back to him, hoping I got the pronunciation correct. When I said it, the pressure in the room swayed.

He said the same word back to me and I turned, found all the spirits pressing in on me, held up my hand, and pushed while forcefully repeating, "Megy."

Like an elastic band, they moved away and then snapped right back. *Damn it.* Was it the wrong word? Was I pronouncing it incorrectly?

Frustrated and more than a little scared, I sat back down, closed my eyes, and tapped into that part of me that spoke to the dead. I focused on all the misty images I saw around me. All were women. When I tried gathering them up again, broken nails scraped down my arms.

I put power in my voice and commanded, "Megy!" Some of the lighter, more insubstantial ghosts disappeared. The rest, though, slowly, resentfully, retreated. They were still in an orbit around me, but at least they were no longer clinging to my skin.

I didn't understand why they were so different from all the

other spirits I'd encountered. They were stronger and angrier. Other than those two ghosts in New Orleans, I'd never felt threatened by spirits before.

Was this an asylum for supernatural creatures? That seemed unlikely—and terrifying. What was it about these ghosts then? How did they have the power to ignore me?

I reclined on the couch, desperate for sleep, as I considered. Could it be the vampires? They were what was different here. Could ghosts feed off vampires? Who could I ask?

Eventually, I did fall asleep but far too soon, Clive was waking me up.

"Sam, darling, we need to get ready." Voice low, he kissed my forehead and went to the closet to pull out a suit.

"Do we, though?" The last thing I wanted to do was go chat with impossibly beautiful deadish people who were hardwired to hate me when I was sleep-deprived and more than a little unnerved by a horde of supercharged hostile ghosts. So far, Budapest sucked.

He turned. "You don't have to, if you'd prefer not." His brow furrowed. "Is everything all right?"

Not really, but I couldn't do that to him. This was a big opportunity and I wanted it for him. "Yep. Just tired. I've been a little keyed up about this trip, so sleep has been evading me."

After living together in the nocturne, we'd learned to speak barely above a whisper. We both had excellent hearing, so it wasn't a problem. If another vampire was intent on eavesdropping, they'd probably just hear a murmur of voices. When we had to communicate something sensitive, though, we spoke mind-to-mind.

"I'm sorry." He pulled me into his arms. "They can wait to meet you. I'm not sure of the schedule, but I'll find time and we can walk around the city. It's been weeks since you've been able to go for a run. I'm sure that isn't helping your restlessness."

"I'm okay. No worries. Besides, I want to meet the players. How else am I going to be able to talk shit about them?"

Laughing, he pulled me toward the bathroom. "Let's get

cleaned up and see if there's anything I can do about all that pent-up energy of yours."

I pulled away, searching for voyeuristic ghosties. A few were still hanging around.

"Sam?" Clive paused, expression concerned.

"I'll be right in," I said.

I could tell he thought something was up, but he nodded and went into the bathroom, turning on the shower.

This time, I led with anger, not fear; anger born of horrible embarrassment. I did not want creepy people from the other side watching Clive and me. I gathered them in my head again, uncoiling that metaphorical golden thread in my chest—my magic—looping it around them and shouting *MEGY!* Thankfully, they did, and I relaxed as I walked into the bathroom.

One very long and exhilarating shower later, I was blow drying my hair again and Clive was in the bedroom getting dressed. Hair up or down? I wanted to make a good impression. Why, I'll never understand.

I was finishing up my makeup when I heard, "Darling, this dress is lovely. Is it new?"

I went into the bedroom, still wrapped in a towel. "Yeah. I asked Audrey to go shopping with me, as she knows what's expected at these kinds of vampy things."

"That word," he murmured, rolling his eyes.

"Thing? Anyway, Audrey said most of you guys would be wearing black, so I should wear color."

"And she was right. This will be stunning on you," he said, giving me a kiss. "It matches your eyes."

The dress was dark green, with a fitted, sleeveless bodice. Baring my arms still made me uncomfortable, but it was summer, and I needed to woman up. The dress flared at the hip, the fabric imperceptibly moving from solid green to a very subtle green floral with hints of blue. The skirt hit just above my knee. Audrey had even found forest green stilettos to wear with it. I wore the blue diamond art deco earrings and bracelet Clive had given me that matched my wedding ring.

Once I'd strapped on the shoes, I looked in the mirror. "Too much?"

Clive came up behind me, wrapping his arms around me and resting his chin on my shoulder. "Perfect."

I looked down at the large diamonds on the cuff bracelet. "No one's going to try to steal this, right?" Wearing expensive things made me so nervous. What if it slipped off my wrist?

Clive kissed my jaw. "I think you'll be safe from pickpockets." He moved toward the door. "Shall we?"

"Wait." I ran back into the bathroom to grab the dark green clutch, stuffing my phone, key, and lip gloss inside. "Hey, what's with there being no cell service here?"

"I hadn't noticed." He pulled his phone from his pocket. "I have service."

I checked my phone and sure enough, I had bars. "Interesting. Earlier today, there was nothing."

"We can ask." He opened the door and held his hand out to me.

"Do you know where we're going?"

He squeezed my hand, his thumb brushing back and forth. "I do."

The hall seemed longer than it had this morning when we'd arrived. Maybe it was the high heels. Probably it was the dread.

There were two vamps talking in the large reception area. Clive didn't acknowledge them, so neither did I. I was acutely aware of how much noise heels clicking against marble made and I irrationally began to hate them. I slowly let out a deep breath, trying to force myself to calm the fuck down.

Was I willingly walking into a room with some of the most powerful vampires in the world? Yes. Did that make me an idiot? God, yes. Such an idiot. The things we did for love.

Clive paused before we hit the open door. Tugging my hand to pull me closer, he kissed me. *You're not an idiot.*

Stop reading my mind!

I wasn't trying to. You're projecting rather strongly right now.

Shit.

Put up your mental blocks. When he started to move forward, I stopped him. I needed a moment to erect them. Picturing walls hadn't worked. Remembering what Thoth, the Egyptian god, had taught me, I once again imagined my mind getting a rainbow candy-coating. Did Thoth recommend a candy-coating of my brain? No. That would be silly. I was the one who'd interpreted his wise words as my needing to skittle-fy myself. To be safe, I did it twice, hoping to keep the likes of Cadmael out of my head.

Finally, I nodded and we started moving again. It was showtime.

FOUR

The Guild: 0/5 Do Not Recommend

When we'd first arrived and I'd seen the interior, I'd thought it beautiful, which had mostly been relief after seeing the outside of the building. Now, though, the unending white marble felt cold and austere, more like a mausoleum. As this place housed vampires, I wondered if the designer had been screwing with them.

The room we entered was a large rectangle, with a six-foot-tall fireplace on the opposite wall. Crystal chandeliers hung from the white coffered ceiling. There was an oversized portrait above the fireplace and a few landscapes in muted tones that looked like afterthoughts on the walls. The portrait quietly, sneakily drew attention. The man had magnetic eyes, black with sparks of red in them. His brows were like violent slashes across his face. Dark hair, with a short beard, he wore a permanent expression of hostility and superiority.

With more difficulty than it should have required, I tore my eyes away from the painting and surveyed the people. Audrey was right. All the vampires were in black, all except for one woman. She wore a dark red cocktail dress in this huge white room, looking like a drop of blood on a sheet.

Wait. I was wrong. One other person eschewed black. Cadmael

stood to the side of the door. He was a tall, raw-boned man. His brown skin was taut over prominent cheekbones. His long, thick black hair lay in braids down his back. Even in what was probably a very expensive pair of chocolate brown trousers and matching shirt, he looked more Mayan warrior than modern vampire.

"Cadmael," Clive said with a bow of his head. "It's good to see you again, my friend. You remember my mate, Samantha."

Cadmael nodded, his expression impassive. He didn't like me any better than I liked him. Of course, I didn't like him *because* he didn't like me, so, as I said on the plane, he'd started it.

When I felt a push against my candy-coating, I glared at him. I wanted him to know I knew what he was doing, and he was an asshole for trying it. I then looked away, as I wasn't trying to start a brawl with a vampire who felt older and more powerful than anyone else in the room.

They talked for a bit, Clive asking about Cadmael's home. In a room filled with vampires, no one talked about anything they didn't mind being heard by all.

While they chatted, I glanced around. There were more people here than I'd expected, mostly men, and far more of them than I'd anticipated were humans. A couple of the humans carried trays with goblets of blood, but others appeared to be standing at the ready should anyone require anything.

I'd need to ask Clive later, as it wasn't terribly important, but there seemed to be a hierarchy within the humans. The ones in black suits with white shirts, like the ones holding the trays, seemed to be the servants. The ones wearing black suits with black shirts appeared to only answer to one vampire. Perhaps they were the vampire's own personal assistants, rather than the Guild's employees.

Regardless, each of them had found an inconspicuous way to show their disdain for me. The one favored by most was a scan of the room where they'd close their eyes as they passed over me. Ooh, snubbed by Renfields. I'd try somehow to survive.

Opening my mind to the vamps, I hovered over their green

blips in my head, not trying to delve deep, not trying to call attention to myself. I couldn't let them know what I was able to do. If they knew I was a necromancer and that I had power over vamps, it'd be an instant death sentence. Right now, I was scum they preferred to pretend didn't exist. I wanted to keep it that way.

Pretending to study the painting beside me, I touched the blips, listening to current thoughts, not delving into memories. They'd all noticed us. I was pretty universally reviled, as I'd assumed, but what I found interesting were the varied reactions Clive received.

It was like working behind the bar in The Slaughtered Lamb. Quiet voices overlapped, but I began to pull out the threads. Some were happy to see him. One, the woman in red, was very happy to see him, though she didn't know who he was. Most were wary, wondering if what they'd heard about the Battle of Alcatraz was correct. Had he really killed so many of their own kind? And why wasn't the Guild punishing him for it?

The voices I focused on, though, were the ones who not only believed retribution was in order but wanted to be the one to hand him his final death. One in particular worried me. I turned from the painting and watched a pale, sandy-haired man walk across the room toward Clive.

Incoming.

Clive glanced over at me and then his attention moved to the man approaching.

Sebastian stepped up, cutting off the other man's path. "Clive, Samantha. It's good to finally have you here." His head tilted as he regarded me. "Clive said you had a broken leg."

Cadmael turned to study me.

The angry vamp paused to speak with someone.

"All better now," I said, distracted by a possible impending assassination attempt. "It's nice to finally be out of the cast." I looked down at myself. "I'm not sure heels were a good idea, though."

Clive glanced at my shoes as well. "Are you in pain?"

"No, no." I patted his arm. "I'm fine. Just little twinges here and there."

"How was your leg broken?" Cadmael asked.

"Oh." I shook my head, unsure of what to say. Would they all attack if they knew my leg had been broken when I was fighting Garyn?

"Haven't you heard the story?" Sebastian asked, a sly smile playing over his lips. "She challenged Garyn."

It was subtle, but obvious. A tightening of a shoulder, a tilting of a head. Everyone in the room was listening.

Who are all these people and why is he doing this to me? I asked Clive mind-to-mind.

Guild members, candidates, their minions, vampire and human. As to why, I'll find out.

"What I've heard," Sebastian continued, "through secondhand sources, is that it was quite a battle. Samantha had the upper hand but didn't want to destroy the fae-owned nightclub and so pulled a punch, giving Garyn the advantage. She swept Samantha's leg and broke it."

Sebastian looked overly pleased at sharing the story. Was he happy someone had finally smacked Garyn around or was he painting a bigger target on my back?

Clive clearly didn't know either. I felt his mistrust. "I know none of our people would be so indiscreet as to pass on that story. Are you in communication with the fae?"

Sebastian smiled. "I have ears everywhere."

Ah, so he was throwing me under the bus to boost his own rep. Got it.

"Just the leg?" Cadmael asked.

I shook my head. "Cracked ribs, concussion, fractured ulna. We know an excellent healer who took care of those problems right away. She did what she could with the femur, but time was needed."

He grunted in agreement. "Healing can be slow for some."

Is he helping or piling on with Sebastian? I asked Clive.

Not sure, Clive responded. *I would normally assume helping, but we both know how he feels about werewolves.*

I turned back to Sebastian. "Thank you for your help this morning. Our new room is much more comfortable than the first."

The smile dropped from his face. "József was reprimanded." Back stiff, he said, "Come. Let me introduce you to the others."

Does everyone one here know how *he was reprimanded?* I asked.

Anything less than death would be considered an insult.

Oh.

Sebastian led us across the room to two men and two women. "Clive, I believe you know Oliver, Frank, and Delores." Gesturing to the woman in the red dress, he said, "You may not have met Ava, though. She's a late entry for North American Counselor."

"It's good to see you all. Thank you for your patience," Clive said.

The first man, light-haired and blue-eyed, nodded. "It's always good to see you, Clive. We were sorry to hear about your mate's injury." He looked at me, holding out his hand. "I'm Oliver. I hope it isn't paining you too much." He had kind eyes, which wasn't something I normally said about vampires. "I've broken quite a few bones over the years, and it always hurts like hell."

I grinned. "I can attest."

The other three apparently intended to ignore me, so Clive took over.

"Sam, this is Frank," he said. "Frank is the Master of Chicago."

Frank barely glanced my way, giving a brief nod. He was shorter and heavier, with thinning dark hair and a beaky nose. "I'm surprised to see you here," he said to Clive. "I'd heard you were dead."

"All indications to the contrary," Clive responded.

Frank tipped his head, still studying Clive. "One with so many enemies often doesn't live long."

Clive's smile was sharp as a dagger. "Strangely enough, they keep losing their heads." Clive glanced back at me and gestured to the woman beside Frank. "And this is Delores," he continued.

"She's the Master of Mexico City and has been even longer than I was the Master of San Francisco."

Delores was petite, her dark hair pulled back in a bun, leaving her delicate face unframed. She wore a long-sleeved black dress that hung to the floor. Two small pearls at her ears were her only adornment.

"Now, now," she began, "you know it is impolite to discuss a lady's age." She made *tsking* sounds but never looked in my direction. Her indulgent smile was all for Clive.

He bowed his head. "Apologies." He turned to the last woman, the one in red, and paused. "Ava, I'm afraid you have me at a disadvantage. Which city are you the Master of?"

Delores' lips twitched, but that small movement said volumes about the woman in red. Frank cleared his throat and Oliver raised an eyebrow. Interesting.

"Allow me," Sebastian said. "Ava comes to us from Savannah, Georgia."

"Savannah?" Clive said. "Has something happened? I thought Marcus was the Master of Savannah." He looked between Ava and Sebastian.

Ava, tall with big brown eyes and long blonde hair, beamed, her red lips curling up as she took Clive in. Sebastian, for his part, looked uncomfortable.

"Marcus continues as the Master of Savannah," Sebastian explained. "Ava is one of the up-and-coming of our kind, and quite powerful in her own right."

Ava laid her hand on Sebastian's forearm, her focus still on Clive. "We need to grow and evolve to survive in this modern world. So many older vampires"—she glanced at all around her—"no offense intended, are out of step with today's science and technology. It's good to have new blood to lend a modern perspective, don't you think?" Her smile was slow and seductive, and totally oblivious to the two vampires beside her who looked as though they wanted to slit her throat with a modern knife. Oliver appeared to be playing chess in his head, ignoring all this nonsense.

"Interesting," Clive responded. "I haven't had any problems staying current, nor have any of our friends here, but perhaps that's not so of others you've met."

She blinked and smiled, but a small line formed between her brows. As I was nosey, I took a moment—they were all ignoring me anyway—to dip into the mind of that one. I almost starting laughing. She was trying to mesmerize Clive. I could hear her repeating over and over, *You love me and want what I want. You want to protect me and give me whatever I need.*

Uh, Clive, the lady in red is trying to enthrall you, I told him.

I'm well aware. Just trying to decide what to do about it. She seems to have ensnared Sebastian.

Is she like Garyn? Can she mesmerize other vampires?

Nowhere near as powerful and rather clumsy with it. I have no idea how Sebastian has been trapped by her.

"That's an interesting perspective," Clive said. "I've been a Master for a very long time and have trained countless novitiates over the centuries."

Delores perked up. She felt the slam coming. Even Oliver had stopped staring into space and was watching the exchange.

"It's a very common cognitive bias neophytes fall prey to. Are you familiar with the Dunning-Kruger effect?"

Oliver did his best to hide his grin. Delores didn't try. Frank looked as confused as Ava.

Sebastian cleared his throat. "Yes, well, has everyone had an opportunity to slake their thirst?"

Clive surveyed the room. "I thought you'd have refreshments for my mate, but I see nothing." His voice was pleasant, but we all heard the rebuke.

Sebastian gave an almost imperceptible shrug of one shoulder. "An oversight, I'm sure." He turned his attention to me. "If you require sustenance, I can escort you to the kitchen."

Banishing the underling to the kitchen, eh? "Don't trouble

yourself. I remember the first room we were shown to when we arrived. I'll take my chances in town. Strangely, I prefer my food free of bodily fluids."

Delores barked out a laugh but Ava appeared horrified by my coarseness. Yeah, whatever, sister.

Clive turned, giving Ava and Sebastian his side. "Oliver, how is Toronto? It's been too long since I visited."

While they chatted about people and places I didn't know, I looked for the sandy-haired asshole that hated Clive. He didn't appear to still be in the room. Frank and Delores, at intervals, called over and spoke with minions, as they clearly didn't care about Toronto, or even pretending to be interested in the conversation. Ava sulked, occasionally forgetting herself and glaring at Clive. She caught my eye once and I smiled innocently. I preferred being invisible to vampires, especially an entire room filled with them.

My gaze returned to the portrait over the fireplace.

"Sebastian?" I interrupted his whispered conversation with Ava. She looked annoyed, but he covered it well.

"Yes?" he said.

I pointed. "That painting is rather...potent. Who is he?"

Sebastian glanced over his shoulder and then back at me, shaking his head. "We have no idea. There were bookcases just there." He gestured to the fire. "We tore them out, as we did everything else during the remodel, and found the stone fireplace and portrait. They'd essentially been walled up."

"He's creepy," Ava said.

"Yes, well..." His shoulder twitched in what could be construed as an unconcerned shrug. "Other than some dust, both the painting and the fireplace were in perfect condition. We tried removing the portrait, but it seems to have been spelled in place. None of us, nor a wicche we keep on retainer, were able to make it budge. So, he's become a part of the décor."

Sebastian went back to talking with Ava.

The lights flickered and I looked up at the chandeliers. Unfortunately, no one else did. *Shit*. Was I the only one seeing this? Staring into the middle distance, I tapped into my necromancy again and found the room was not only filled with vampires but with ghosts as well.

The lights flickered once again and went out, the fire casting the only light in the room. No one was reacting, so it was okay. No reason to panic. A ghostly woman in a long gray dress bustled past me, her hand clamped around the frail wrist of a gaunt old woman in a threadbare nightgown. The old woman grabbed at me. Her curled, arthritic hands clutched my wrist, her ragged nails scratching my skin. Her eyes, a milky white, rolled back in her head as she was yanked on.

It was official. I hated it here.

I saw movement out of the corner of my eye, so I turned to the fireplace. It wasn't the fire that had caught my attention, though. It was the man in the painting above it. Like something out of a nightmare, he turned his head and glared at me. Red lights fired in his black eyes. His lips raised in a snarl as he spat out some kind of Hungarian curse at me.

He gripped the gilded wood framing him and leaned out, reaching for me. His blood-soaked hands dripped on an oblivious Ava and Sebastian, the only ones standing between him and me. I took a step back, heart racing, as every vampire in the room turned to stare at me.

FIVE

It's Time to Go

"Darling?" Clive murmured. "Is everything all right?"

Pull it together. They can't see ghosts and you look like a crazy person. "Of course," I replied overbrightly. Ignoring the black-eyed creep leering at me from the portrait, I placed my hand on my stomach and added, "It's been too long since I've eaten. I think my system is going into overdrive." I leaned in and kissed him on the cheek. "Have a good evening. I believe it's time for me to visit the town and taste the local cuisine."

Turning to the rest of our group, I said, "It was lovely to meet you all. I wish you a good evening as well. Please, excuse me." Trying not to appear as though I was hurrying, I plastered a pleasant expression on my face as I made for the door.

Sam?

I'm good. I just need to get out of here, breathe some fresh air, and eat something.

All right. If you need me, just call.

Of course. Good night, love.

Cadmael studied me as I walked past. I could do stoic too and my candy-coating hadn't been cracked, so he could just wonder. It wasn't easy to take long strides in stilettos, but I did my best. Once I passed the entry and hit the hall, I paused to unstrap the shoes and carry them in my free hand so I could walk more easily, run if I had to. The sandy-haired vampire was out here somewhere, and it would be easier to use the stilettos as weapons if they were in my hands.

I made it halfway down the hall when the wall sconces flickered.

That same woman in the long gray dress grabs my shoulder and spins me around. She says something, but I don't understand her. Shaking my arm, she shouts in my face, spittle foaming on her chapped lips.

I say something in Hungarian. Unfortunately, as I don't speak Hungarian, I have no idea what I said. I try to unsheathe my claws, but nothing happens; my hands remain clasped in front of me because this isn't me. I'm living someone else's experience and have no ability to protect myself. I tremble. I'm not sure if it's her or me, but I assume both of us.

The woman's expression changes from anger to confusion and then she marches me down the hall two doors. She unlocks it, shoves me in, and then locks it again. Pressing my face to the small square of glass in the door, I watch her walk away.

When I turn, I see a room very like the one that creepy Renfield took us to when we arrived, minus all the cobwebs and mold. It's small with used-to-be-white walls and stained tile floors. A very thin pad is rolled up on a metal bed frame.

As I walk across the floor to the window, cockroaches scurry out from under the bed and squeeze between the cracked baseboard. I'm trying hard to hold it together, but it's difficult to reason with abject terror.

I look out the window and see a very different Budapest. All the modern buildings are gone. The town is smaller, the government build-ings even grander by comparison —

The door swings open, bouncing off the wall, as three people burst through the door: two women in gray dresses and one man in a white coat. The women say something to me and I respond, and then each one grabs an arm, dragging me to the bed.

MEGY! I scream it over and over, but nothing changes. I'm trapped

*in a nineteenth century mental asylum. The women are talking to me
again as they strip off my dress and take my shoes.*

*Shivering in nothing but a slip, they force me onto the bed and then
strap my arms and legs down.*

Nonononono, I can't be held down. Please, no.

*The man in the white coat leans over the bed, studying me. He has
thinning dark hair, a trim mustache, and intense eyes. Expression mildly
disgusted, he gazes at me as though I'm a bug to dissect. Beneath assess-
ment, though, there is a kind of glee that terrifies me. He has a new test
subject, and his brain is racing with the possibilities.*

The women move back, and he smiles down at me.

I opened my mouth to scream, but I was standing in the hall
again, my room key in my trembling hand. Chanting *megy, megy,
megy* in my head, I changed my grip on the shoes and then
fumbled the key, dropping it on the carpet. The back of my neck
prickled. I was being watched.

Scooping it up, I unlocked the door and bolted inside. As I
slammed the door shut, I saw a dark-haired vamp with a thick
mustache at the far end of the hall, watching me. Pressing my head
against the back of the closed and locked door, I let out a deep
breath, praying the ghosts were done with me for the night.

Too tired and hungry to fight them off, I needed out of this
place now. I peeled off the dress, secured the jewelry, and changed
into jeans, a t-shirt, and running shoes. I grabbed my little crossbody bag, stuffing my phone, wallet, and key inside.

Rattled, I almost left without protection. Finvarra, the fae king,
still wanted me dead. I wasn't going to make it easy for him, so I'd
brought my axe to Budapest with me. I'd won it when I bested his
dwarf assassin. I put on the leather straps, securing the axe like a
backpack, before donning a light jacket over the top. With my hair
down, no one would notice.

I did my best to brace myself for whatever was out there and
opened the door. The vamp was gone. I closed the door, checked to
make sure it locked, and then followed the directions Clive had

mumbled this morning. He hadn't told me how to get back in, but I was strangely okay with being barred from this place.

When I got to the main hall, I turned left, away from the entry area and meeting rooms. After twenty yards or so, the carpet stopped and there were no more dim wall sconces. The floor was the cracked tile of the asylum that had almost been white a hundred years ago. The walls carried the filth of decades of disuse, black splotches of mold growing rampant. The remodel clearly hadn't made it this far.

A framed black and white photograph hung on the wall. I almost walked past it, but something about it made me stop. An older version of the man who had just leered down at me while I was strapped to a bed now stood on what looked like the steps of this building when it had been new. He wore a white coat and a stern expression. Head tilted, he smiled manically. Behind him in the photo, blood dripped from the windows, spattering his white coat.

Stumbling back, I hit the opposite wall, staring at the photograph. The blood red was gone. It was once more a grainy black and white photo featuring a stern-looking man in a white coat standing in front of the asylum.

Not wanting to turn my back on it, I kept glancing over my shoulder to make sure it hadn't started bleeding again. At the end of the hall, I found a dented metal door. Concerned as to what had put the dents in it, I paused, trying to decide if this really was the best way out. Stomach growling, I decided Clive wouldn't have sent me into danger and if this turned out to be a horrible mistake, I could call him for an extraction.

I had to yank hard, but the door finally gave way on a screech. It was pitch-black and the smell of cold, wet earth was overwhelming. I pulled out my phone and hit the flashlight. Okay. Stairs down, to what must have been an underground tunnel from the asylum to town. I let the door close on another metallic screech and headed down. This was probably one of the ways they'd moved patients in and out of the facility.

It had been common, from what I'd read, to have girls and women committed when they didn't behave the way their fathers and husbands deemed appropriate. Not because they were mentally ill, but because they weren't as biddable as the men would have preferred. This tunnel was probably how they'd been secreted in.

The lower tunnel was narrower than the one above, and unfinished. There were timber crossbeams at intervals to stave off cave-ins, but as I was stepping over large chunks of dirt, they hadn't been entirely successful. I was never using this exit again. There had to be a better way in and out. This route was probably Sebastian's FU to having a werewolf stay in the Guild.

The screech of the heavy door at the top of the stairs brought me up short. Who was following me? I thought of the sandy-haired vampire in the meeting room and then of the mustachioed one I'd seen lurking in the hall outside our room.

Searching my mind, I found his cold green blip descending the stairs. I tried to figure out who it was, but he was too powerful. I couldn't easily slip into his mind, and he was coming up behind me. Turning, I used my flashlight, but he was too far back. I saw eyes glowing, but nothing more.

Time to run. Not wanting to trip on clots of dirt, I kept the flashlight trained on the ground and sprinted. Were vampires faster than me? Mostly yes, but not by much. Of course, that was when I'd been in top form. Ten yards in, my thigh began to twinge. *Damn it!* Maybe a quarter of a mile later, my limp more pronounced, I hit the steps going up. Leg aching, I dragged open another rusting door and rushed down a short corridor, leading to yet another door.

Behind this one, though, I heard the low murmur of voices. I checked my mind and found the vampire climbing the stairs. Blowing out a breath, I opened the door a crack and saw a darkened passage. Slipping through, I glanced up and down a short hall. The walls were spray-painted in words and symbols I didn't recognize. The lock clicked as the door closed behind me.

I brushed off my clothes and straightened my hair as I limped toward the noise. Turning a second corner, I bumped into a man in an apron. He said something to me in Hungarian, seeming concerned as to where I'd come from.

"English?" I asked.

He looked irritated and then said, "Why are you here?"

"Sorry. I was trying to find the restrooms." At his blank gaze, I clarified, "Toilets."

He nodded and pointed me in the opposite direction. I thanked him and then arrowed across the bar in the direction he'd pointed. I didn't want to wander around Budapest looking like what I was, an asylum escapee.

Staring at my reflection a moment, I decided I didn't look crazy, just scared. I searched for the vamp again and felt him passing by the restroom door. Tensed, waiting for the attack, I sensed him moving farther away into town. Maybe he hadn't been following me after all. Perhaps I'd instead made a fool out of myself for his entertainment, and he was just heading into the city. I'd messed up my leg for nothing. Idiot.

I went back out and took a moment to look around the bar. It was a ruin bar. I'd heard of them. Some enterprising people in Budapest had taken derelict buildings, empty lots, and warehouses, with crumbling walls, collapsing roofs, and graffiti, and turned them into bars. They hung fairy lights, added some plants, and brought in mismatched furniture from street sales. Add some alcohol and voilà! A bar.

I checked the sign as I left The Bloody Ruin Asylum & Taproom. It closed at three. Granted, I had no idea how to get back into the tunnel, but I could call for directions, or better yet, a different route. It was late, but I was hoping someone was still serving food.

I was on the Buda side of Budapest, which was hillier. There used to be two separate towns, Buda on one side of the Danube River and Pest on the other. In 1850, the cities had been merged into Budapest.

There weren't many shops and restaurants on the Buda side and those that were had already closed. Now what? I walked farther, passing a wooded area, and finally saw the Danube, a wide black expanse snaking between streetlights on either bank.

My leg hurt but my best chance for food was the other side of the river, so I limped to the nearest bridge and crossed. The Pest side was flatter, with a huge downtown retail area. I wanted to return during the day so I could sightsee properly. Right now, I was just looking for open restaurants. Most closed at eleven or midnight. I found one that closed at one, but they'd stopped preparing food at eleven. It was just the bar that was open.

The host took pity on me and pointed down the road at another restaurant. The sign on that one said they were open until two, so I held out hope.

The host said something in Hungarian.

"Do you speak English?" I'd downloaded a translation app, so there were options if she didn't.

"Yes." Her expression, though, said she'd prefer not to be tested on it.

"I'm sorry. I know it's late. Can I still get food?" *Please-pleaseplease.*

She was about to say no—I could see it—and then she paused. "I'll ask kitchen." She turned and went deeper into the restaurant.

There was a chair by the door, so I sat and began rubbing my thigh through my jeans. "Come on. We're still friends, right?" I murmured to my leg. "It was just a little running. Did Doc Underfoot warn me not to do it? Of course he did, but I had a vampire on my butt. I'm sorry and I'll try not to run anymore. Please don't seize up on me."

The host came back. "He said he can"—she paused, clearly trying to find the right words—"bunch what is left to make meal. Different from menu."

I nodded and stood, so very grateful. My leg buckled, but I caught myself. "Great. Thank you so much."

She looked down at my leg and then checked a piece of paper

in her pocket. "He has sea bass, lamb, or chili shrimp and whatever vegetables he can find."

"Yes. Thank you. I'll take it all, please. I'm very hungry." I patted my stomach. At her confused expression, I added, "I can eat a lot."

She didn't seem convinced, but she waved me in. Oh! It was beautiful, three stories high, with a glass roof. There was a huge light fixture in the center of the open space. Long black poles radiated from the center and at the end of each was a round glass ball illuminating the room. There were plants everywhere. Vines dripped down from the balconies above. Tall potted plants with oversized leaves were placed throughout the restaurant, creating intimate eating areas in the open expanse.

She led me to a secluded table, far to the side. I heard the low hum of voices, the clink of glasses, and then caught a glimpse of a bar at the far end of the building. The tables and stools over there were full, but it was quiet and dark where I was, which was perfect.

"To drink?" she asked me as I sat.

"Water's good."

She nodded and left.

My stomach grumbled. Whatever the chef was willing to let me have would be wonderful. It didn't take long before the woman returned with a tray as well as a man holding a second tray. They placed the plates around me on the table and then paused, as though believing my ordering everything had been a misunderstanding.

"Thank you both." I nodded, trying to convey that she'd understood me perfectly. "It all looks wonderful. I appreciate you making an exception for me tonight."

The man looked at all the food again and then at me before scratching his cheek and walking back to the kitchen. The woman returned to the podium by the front door. The food servers had probably already left for the evening. Thank goodness the host was willing to do double duty.

The sea bass was delicious, in what tasted like a ginger broth, with rice on the side. I inhaled it all and then slid the empty plate under the lamb dish. A couple of groups of people had already passed me on the way to the bar. Since I'd received some funny looks, I was now trying to hide empty dishes.

The lamb shawarma came with some kind of spicy tahini dipping sauce, and pita triangles. It was amazing and my body finally stopped shaking from running when I was already starving. By the time I finished this plate, I was feeling more myself.

Tucking two plates under the chili shrimp with cherry tomatoes, celery, and what looked like sautéed clams, I continued my feast. They'd even given me some bread to soak up the chili sauce. I took my time with the third plate, savoring every bite.

When I was done, I pushed the plates away, finally feeling content. The man returned with a dessert plate holding a brownie in sauce. Raising his eyebrows, he handed it to me.

I smiled and nodded. "Thank you!"

Shaking his head, he walked back into the kitchen.

I took a bite. Mmm, amazing. The sauce was an interesting mix of coffee and cherry, with a hint of lemon. It made me very happy.

The host returned with the check and I pulled out my wallet, handing her my card. I had no idea how many Hungarian forints there were to the dollar, and I didn't care. I needed the food, whatever they were charging me. After adding a big tip, I put my card away and struggled to my feet. My leg had started to stiffen. I needed to take a nice, leisurely walk back. No pushing it this time.

I paused a moment to check for vampires. It wouldn't do to walk out of the restaurant directly into one. Unfortunately, I found a cold, green blip far closer. Glancing up, I met dark eyes staring down at me from the interior third-floor balcony.

SIX

Well, Shit

It was the dark-haired, mustachioed vamp who'd been staring at me in the hall of the Guild. Apparently, he was the one following me. Fine. Fuck it. I couldn't run again. If he wanted to attack me, I'd kick his ass. Possibly.

When I looked up again, he was gone. Asshole was just going to lurk and make me twitchy. I said goodnight to the host and left at the same time as a larger group. Thankfully, they seemed to be happily drunk and didn't notice my trailing behind them.

When they eventually turned into the lobby of a hotel, I continued on to the bridge back across the river. In the wee hours of the morning, the bridge was empty. If he was going to attack, it'd probably be here.

Monitoring him in my head, I loosened my jacket so I could grab the axe quickly. I doubted he was expecting an axe or claws. A normal wolf took time to shift. I was a Quinn, though, the origin line of werewolves, and could shift with a thought. Of course, I was still recovering from my last brawl with a vampire, so I wasn't getting delusional about my chances.

When I reached the center of the bridge, I braced for him to fly at me, but instead he kept pace, half a bridge away. Why the hell was he just following me?

My thigh was throbbing, but it felt a little stronger after I'd rested and eaten. I could make it back to the asylum. I decided this time I'd just climb the fence and deal with the barbed wire. Or maybe I should wait for my vamp stalker to catch up so I could trail him back into the Guild. Presumably, he knew a way.

He didn't attack and I didn't stop. By the time I made it back to The Bloody Ruin Asylum & Taproom, I understood the name. The former asylum—current Guild headquarters—loomed on the hill, high above the bar, with broken windows and walls stained with what looked, from the distance, like blood. It rose over the surrounding trees like a zombie lurching toward town.

I'd almost walked past the ruin bar because, though the sign had said it was open until three, that was clearly just one of its many possible closing times. It was a little after two and the place was locked up and dark. Super.

Checking again, I found the vamp moving closer, though still a block or so away.

I was just reaching for my phone to call Clive when I heard angry Hungarian words snarled at me. *Damn it.* My focus had been on the vampire tailing me and the creepy building haunting me, not the stupid wolf rolling up on me.

Like the asylum, he loomed. Unlike it, he didn't scare me. "I don't speak Hungarian."

He was probably six foot four, with dark brown hair, brown eyes, and pale skin. Voice deep and menacing, he sneered, "Get. Out."

I nodded. "Understood. I'm in your territory. Sorry about that. I didn't know there was a pack in Budapest. It's not like I can consult a directory of European Wolf Packs, though that would be super helpful."

His anger seemed to be tilting into confusion. Perfect. It was my goal in life to keep my enemies off balance.

"So you see, I couldn't call and ask for permission, as I wouldn't have known who to call. Let's just get this over with now. Can you tell your Alpha I'm visiting with my husband, and we promise not to start any shit with the wolves. Okay?"

Growling, he reached out to grab the front of my jacket. I blocked his arm while grabbing his wrist and twisting it behind his back. I shoved him down and leapt on his back with my knees. He roared quietly. I think we were trying not to call attention to ourselves. There were lots of apartment windows overlooking our dustup.

He tried to buck me off but I wasn't moving, and neither was his arm. In fact, I jammed it farther up to get him to stop struggling.

"Listen, you don't like me in your territory." I leaned down, dropping my voice even more. "I get it. I won't be here long. You're going to need to relax, though. Okay?"

When I smelled another wolf, I straightened up and found a gun leveled at my head. *Shit!* No wonder that takedown had been so easy. I stared into the eyes of the wolf with the gun, letting mine lighten to gold. I was fast and I knew it. Still, a gun aimed at your face was off-putting.

I grabbed the gun, yanking it out of his hand while backflipping off the downed wolf to give myself some room. If I had to fight two or more wolves, I needed some space to evaluate the situation.

Pocketing the gun, I drew the axe over my shoulder in my right hand and unleashed the claws on my left. They could come at me if they wanted, but they'd leave bloody.

The vamp was nearby, because of course he was. My gaze flicked to the right and I saw him in the deep dark between two buildings, leaning against the wall and watching.

The wolf I'd had pinned was getting to his feet. Neither had noticed the vampire. Both were staring at my claws with looks of disbelief.

The new wolf, who'd recently been divested of his gun, was shorter than his buddy, with light hair, a thick beard, and close-set brown eyes.

The taller one whispered something and then the bearded one finally tore his eyes from my claws and said, "Kin?"

Kin? As in family? "Quinn? Are you asking if I'm a Quinn? Because yes, I am."

The bearded one took out his phone and swiped through it. A woman answered and they spoke in Hungarian for a moment before she said, "I am Viktoria. László, the Master of Budapest, asks that I find out who you are and why you're here."

"Sure. I'm Sam Quinn. I'm from the U.S. My husband and I are just on a quick trip. He has business here. I won't cause trouble in your territory, and we'll be gone before you know it."

She translated my response into Hungarian. László, the taller one, asked something and she said, "Which hotel are you staying in?"

My gaze darted to the vampire. He'd moved farther into the dark, but he watched, eyebrows raised, no doubt waiting to see if I'd spill vampire secrets. "We're not. We're staying with friends in a private residence."

Hungarian in both directions and then, "Where?"

I could have lied to buy time, but I didn't want to start down that road. "I'm sorry but I can't tell you that."

"Why not?" Viktoria asked. She didn't wait to translate for László that time.

"Just as I'm sure you wouldn't want me to share information about your pack, I cannot share information about our hosts. As I said, we won't be here long, and I'll try not to do anything to bother you while I'm in your city."

Hungarian flew back and forth and then László sniffed me and spat, "Vámpír."

"Well, if you knew, why did you ask?" Stupid wolves.

"László says you reek of vampires. He thought perhaps you'd been fed on, but now he sees that you welcome the leeches."

I'd been so hopeful I was getting out of this unscathed. "First of all, rude. Do I love all vampires? No. I'm not stupid. But then again, there are a lot of really shitty wolves too, so maybe take it down a notch. My husband is a vampire, and his business is his own, not yours."

"Thank you, darling. I appreciate your loyalty." Clive had clearly done that trick of his, seeming to appear out of thin air, causing both wolves to flinch.

When he wrapped his arm around me, I kissed him on the cheek. "I wanted to tell them that you were bigger and stronger and could kick their asses, but it felt a little childish. I was thinking it, though."

Clive's lips twitched. "And that warms my cold, dead heart." He spoke to the wolves in Hungarian and the men snarled something back.

On the phone, Viktoria said, "You are visitors in our city and László, as Master, has every right to know who you are and why you're here."

"And I told him what I could," I said.

László let out a stream of very angry Hungarian words and Clive responded. They went back and forth a few times, Clive remaining calm. He nodded at whatever the wolf had said and pulled the gun from my pocket, returning it to Budapest's Master. With that, Clive tipped his head to László and then turned us around to walk away. I glanced over my shoulder and found the Alpha glaring after us.

"What was that about?" I asked.

In a moment, Clive responded.

At the corner, his gaze traveled over me, checking to make sure I was okay. I glanced back again and found the street behind us now empty.

Lifting my axe, I said, "Can you help me put this back?"

He swept my hair over my shoulder and had the axe secured a moment later. Taking my hand, we continued down the same road. *You're limping.*

I know. There was a stupid vampire following me when I was in the tunnel. I thought he was going to attack me, so I ran.

Clive paused a moment, the pain lessening significantly, and then turned his back to me. "Climb on." Clive could hurt others with his mind, but he could also draw the pain away, which he did for me now.

The throbbing had stopped but my leg was still injured, so I took the piggyback ride. Clive was careful not to grab where the break had been.

Do you know who followed you? he asked.

No. I saw him lurking at the end of the hall to our bedroom, but when I came back out a few minutes later, he was gone. I felt a vampire following me in the tunnel—he was too powerful in that moment for me to try to read him—so I ran in case he was one of those vamps who hates werewolves or the super angry one from the meeting room.

The one following you didn't try to hurt you? Clive's voice in my head was cautious. I didn't think he knew what to make of the strange behavior either.

No. He followed me to the restaurant and then apparently watched me eat, because I saw him as I was leaving. Then he followed me back over the bridge. He was tucked between two buildings when the wolves attacked. He didn't do anything, though. Just watched.

Have you acquired a new admirer?

Doubtful, I scoffed.

What does he look like?

I only got brief glimpses of him but pale with dark hair and a large dark mustache.

A mustache, Clive repeated, shaking his head.

Do you know who it is?

Unfortunately. The only vampire I can think of with a large mustache who is currently in residence at the Guild and we've not yet seen is Vlad.

Should I be worried?

He's referred to as the Impaler for a reason, darling. His mass murdering skills are rather legendary.

So I should be worried?

One should always be worried when Vlad is involved. He patted my good leg. *My guess, though, is that he was just interested in you and so followed.*

He turned down another road. *Who is this angry vampire you're referring to?*

Oh, I responded, *yes. You need to watch out for that one. He wants to kill you. When we first arrived, you were talking to Cadmael and I was scanning the room, making sure no one was planning to jump me. Anyway, I caught this guys' stabby thoughts about you. He started toward us but then Sebastian showed up and the guy disappeared.*

Interesting. Clive turned down another road, this one headed back toward the river. *I hadn't noticed him. What does he look like?*

Tan. Sandy-colored hair. I think his eyes were brown. He's about my height. No. I was wearing heels last night. He's maybe six feet tall. I mean, the rest of the description is black suit. You guys don't branch out in your choice of clothing—except the lady in red and Cadmael.

Internally smacking my forehead, I said, *Oh, shoot. I just remembered. Give me a sec.* I thought of the angry man's face and pushed the image into Clive's mind. I'd only recently tried doing this and had found it worked.

Thomas. He's one of the Australian Counselors. Odd. I didn't realize there was any ill will between us.

Is he connected to Garyn in some way? I wondered. *There have got to be a ton of vamps gunning for us because of that whole mess.* It wasn't right that people kept attacking us and then we were blamed for defending ourselves. Jeez.

Not that I know of. Thank you for the warning, though. I'll speak with Cadmael and try to determine what's going on there.

Good. I adjusted my arm around his neck. Thank goodness he didn't need to breathe. *Now tell me what all that was about with László.*

He has a very healthy and understandable hatred of vampires. What I got was that humans were being found in the city minus quite a bit of their blood, often with bite marks on their necks. He said they smelled of vampire, but I have to imagine there's something else going on. The Guild is committed to secrecy. I find it highly unlikely that its members are wandering around Budapest at night preying on its citizens, especially in such an obvious way. Bite wounds left on necks? He shook his head.

My stomach clenched. What if Clive was wrong about these Guild guys? Was I encouraging him to join a group of predators? I mean, yes, vampires, but that didn't mean they were psycho killers. Not all of them, anyway. Shit.

Instead of dismissing it out of hand, I said to him, *how about if we investigate his claims? I'm a lone wolf in his territory. László could have gone for the immediate kill, but he didn't. He got a translator to find out who I was and why I was here. Yes, he came on strong, but he's supposed to show strength to a potential threat. It wasn't until vampires entered the chat that he actually got pissed off.*

Do you have a feeling about this? Clive asked. He knew I sometimes picked up on impressions from vampires without even realizing I was doing any kind of necromantic eavesdropping.

I don't know. Not for certain. I love the idea of you being a Counselor. You'd be wonderful at it. So far, though, I'm not impressed with the Guild.

He rubbed my leg on a sigh. After a long pause, he finally said, *I find myself uncomfortable with this conversation.*

I hugged him more tightly and kissed his ear. *It's probably like you said. Someone else is attacking the humans and casting suspicion on the vamps.*

I'm finding this conversation uncomfortable, he repeated, *which tells me I want this too much. In order to protect you—protect us—I can't allow desire to cloud judgment.*

I hated that Clive was doubting himself. *It's only our first night around here. We'll keep our eyes and ears open, and we'll figure out what's going on. Okay?*

One of the things I love about you, darling, is your unwavering support. This isn't only about me, though. We need to decide if this is a good fit for both of us. Even if I am offered the job, it has to be right for both of us or I turn it down.

I breathed in his scent. Home. He was my home. *I love you, you know.*

Thank goodness, he said, looking up and down the empty road at the next intersection.

I wasn't sure where Clive was taking us, but he was definitely heading away from the asylum.

Hey, does this mean we don't have to go through that tunnel again, because yay.

The wolves are following us to see where we're going. I need to lose them before we double back.

I'll get down, I said, starting to move.

He held me tighter. *We're faster if you stay there. Don't let go.*

When he turned the corner down a narrow alley, he took off. I had to close my eyes; they were tearing up from the speed of the wind. The scent changed. We were out of the neighborhood and in a wooded area. A moment later, we were airborne. I opened my eyes to watch us fly over the high fence and then he was streaking over the asylum property to the front door.

SEVEN

Sam!

I worried we were going to smash into the front door, but it opened as he hit the steps. He slid to a stop across the marble entry as the door was closing. Pulling me around his body, he set me on my feet, holding me steady until I could stand on my own. A twinge of pain broke through Clive's pain removal, but then it was gone.

Should we tell them to be ready, that Vlad will be returning soon? I asked him.

No. Vlad's business is his own. He may not want the Guild to be aware of his comings and goings.

He placed his arm around me, surreptitiously taking my weight so my limp wasn't too pronounced. He knew I wouldn't want to be carried in front of a bunch of vampires and their minions.

"How was dinner?" he asked, which was a nice, bland question when we knew there were always people listening.

"Excellent. I found a place willing to feed me even though I was arriving so late. If you have time while we're here, I'd like to take you. It's across the river."

We turned down the side hall toward our bedroom. "It's a date. I'll check with Sebastian on the schedule going forward."

Once behind closed doors, he picked me up and carried me to the sofa. "We haven't even been here twenty-four hours." He shook his head, rubbing my sore leg. "I selfishly want you with me, but neither the Guild nor the town are safe for you." He brushed the back of his hand over my cheek. "Our plane is here. You don't need to stay, darling. I'm sure Fergus misses you terribly."

I put my hand over his and squeezed. "No fair bringing Fergus into this. Partners stick together and my leg'll be fine. I just need to rest it. Not to mention I wanted to come. All these places you've visited countless times and I've never been. I wanted to see Budapest."

"And instead, you're stuck in a vampire-infested, rotting asylum in a town filled with wolves who will attack on sight because of me." He gave me a look that had me smiling.

"Cheer up. It's an interesting new experience. Is it a good one? No, it is not. But it's new."

When he leaned in to kiss me, his phone buzzed. He closed his eyes a moment. "I believe the meeting is reconvening." He gave me a quick kiss and stood.

"How's it going? Are the other kids playing nice?" I struggled to extricate myself from the axe holster while sitting on a couch. Suddenly, Clive was there, easing it down my arms and placing it on the coffee table.

"For the most part," he responded. "Frank and Delores often bicker with one another, and both tend toward solutions to hypothetical problems by punishing all involved. Ava has no idea what she's talking about but does so love to throw around platitudes in an attempt to cover her ignorance. Oliver sits quietly, ignoring everyone, until he's asked a direct question. When he is, he gives a complete and reasonable response."

"So you're the star pupil, huh?" I said, grinning. "I knew it."

"Let's not go too far," he said, bringing me an armload of water bottles, protein bars, and assorted snacks.

"Where'd you get those? I checked. None of the food stores

were open." Thank goodness. I didn't have to go through that tunnel every time I was hungry.

"Darling, humans are employed here. There's a kitchen and I raided it for you."

"That reminds me," I said, "why do some humans wear white shirts and some black?" The Renfield situation bugged me. I was sick of the little shits giving me dirty looks, and I needed to know what I was dealing with.

"Ren—oh, the human servants? Just as the nocturne back home has Norma, the human liaison, the Guild also has humans who can deal with situations, bring in supplies, whatever needs doing during daylight hours. The ones in white shirts want to be given the dark kiss and so are trying to prove their worthiness, mostly to Sebastian. If any of the Counselors take a liking to a white-shirted Renfield," he said on a grin, adopting my term for them, "they may offer to take on the responsibility, with the promise of eventually turning them. The ones in black shirts already belong to a specific vampire. They have been claimed and are beginning to be fed blood by their Master. Not enough to turn them, but enough to give them some enhanced abilities and to create a stronger allegiance.

"The white shirts should help you or answer your questions. I say *should* because most of them, like the dead one this morning, are going to be hostile toward you, believing it makes them more —I don't even know what—trusted? appreciated? by a vampire protector. You're smarter and stronger than either type, but I recommend staying away from both. Weak men desperate to prove themselves to other men rarely make good decisions."

He dropped a kiss on my nose and then headed for the door. "Try to get some rest." He tapped the side of his head. "If you want to eavesdrop, feel free." He left as his phone started buzzing again.

I grabbed one of the bottles of water and took a big swig. I considered changing into my pajamas, but I didn't feel safe here. Locks were child's play to vampires and, for all I knew, the

Renfields had copies of the room keys. No. I needed to stay fully clothed and able to defend myself.

Tipping over, I reclined on the couch, putting my head on a pillow. I was so damned tired.

The lamp on Clive's side of the bed flickered. I didn't have the energy for this. I had to stay and let my leg heal, so the ghosts could fuck right off. "Listen, if you want to play with the light, could you just turn it off completely? The flickering is going to give me a headache."

The light went out. Cool.

I was starting to locate the green blips in my mind, wanting to find my guy and listen in on the vampy drama, when I heard him shout, "Sam!"

I was up and running across the room before I had a moment to evaluate the likelihood of Clive shouting for my help. Halfway down the hall the sconces flickered and went out. The hall was pitch dark, but I kept going. Clive needed me.

A few steps later, I realize that the sound is all wrong. The hall is carpeted and yet I hear the echo of my shoes slapping against stark tile. There's a sickly, yellowish light. The electric sconces are gone. A gas lamp stands on a side table that wasn't there a few minutes ago.

I'm surrounded by the same industrial white tile floor of the asylum, the white walls, the white metal doors with scratches and dents. A scream makes me jump. I turn to see an old woman through the small square of glass embedded in her door. Her withered face fills the glass as she curses at me in Hungarian.

Frantically rattling the knob, she bangs her head against the door, over and over again, making the glass crack. Blood trickles down her face as she shrieks.

A wail behind me makes me jump. I spin to the door opposite the screamer's and find a woman whose face is burned. It looks as if hot grease was thrown on the left side of her head. The wound isn't new, but it's angry and red. The desperation in both women's eyes makes me break out in a cold sweat.

"Nem, Apa!"

Wait. I know that one. Nem means no. Apa? I'm walking again. The voice seems to be coming from the reception area. Isn't apa father? *Or is that Korean? I remember something in a book…*

Another woman bangs on her door and curses me with words I don't understand.

I move faster to the end of the hall and turn right, almost running into a gurney left against the wall. The woman strapped on it stares blankly up at the ceiling, her jaw hanging open, revealing discolored teeth. The stench of death overwhelms me. She's been left here to rot for hours.

Another woman, this one an attendant in a long gray gown stained with sweat rushes past me and down the hall I just left. She makes a fist and bangs on the cursing woman's door, shouting something in response, and then goes down to the screamer's door, taking a large ring of keys out of her apron pocket.

She pounds the door, shouts something, and then unlocks the door and opens it. The screaming gets louder before it cuts off with a crack.

Stomach twisting, I turn back to the entry. A teenaged girl, well-dressed, is clinging to an older man in an overcoat. They appear to be the only two people who don't work here, the only two not wearing some type of uniform.

The man in the overcoat has the same blue eyes and reddish-brown hair color as the teenaged girl, who has succumbed to tears, her words lost in sobs. He yanks his hand away from her with a look of disgust as he turns to speak with the man in the white coat.

It's the leering man who was leaning over me in that nightmare, the one who was standing on the front steps of this building in the bleeding photo. The man in the overcoat hands the white-coated man an envelope and shakes his hand. The white-coated man nods to a woman bent over the counter, writing something behind the reception desk.

She, like the other attendant, is wearing a long gray dress, this one with stains at the hem. Moving forward, she speaks quietly to the teen, hooking an arm tightly around the girl's shoulders and turning her toward the hall where I'm standing.

Two men, also dressed in gray, stand in the entrance to the hall on the opposite side of the reception area. Presumably, that's the way to the men's dormitory. I don't like the way the men are watching the girl, their gazes predatory.

One of them pushes off the wall with his shoulders, sauntering over to the desk and checking the book the female attendant was writing in. Grinning, he taps something on the page and turns to the other attendant, nodding and walking back to the men's side of the building.

The teen struggles with the attendant, trying to get the attention of the man leaving her at the asylum. "Apa! Kérem," she pleads.

He never looks back, striding out the door into the night.

"Shh, Léna. Mi gondoskodunk rólad." The doctor? Director? Superintendent? The man in the white coat shakes his head, pocketing the envelope and walking into an office behind the reception desk.

The girl— Léna—screams and I follow her. She's taken to the room Clive and I were first taken to. The cell is white with only a thin, soiled mattress on a metal frame. Terrified, the poor girl is looking everywhere at once, clearly trying to find an escape, to find anyone who can help.

Her gaze slides over me. Everyone's has.

Two female attendants strip off her coat and shoes, throwing them out into the hall. One pulls off Léna's ring and pockets it, ignoring the girl's tears. The other takes the silver comb holding back her hair, letting it fall loose to her waist.

The ring thief goes out to the hall and returns with a pair of large shears. Léna's eyes get big as she fights to get away. The comb thief wraps her meaty arms around the waifish Léna, holding her in place while the other hacks off her hair to above the shoulders.

Léna closes her eyes tightly, as though this is all a bad dream and she'll wake soon.

One of the women laughs and the other rolls her eyes. They strip off Léna's dress, leaving her shivering in only a chemise and drawers, then march her barefoot down the hall, dropping her dress on the pile they've created of her belongings.

I follow them down the hall, unable to break away. They turn right down the larger main hall and go almost to the end before slipping through a door on the left and down a flight of stairs. Léna is stumbling, but they have her arms locked in their own as they drag her down.

At the bottom, they push through another door and take her down a cold, dark passage. The sounds coming from behind the locked doors fill me with dread. This poor girl shouldn't be here. No one should.

They take her to the door at the end, one of them kicking it open. A large metal tub sits in the middle of the room. One of them turns the faucet while the other seems to give the girl instructions.

I watch the women, looking for any sign of sympathy, even simple concern, and find none. Dead eyed, they wait for the bath to fill and then force the girl in. She squeals at the cold, but they ignore her, shoving her down into the icy water.

One takes a thick bar of hard soap and scrubs the girl, while the other holds her in place. When they finish their cursory wash, they dunk her under and then drag her up, her underthings plastered to her frail body.

Like this, it's clear to see that Léna is pregnant. She presses her hands to the growing mound, trying to hide, but the women see and jeer. They drag her out of the bath and take her, shivering and wet, back through the hellish passage, to the stairs, and return her to her room, where they push her in and lock the door.

I'm not sure how long I stand in the hall outside her door. I want to leave, but I can't make myself move. Eventually, I hear footsteps. Not the female attendants. I've learned the sound of their treads. These are heavier.

The two male attendants come around the corner, looking up and down the hall. Seeing no one, the one who'd looked in the reception book takes a ring of keys from his pocket, unlocks Léna's door, and the two slip in.

I'm in the room with them. The girl's curled up tightly on the filthy mattress, trying to get warm, tears still fresh on her cheeks. When the men walk in, she jumps up, cowering on the far side of the bed, her arms out, warning them away.

I know what's about to happen and I scream for her. Running at the men, my claws out, I try to rip their heads off, but I rush through them, *slamming against the far wall instead. Howling, I try again to slash at them, but I'm not there. There's nothing I can do to stop them.*

EIGHT

I Hate Everyone. No. Not Everyone. Mostly, It's This Guy

S *nap.*

Blinking, I stared into the eyes of a smirking white-shirted Renfield whose fingers were still hovering in front of my face.

"Do you need something?" he asked in heavily accented English. "You've been standing here for a long time. Is there something wrong with you?"

I glanced around. I was back in the hall, the beautiful walls, the moldings, the light fixtures. I wasn't trapped in the asylum with Léna. *Oh, God. Léna.* Ignoring the Renfield, I ran back through the open bedroom door, slamming it on the way to the bathroom. I barely got the seat up before I was vomiting.

Sam? What's wrong?

Nothing, I said, climbing to my feet and holding a washcloth under the cold water. *Just had a bad dream. I'm okay. How's your meeting?*

Tedious. That's why I was checking in on you. If you asked me to return to our room now, you'd be doing me a favor.

I held the cloth to my face, trying to breathe through the aftershocks. Every time my thoughts returned to that poor girl, more tears streamed down my face. *No way. I'm not encouraging you to play hooky. I mean, you're already doing the Counselor gig on the down low for the vamps who call you. I want you to have the job for real. Don't worry. I'm good.*

All right. I'll swing by the kitchen on my way back to you. Perhaps they have cake.

Thank you. I'd love cake. And if I'm asleep when you return, I'll have it for breakfast.

Sweeter dreams, darling.

After brushing my teeth, I went back to the bedroom, wrung out and unable to stop thinking about Léna. Was her father punishing her? Hiding her in the asylum and punishing her for being pregnant? Who was the baby's father? Had he faced any consequences? As I already knew the answer to that one, I punched the pillow a few times and lay back on the couch.

Remarkably, I must have eventually fallen asleep. I woke, lying on the bed, Clive's arm around me. We were on top of the covers and he'd left me fully clothed, though he'd taken off my shoes. He probably hadn't wanted to wake me by trying to undress me.

Stomach growling, I checked the time. It was late afternoon. Perfect. There was time for me to get food before shops closed. Wait. I shot up in bed. Had he found me cake? And then I saw a plate on my nightstand with another plate flipped over on top of it, creating a safe pocket of possibility.

Excited, I lifted the top plate and found a slab of five-layer sponge cake with a chocolate buttercream frosting. There was even a fork. Scooting back on the bed, I leaned against the headboard and ate one delicious bite after the next before giving Clive a chocolatey kiss on the cheek. Good husband.

Feeling much better about today than yesterday, I took a shower and tied my hair up in a braid. According to my phone, it was warm out, it being summer and all. I put on a pair of green shorts—baring my body was still uncomfortable for me, but I was trying—a matching t-shirt, and my dark gray running shoes. If my life had taught me anything, it was to always be prepared to run.

I strapped on the axe and added a light denim jacket over the top to hide my weapon. I picked up my little handbag, gave Clive another kiss, and headed out. Did the tunnel suck? Yes. But it wasn't as creepy during the day when all the vamps were resting. I also didn't know of any other way of leaving besides walking out the front door of a condemned, abandoned building and scaling a tall fence, all in plain view of anyone who happened to be walking by.

Nope. Tunnel it was. Hopefully, the waiter who had caught me sneaking around The Bloody Ruin Asylum and Taproom last night was off duty. It would be highly suspicious to be found in an employees-only area twice.

The Guild was quiet. I knew some of the Renfields were probably awake, doing human liaison stuff, but I assumed most slept during the day in order to serve their fanged masters all night. The ghosts had had to expend a lot of energy last night, so they should be resting as well. Perfect.

Superimposing Léna's memory with what I was seeing now, I found the door down to the lower level with the creepy cells and the tub room. I hadn't noticed it last time because the door was barely discernable and I'd been focused on the mold bloom on the right, not the door on the left.

Regardless, I kept going to the horrible screeching door. With any luck, the noise would wake that punk Renfield who'd snapped his fingers in my face last night. Granted, he did pull me out of Léna's memory, but he sneered while doing it. Ergo, ipso facto, he's a punk who does not deserve a solid eight.

The stairs and tunnel weren't as scary this time. I knew what to expect and I didn't have a vamp on my tail. Of course, now that the idea had popped into my head, I had to check... The vampires all seemed to be down for the day, all except one who was stirring. I paused in the tunnel to see who it was. Clive should know that one of these people could move around during the day. The vamp felt familiar, like a mustachioed green blip.

I didn't know why Vlad was up and around, but as he wasn't following me, I didn't care. I lucked out when I emerged into The Bloody Ruin again. No one was paying attention as I slipped out of the hall into the bar. Trying to look like I belonged there, I walked through the bar and out onto crowded streets.

Quite a few people were headed up Castle Hill toward the Buda Palace, which I planned to visit while I was here. Right now, though, I was heading across the bridge for food. The Danube sparkled in the late afternoon sun beneath me. The Parliament building dominated the skyline, sitting on the opposite bank of the river. It speared the cloudless sky.

During down times at The Slaughtered Lamb, I'd been reading about the best places to visit in Budapest. The Parliament building topped most lists. It was stunning, an enormous neo-Gothic structure, much like its counterpart in London. When the Habsburgs ruled, they brought a strong western European influence with them, resulting in opera houses and cafés that would have looked at home in Vienna.

Hungary's parliament building had a center dome with two symmetrical halls running out from the center. Every window, wing, and courtyard was designed to strain heavenward.

The rest had done my leg good. No limp today. I was aware of it, aware of a gingerness in how I walked, but it wasn't paining me. On the contrary, my whole body relaxed, happy to get out and move. I passed an ancient church, modern shops, busses, cars, pedestrians. Budapest was hopping and it was exhilarating to be a part of it.

The downtown retail area was filled with every kind of shop, restaurant, and bar. Wide avenues were reserved for foot traffic, and I fell in line with all the others. I looked up restaurants nearby and found one with a Michelin star rating only a block away.

When I entered, the host, a dark-haired woman in her thirties, wearing a black dress and a perfect red lip, welcomed me in English. How did she know?

Glancing at my shorts and running shoes, she asked, "Do you have a reservation?"

Dang. The food smelled amazing. I didn't want to leave. "I don't. It's just me. Do you have a small table somewhere? I promise to eat a great deal of food, spend a lot of money, and leave quickly so I can continue sightseeing."

Eyebrows raised, her lips curled up. "How could I refuse such a generous offer?" She held up a finger. "One moment. Let me check."

She moved away from the front desk and I picked up a leather-bound menu, wishfully perusing. My stomach growled, but thankfully no one was close enough to hear it.

She returned a few minutes later. "It's on our terrace. I had them set up a small table for one in the corner. Does that work?"

Nodding eagerly, I said, "Yes, please."

She glanced at the menu in my hand, so I tried to pass it to her. "Keep it and come this way." We passed through the beautiful restaurant's, rough stone walls, white linen tablecloths, copper, wood, marble, a marriage of history and modernity.

When she took me upstairs and opened the door to the terrace, I held my breath a moment. The seating was basic, small wooden tables, metal chairs with funny, fluffy backs. That wasn't what had caught my attention, though. Glass walls and an open roof meant an unparalleled view of Budapest.

The only empty table on the terrace was at the end of a row of tables, butted up against the window. It would be uncomfortably narrow for two people, as there was a post behind the chair, keeping it from moving back. Since no one was with me, though, they'd pushed the table into the bench opposite the chair, giving me more room and a spectacular view in two directions.

"Your waiter will be right with you," she said and then headed back down to the first floor. I looked out over the rooftops of Budapest and fell a little in love. Directly in front of me were the twin spires of the ancient church I'd passed. Pulling up the map app on my phone, I discovered it was Our Lady of the Assumption, founded in 1046.

Sometimes it hit me at strange moments. Clive and that church were about the same age. To have lived through architectural movements, social eras, to have participated in them, and to still be here now was mind-blowing. I sometimes got overwhelmed by the now, and he'd lived through now, then, and way the hell back then. I understood why some of the really old supernaturals went crazy.

Lost in that thought, I jumped when the waiter spoke to me. "I'm sorry." I gestured out the windows. "My mind was elsewhere. What did you say?"

He nodded kindly, taking a moment to gaze at the view with me. "Have you had a chance to look over the menu?"

I'd already studied it downstairs. Handing it to him, I said, "I'd like the experience, please."

He tucked the menu under his arm. "Of course. Your first course will be right out."

The *experience* was a twelve-course meal set by the chef. It included dishes like smoked eel, foie gras, white asparagus, guinea fowl, and venison, each plated with its own sauce or accompaniment. It all sounded very fancy and delicious, and I was here for it.

While I waited, I texted Fyr. For a man who worked late nights, at either The Slaughtered Lamb or Stheno's place The Viper's Nest, this was still early morning. I didn't want to wake him. I just wanted a Fergus update when he had the time.

I received a text back almost immediately of Fergus and Alice, two impossibly large dogs lounging on the sidewalk at Fyr's feet.

> Fyr: Coco and I decided to hit the café around the corner. The barista loves the dogs and always gives them treats. How is it there?

> Me: Thank you for taking care of my boy! He looks happy. Things here are fine, except for all the vampires:) Budapest is beautiful. I'll send you guys some pics. I'm wandering around today.

> Fyr: Sounds good. Protect your neck.

Grinning, I put the phone away as my smoked eel arrived.

While I ate, I stared over the ledge, people watching those down on the street, and caught sight of a man in a black suit with a black shirt. On its face, that wasn't too weird, except it was a hot summer day and he looked like an annoyingly familiar Renfield. He stood across the street, in the shade of an awning, sneering up at the patio where I sat. Why the hell were they following me? If he thought he was going to intimidate me or make me lose my appetite, he was going to be sorely disappointed.

After another amazing meal, I paid and left, resigned to dealing with the creep across the street, but he wasn't there. I scanned the street in all directions but didn't see him. Great. Was he going to ruin my afternoon of sightseeing by skulking around?

Whatever. I began to wander, touring parliament and nearby parks. Budapest was known for their thermal baths. The city sits on a geographical fault line. Buda Hills crash up against the Great Plain, causing more than one hundred thermal springs to erupt. Consequently, there are huge palaces of mineral baths all around the city, overflowing with people relaxing in the hot water.

As that really wasn't my thing, I kept walking, enjoying the ease with which I could now move without the cast. Budapest was an amazing combination of awe-inspiring architectural master-pieces and plain, squat structures, depending on whether the building was designed while Habsburgs ruled or the Soviet Union.

Around the time I was wandering the Great Indoor Market Hall, tasting samples from a local butcher, I scented a wolf. Even over the chaotic scents of produce, meats, and spices, the wolf scent hit me hard and put me on edge. The hall was enormous and filled with people, so I couldn't pinpoint the wolf at first. As no one had jumped me, I continued as though I hadn't realized I'd gained another stalker.

After purchasing a substantial number of meat sticks from the nice butcher—don't judge me!—I headed for the door and caught the scent of a wolf again. A woman in jeans and a tank top stood at a stall of peppers and spices, which was smart. It almost hid her scent. There weren't many female werewolves in the world. As this one was following me, it only made sense that she was the one who spoke English on the phone last night.

I stepped up beside her and said, "Viktoria?" She had short reddish-brown hair and blue eyes that looked quite annoyed.

"I told him it was pointless to follow you," she said, "but we had to try."

"Understandable," I said, opening my bag. "Do you want a meat stick?"

Sighing, she looked in the bag, pulled one out, and said, "Where are we going now?"

NINE

The Fisherman and the Mermaid

Viktoria turned out to be an excellent tour guide. "In 1896, Hungary had a celebration of our one thousandth anniversary," she said, leading me around town. "At that time, Hungary was under Habsburg rule. The buildings and monuments were constructed to incorporate the number ninety-six. The opera house across the road has a grand stairway with ninety-six steps. Domes were built ninety-six meters high."

"Have you lived in Budapest all your life?" I asked.

Viktoria shook her head.

I guessed we weren't sharing private information about ourselves, which was fair. I wasn't sure why I liked her. Perhaps it was only because I'd never been able to chat alone with another female wolf before.

We walked in companionable silence for a few blocks, though my stomach began to twist. Was it the eel at lunch? The meat sticks? It felt like the blood had drained from my head and I was about to pass out.

We stopped in front of a huge Moorish building. "This is the Great Synagogue," Viktoria said. "And that over there is the Tree of Life memorial. It's dedicated to the half a million Hungarian

Jews who were killed in the Holocaust. They chose that spot because it sits on top of a mass grave."

"Oh my God," I murmured. No wonder I was getting light-headed, a necromancer at a mass grave. I did my best to breathe through the worst of it as my stomach cramped harder.

The tree was a weeping willow made of a silvery metal. She waved me forward, clearly impatient with the way I hung back. "Each of the metal leaves on the tree bears the name of a Jewish Hungarian killed by the Nazis. Come. Take a pebble, say a prayer, and add it to all the others in the base."

I did, coiling my magic around the pebble, wishing that those who had had their lives stolen from them found peace on the other side, away from the hatred and bigotry, the sadism and indifference.

"The tree symbolizes the mourning of this nation," she said.

Nodding, I considered taking a photo for Clive, as I had at the other spots we'd stopped, but I couldn't. Some things were too important, too profoundly moving to take pictures of.

We wandered back the way we'd come, both lost in our own thoughts.

"Can I ask you something?" I finally said.

She shrugged one shoulder. "You can ask."

"You don't actually believe I need to be watched, do you? That I'm going to do something to hurt the people of this town?" I kept my eyes on her, but she was looking out over the Danube.

"Do you see that?" she asked.

I followed her gaze. "The island in the river?"

She paused. "Part of the island is industrial, but the majority of it is a public park. A teenaged girl, pretty but painfully shy, was found over there at the base of the Danube Mermaid statue. She had a bruise on her neck with two small pinprick wounds. She was missing most of the blood in her body and she showed evidence of rape."

My stomach twisted again.

"One of our pack is a nurse," she continued. "He says the girl reeked of vampires. Multiple. Her parents fell apart. She was only fifteen. She disappeared on her way home from a school play and was found out there early the next morning by a jogger."

She turned to me, eyes blazing. "We know there are vampires in this town, but we can't find them. It doesn't make any sense, unless the nocturne has been magically hidden and spelled against us." She shook her head, looking back over the river. "They're blood-sucking demons, preying on the innocent, and you married one of them. We have no idea what you're capable of, so we'll watch."

We were quiet for some time before I finally responded. "My husband believes it must be someone or something throwing suspicion on vampires because they have a code of secrecy, and they stopped feeding on humans when bagged blood was invented."

Viktoria scoffed at that idea.

"Okay, most. Also, vampires can heal the wounds their bites inflict. A swipe of the tongue and no more wounds. It doesn't make sense. Why would they let the marks remain? Why leave evidence when the first rule of being a vampire is no one knowing about vampires?"

"Do you think she was the only one?" Viktoria asked, her voice hard. "Most are found alive and dazed, with no memory of what happened the night before, but the memory is there. Just under the surface. It returns in bits and pieces. In nightmares, the victims relive shadowy echoes that keep them forever on edge, consumed by fear. And they all reek of vampire. We know this town. We know who lives here. It's the leeches."

The horrifying part was I believed her. What the hell was going on at the Guild? "Can you show me where you found her?" I asked.

Jaw clenched, she said, "What's the point? It was last week. I doubt the scent is even there anymore."

"Okay, but I know more vampires than you do. If there's still a trace of her killer, I might recognize the scent."

She gave me an appraising look. "That's true. Wait here." She pulled her phone from her back pocket and walked away. Since I didn't speak Hungarian, she could have stood right next to me, shouting her conversation, and achieved the same level of privacy.

She returned a couple of minutes later. "Okay. I have permission to take you."

We walked back across the bridge and then backtracked over a pedestrian bridge to the island. Viktoria led me across the island, past people lying out in the sun and couples strolling, past a copse of tall trees and into a small clearing and a statue of a mermaid holding a shield.

Viktoria went to the front of the statue, to the fierce mermaid staring out over the river, her shield up to protect the people of Budapest. My guide pointed down to the grass directly beneath the raised shield.

I waved her back. I didn't want her scent muddling things more than was necessary. "I need you to tell me if anyone comes near. I can't have humans catching sight of me."

She looked confused but nodded.

Glancing around and considering how good phone cameras were, I decided to pull my arms out of my jacket and lift it over my head. Kneeling down in the spot she indicated, I shifted my head to my wolf's. I needed a heightened sense of smell and keen eyesight.

Scanning the grassy area first for the smallest clues, I found nothing. Closing my eyes, I dipped my snout to the ground and tried to weave my way through too many overlapping scents. Wolves. Cut grass—the gardeners had mowed recently—Humans. Blood. Decomposition.

A gust of wind almost blew my jacket away, but I held tight with one hand. I heard a gasp, so I assumed Viktoria caught sight of me. I couldn't let her reaction distract me because I'd caught it. Vampire. No. Vampires. And that little shit who'd taken us to that first room when we'd arrived.

The wolves were right. Vampires were killing the people of Budapest.

Shifting my head back, I slid my jacket back on to hide my axe and dropped onto my butt. What the hell had Clive and I walked into?

"Well?" she asked.

How did I answer? Damn it, I didn't owe any loyalty to killers. "You're right. It's vampires. Multiple. The only one I recognized was a human servant I met when we first arrived. I have their scents now. I'll figure out which ones."

"You must tell us where they den!" She pulled out her phone. "The sun is still out. We can go now."

I held up my hand to stop her. "I'm not going to do that. My husband is not part of this. I'm sure there are many others who also aren't. Let me handle this. Clive and I will find them and deal with them. You have my word."

She growled, "We. Don't. Trust. You."

I flopped back on the grass and stared up at the mermaid. "I probably wouldn't either. All I can tell you is that I will investigate and deal with the vampires involved. The human servant is already dead."

"You killed him?" She leaned forward, interest replacing disgust.

"Not me, no. He was an asshole and vampire justice is swift."

"Listen," she said, lowering her voice even more, "just tell me where they are. You and your husband leave tonight. We won't attack until tomorrow. Yes?"

That wasn't going to happen, no matter how much Viktoria wanted it. Still staring at the mermaid, I let out a long breath. Clive wasn't going to be happy because it was going to make me even more of a target, but I had to find the vamps who were preying on humans, stealing them away to feed on, rape, and kill. They had to be stopped. I couldn't pretend I didn't know.

"Tell me about the mermaid," I said.

"The mer—it's a statue. I don't care about that. You have to help us!" she hissed. "They're terrorizing our people."

I was lying on my axe, so it wasn't comfortable, but I stayed where I was. I almost laughed when I realized I was showing her my belly in this position. Deep down, I knew she was right, but I couldn't give the pack the Guild's location. No. I wouldn't do it.

"I hear you," I said, "but that isn't happening. I will find them, and I will deal with them. You don't have to believe that. I won't blame you for not, but I keep my promises." I clasped my hands over my stomach and took deep breaths in and out, steeling myself for what I'd need to do soon.

Wanting a diversion, I asked again, "Does she have a story? She appears quite determined to protect this city."

Viktoria paced and cursed. Luckily it was all in Hungarian, but I got the general idea. Eventually, she burned through the mad and dropped to the grass near me, leaning up against the statue's base.

"There are many stories of mermaids in the Danube," she began. "I'll tell you the one I know well and then you will give me some piece of information that we don't have."

I remained silent.

"The story begins in the dead of winter," she said. "Two fishermen were sitting in fishing huts on the frozen section of the river, repairing nets. The old man told the younger one a story of the Danube Prince, who had many children and lived in a tall castle made of green glass at the bottom of the river."

An underwater castle made of sea glass. I already liked this story.

"The prince was a cruel man," she continued, "often walking the shores dressed as a fisherman so he could capture unsuspecting humans and drag them to the depths of the river, where he stored the souls of his dead."

I was liking this story a lot less.

"Being a cruel prince," she said, "he was no better to his daughters, keeping them prisoners. Sometimes they escaped, though, and fishermen would hear them dancing and singing along the banks and in town."

Oh, good. They got away from him.

"They were cursed to return before daybreak," she said, "when the prince would beat them for their disobedience until the river ran red."

"Jeez," I grumbled, "this mermaid story sucks."

Ignoring me, Viktoria continued, "The younger fisherman shook his head, not believing a word of it, until a beautiful young woman approached the men. She wore a long gown, with flowers wrapped around her waist and woven into her long black hair."

"Pretty," I mumbled.

"She told them they needn't fear," Viktoria said. "She wasn't there to harm or steal from them. She wanted only to warn them that the ice was breaking, the snow in the mountains melting. A great rush of water would soon flood them. And then she disappeared.

"The men rushed to tell the others and though the huts were all washed away, the Danube Prince took no souls that night."

"Yay, flower lady. Wait. Is she the mermaid?" I asked.

"Guess," Viktoria said. "So, spring came and life got back to normal for all except the young fisherman. He had fallen in love with the dark-haired mermaid—"

"Ha!"

"—and searched relentlessly, rowing out into the middle of the river every night, trying to find her again."

"Aww." This story was a real roller coaster.

"One morning," she continued, apparently making her peace with my interruptions, "the old fisherman found the young man's boat washed up onshore and empty. Did the Danube Prince finally collect his soul? Did the young man find the mermaid and run off with her? Or did he, heartbroken at not finding her, offer himself up to the prince?"

Shaking my head, I stood up. "I'd like to introduce you people to the concept of happily ever after."

"That is not life," she said, standing as well.

"Maybe not," I said, "but there's something to be said for hope. We need to believe happy is a possibility to have the wherewithal to keep going."

She rolled her eyes. "Americans. We prefer to see what is and meet it head on. It is the only way to fight for justice. You hide your eyes and dream of fairytales."

"Ouch," I said, heading back for the bridge. "I want to see the Buda Palace. You can come with me or follow angrily at a distance. Whatever works for you."

TEN

One Less Monster in the World

Viktoria followed at a distance, still pissed I wasn't ratting out the vamps, no doubt. I climbed Castle Hill and explored the Palace and Matthias Church. Just outside the church was a courtyard called the Fisherman's Bastion. Since I no longer had my tour guide, I relied on the internet to tell me what I was looking at. Apparently, this was a gathering place for fishmongers back in the day. Now, though, it boasted incredible views, high above the river, looking out over all of Budapest.

Viktoria was still following me but seemed content to keep her distance. I ignored her and watched the sunset.

Good evening, darling? Where are you?

I'm at the Fisherman's Bastion, leaning against a stone arch, watching the sun dip below the horizon.

I wish I were with you.

Me too. I've been taking pictures all afternoon to share with you, so it will almost be like we're sightseeing together.

He was quiet for a moment. *I'm sorry you had to experience the city for the first time all on your own.*

I wasn't. I've had a wolf following me—the woman translating on the phone. I went up to her and introduced myself. She started acting as my

77

guide. She's super pissed off at me now, though. And I have an update for you that you're not going to like.

Are you all right?

I'm fine. It's about the vamps attacking humans in town. I'll explain it all when I see you. My current problem is how I get back into the Guild. The tunnel is one-way.

Yes, I asked about that. Sebastian wasn't terribly helpful, saying we should do what we did last night.

Well, you said it was a super-secret lair, so they probably don't want to advertise that people go in and out. It's cool. I can find a bench and hang out, watching the sunset and the lights sparkle on the Danube until it's dark enough for you to find me.

I don't like you being out there on your own with a hostile wolf surveilling you.

You should ask Vlad how he gets in and out. He might have a secret passage we don't know about. Oh. Speaking of which, Vlad can move around during the day. He was active while you guys were snoozing.

I have yet to see Vlad. He's not terribly social. As for being a day-walking vampire, I know. It's part of what makes him so threatening to others of our kind.

Hmm, creepy.

Indeed. I'll be there shortly. Stay safe, please.

Will do.

Where I was standing was the edge of the upper courtyard. There was a steep drop to another gathering spot below. The stairs down were far to the side. I wanted to just sit on the edge and wait, but I didn't like being in a compromised position where an annoyed Viktoria could shove me off. I'd survive, but a twenty-foot plunge on a recently broken leg concerned me.

I decided to stroll instead. The rest of the tourists were heading back down the hill, but I stayed. I took a picture of the huge statue of St. Stephen, Hungary's first king, on horseback. Taking the wide stairway down, I paused halfway and sat on the stone balustrade, enjoying the view.

I heard a whisper of steps behind me. "Viktoria?"

She stopped a few steps back. "Why are you just sitting here?"

"It's beautiful," I said quietly.

She came down, stopping a little past me before leaning against the thick wall I was sitting on. Her short reddish-brown hair blew in the breeze.

We shared the twilight in silence before she finally asked, "I don't understand. How could you have married a leech?"

Her tone conveyed confusion rather than derision, so I answered her. It was probably stupid on my part, but I thought if she understood, she might trust me to do what I promised: find the men who killed that poor girl. "I married Clive, a man I love very much. The vampire part isn't the important piece—well, I take that back. If he weren't a vampire, he never would have lived long enough to meet me."

"They're evil, sick predators." She shook her head. "I've been watching you all afternoon. You're polite. You step to the side to let others go. You hold doors open. You offer to take pictures for families." She stared at me. "You did it three times."

This conversation was quite odd. "That's the bare minimum of being a decent human being."

"Are you aware of how many people smile after interacting with you? Even the ones who don't speak English, who had no idea what you were saying to them, they smiled and watched you walk away. But you've tied your life to a filthy bloodsucker." She turned her head to stare at me. Her blue eyes were familiar, but I couldn't place why. The look of disgust on her face was all too familiar.

"Vampires, like humans, come in a wide spectrum," I said. "Some are monsters, and some are like my husband. He's kind, considerate, and there's no one I'd trust more at my back in a fight. He'd lay waste to legions to keep me from harm. More than that, though, he'd step back if he knew it was something I had to face on my own.

"Warriors wade in, swords drawn, and that's him. An ancient warrior who's had to suppress that drive to give me the room to grow and learn." Looking down at my wedding ring, I felt so lucky. "The fact that he survives on blood is the least interesting thing about him."

Viktoria turned away, staring out over the hills and river, her brow furrowed. "Then he is a rarity. The rest should burn in hell."

A silence grew between us, but it wasn't uncomfortable or hostile, just sad.

"This isn't only about that poor girl in the park, is it?" I asked.

She was quiet a little longer and then said, "My lover. Mira. She disappeared one evening. We were at that Bloody Ruin bar you were at last night. She went to the toilet and never came back. I went looking and smelled vampire near the toilet door.

"I panicked. Others had disappeared from an area that smelled like vampire. I called László and the pack helped me search. We scoured the town, went up into the hills, nothing."

Hands shaking, she stuffed them into the pockets of her jeans. "We found her the next morning. In an alley. Her shirt was inside out, her bra missing, and she stank of vampires. Multiple vampires.

"I took her to the clinic. They said she was fine. Anemic but fine." Viktoria turned her head to glare at me again. "She wasn't, though. She had nightmares. Every night she woke up screaming and talking about black eyes surrounding her, grabbing her, groping her, and her inability to move, to fight them off and get away. She was stuck in a body that wouldn't move."

She angrily brushed away tears. "It was too much. She couldn't live with the nightmares."

I understood being plagued by nightmares, as well as the impulse to make it all stop. "I'm so sorry. For you and for Mira."

She nodded slowly, staring out at the purpling sky. "They're all monsters."

I thought about it for a while. "Yeah. Some of them. But some of us are too. And some humans and some fae. There are all kinds of monsters in the world. Our job is to battle them when we find them."

"But you won't give us the information to do just that," she threw back at me.

I started to pull up my sleeve and then remembered. "I used to be covered in scars, from my neck to my feet. Horrible, thick scars. A wolf did that to me. He raped and tortured me for hours. There are lots of monsters."

Viktoria watched me. "And did your husband hunt him down?"

I shook my head. "I did. The wolf took me again. I was older, though, stronger. I wasn't a seventeen-year-old grieving her mother anymore. I broke free of his restraints and tore him to pieces." I took a deep breath. "One less monster in the world."

"Good," she said with a growl in her voice, happy I'd killed my rapist. After a moment, she asked, "What happened to all the scars?"

"I've had a very weird life and have met some very powerful people. One of them erased all my scars as a thank you for helping his son."

I studied my bare legs. "This is the first time I've worn shorts in almost eight years. I know the scars aren't there anymore, but I still feel them." I studied her a moment. "Can I ask? I don't meet many female wolves. How were you turned and how did you survive it?"

She let out a gust of air. "Wrong person. Wrong Place." She rubbed her forehead. "I was rebelling, I suppose. My parents were very strict." She glanced back at me. "I'm older than I look. Anyway, my parents adopted me from an orphanage in town. You asked me before if I'd always lived in Budapest. I didn't. I grew up in a village about ten miles to the north. My birth mother was from here." She pointed back toward the Guild. "From that big, condemned building on the hill. I was able to get that much information from the orphanage. They'd apparently told my parents the same. By the time I was looking, the asylum had already been closed down and boarded up."

She shook her head. "My adoptive parents were good people.

Kind, but they didn't know what to make of me. I always knew how I felt about other girls, but I could never tell them. When I was a teenager, I was seen kissing another girl behind the barn.

"The uproar," she continued, staring up at the twilight sky. "My father tried to erase it by marrying me off right away. I refused. There was lots of anger and gossip in the village. They all knew I'd been adopted from the asylum and therefore assumed I'd inherited my birth mother's insanity. Our neighbors, who'd known me all my life, now thought I was sick or possessed.

"Budapest, even more than a century ago, was a big city. I could lose myself here. And I did. Eventually, I even found a night-club and a community for others like me."

She crossed her arms over her chest. "I wasn't alone or broken. There were others like me, and they welcomed me in." She took a deep breath and blinked her eyes rapidly. "I'd found an accepting home. Other than missing my parents, I was happy.

"When I was in my twenties, I met a woman. Beautiful. Long dark hair, golden brown eyes, and a dimple. Just here," she said, pointing to her cheek. "We hit it off immediately. Love at first sight and all that. One night, we were in bed, and she bit me. I honestly didn't even realize it was that hard. I hadn't been thinking clearly. Anyway, after she left, I realized there was blood on my thigh, but all I could think was that I needed to tell her to be more gentle next time."

She blew out a breath. "I never saw her again. Heartbroken, I tried to understand what I'd done to drive her off. At the next full moon, grief turned to betrayal. She'd bitten me and run, leaving me to shift into a beast. Into this monster. So, I was different and alone all over again. Thankfully, László found me running in a panic in the hills. He brought me into the pack. Strange as it was, I'd found a home again. Acceptance."

"I'm sorry," I said. "Shifting all on your own, with no idea of what's going on, is terrifying. I'm glad he found you."

She nodded, lost in thought. "But you, even though you have packs the world over that would honor you and your abilities, you have these powerful friends who feel indebted to you, you still choose a leech as your mate." She couldn't get past that.

I looked at my wedding ring again and a calm came over me. "Clive is wily and patient. He watched over me for years, giving me little pushes, helping me to stand on my own two feet again, training me to defend myself. If I hadn't wanted him, he would have accepted that, but he still would have looked out for me while helping me defend myself. Regardless of how I felt about him, he needed to make sure I was never hurt again."

She studied my ring as I had. "And how long did he wait for you to heal?"

"Seven years," I said.

"I would have waited centuries for you." Clive descended the steps silently, stopping beside me and wrapping his arm around my waist. "That's quite a drop," he said, looking over the balustrade. "Fifty feet would do more than break your leg."

ELEVEN

Robin Hood & Little John

"I 'm perfectly safe and have excellent balance. Viktoria, this is my husband Clive. Clive, Viktoria of the Buda Pack."

Clive nodded. "It's good to meet you. The other members of your pack aren't pleased to have us in your territory. Do you feel the same?"

Viktoria stared at him a moment, braced for attack, and then slowly relaxed her stance. "About bloodsuckers? Yes. You?" She glanced at me again. "Probably. László is Alpha, though. We protect the people of Budapest, and vampires are a plague." She stared at him as though challenging him to disagree.

"We can be," he said. "It is our eternal shame."

She kept her eye on him, wary. I may have told her all sorts of lovely things about him, but vampires caused her lover's death and that wasn't something one made peace with easily.

He nudged me toward him, off the wall, glancing at the bag in my hand. "Good. You found a butcher. I'm afraid we need to get back now." He looked at Viktoria. "It was good to meet you."

"Can you give me your number?" I asked. "When I know anything for certain, I'll contact you."

She thought about it a moment and then took out her phone. Once we'd exchanged numbers, Clive gave me his back again. I climbed on and he gave Viktoria a shallow bow. "Good evening."

He moved so fast, I couldn't track it, though I knew he'd leapt over the wall and raced into the night.

Show-off.

Not at all. I didn't want her to follow us and by our leaping from a fifty-foot wall, she couldn't. If any pack members were watching, they'd know it was impossible for her to follow us.

I kept my head down and my eyes closed. The speed and movement made me seasick. *Is it any wonder I love you?*

Only to the rest of the world. Hang on tight. We're going over the fence again.

A moment later, he was sliding across the marble entry floor like he was wearing socks on a freshly polished floor.

A Renfield closed the door. "The gathering will begin in twenty-three minutes."

Clive helped me down and then took my hand. "Noted. But as we're not clocking in for work, I don't believe we need to be quite so precise with our arrival."

We made a point of walking leisurely back to our room, me swinging my bag of meat sticks. It was a message to the minion that we didn't take orders from him.

I like the shorts. Your legs are warm from the sun.

I feel uncomfortable when I think about it, or when that Renfield looked at my legs, but for most of the day, I forgot about them.

Progress. Hopefully, you didn't burn.

I looked down as I walked. *I don't think so. I need to tell you about a teenaged girl they found in a park, bled dry with bite marks in her neck…*

As I got changed, Clive sat on the couch and listened, his expression darkening. *You're sure?*

Nodding, I told him, *I recognized the Renfield's scent as well as a layering of vampires. I didn't know the vamps, but I haven't met everyone yet.*

Sam, this makes no sense. This is the Guild. They make the rules everyone has to follow. How can it be Guild members flouting secrecy and killing humans in their own backyard?

Maybe it's one of those do-as-I-say-not-as-I-do type deals. I went to the couch and sat beside him. *There's something rotten here. I felt it before we even entered this place. Maybe it's only a few people and the rest of the Guild isn't aware.*

Clive shook his head. *It would be impossible to hide something like that. We'd all smell the humans and the blood, the sex, if the wolves are correct about the assault.* He stared at me as though willing me to be mistaken and then his shoulders slumped. *I want it too much.* Nodding slowly, he said, *Perhaps all didn't participate, but they knew and did nothing. All right. We know now. Let's figure out who and stop it.*

Leaning forward, I gave him a kiss. *We'll do just that.* Standing, I went back to the closet and began speaking aloud again. "Audrey said pants were okay to wear." I held up a pair of charcoal slacks.

"You can wear whatever you want. Leave the shorts on, if you'd like. I've told you. You aren't a vampire and therefore needn't follow our rules."

I stepped into the trousers. "I don't want to embarrass you."

"Hush. After all the lovely things you said about me to the wolf, I'd be one of those monsters to criticize your ensemble." He put his feet up in the coffee table, his attention focused on partially clad me.

"You eavesdropped? Rude." I pulled on a soft cashmere sweater in sea glass green. It reminded me of the mermaid's story and my hope that she and the fisherman had found their happy ending.

"Unintentionally. I'm attuned to your heartbeat and was listening to find you."

I put on a tumbled sea glass necklace, earrings, and bracelet set.

"Pretty. I haven't seen those before," Clive said.

"I found them in the window of a little shop right after I'd purchased the sweater. Audrey said she thought they were perfect." I was starting to feel a little less weird about spending money. Were they gems? No. But they were lovely and made me happy.

I stepped into charcoal gray suede heels that matched the trousers and turned back to Clive. "Okay?"

He stood, gathering me up in his arms, and kissed me. Eventually, he leaned back, his thumb brushing over my cheek. "Perfect. You got some sun on your face too. Sunkissed, that's what you are."

Grinning, I said, "I'm pretty sure I'm vampire-kissed." I picked up my phone and stuffed it in my bag. "Ready when you are."

By the time we got to the meeting room, it was quite crowded. I heard Clive swear under his breath but couldn't see what had upset him. The voices in the room were louder than last time. If vamps drank alcohol, I'd wonder if some of them were drunk.

The lights flickered as a Renfield came by and offered Clive a goblet of blood. "Master thought you'd prefer this to our other offerings this evening. If not, please feed at your leisure."

Clive glared at the Renfield, taking the goblet from his tray. "I don't care for tonight's fare." He tipped the cup to his lips and swallowed it down before returning it to the tray, all while blocking me from the room.

"We have our answer. Let me deal with this, love," he said. "I promise I'll put an end to it." Clive's expression was so strange, part fury, part concern.

"Deal with what? What's wrong?" I asked, looking over his shoulder.

Clive's eyes went vamp black as the color drained from his face and he clutched his stomach.

What is it? I grabbed his arm, trying to lead him away from all the others.

Poison. The blood was poisoned.

I went lightheaded. *What do we do?*

Try not to die, I suppose. Jaw clenched, his fangs poked out from between his lips.

That's not funny! Will my blood help? It might help dilute the bad blood. Bite me.

He lurched to the side, but I caught him and kept him upright. *Do it. Drink my blood.* I wrapped my arms around him and felt a slight prick in my neck.

Looking over his shoulder, I flinched. The women from the asylum, threadbare gowns stained in ways I didn't want to think about, stared at me with blank gazes, mouths agape. One woman, who was missing patches of snarled hair, tugged mindlessly at a greasy hank and pointed at the other side of the room. Another scratched at her arm with torn nails, ripping at her skin. Blood dripped on the floor at her feet. The screaming woman I'd seen the day before opened her mouth, teeth gray and rotting, but made no sound. Instead, she lifted her arm, pointing as well.

Chills ran down my spine. The lights flashed and the asylum patients were gone. What was in their place, though, was far worse. This had been what had caused Clive to swear as we walked in.

Standing like zombies in the room were humans, women and a few men, stripped naked to the waist, with vampires groping them while they fed. This was what they'd done to Viktoria's lover Mira, to that poor teenaged girl whose body they'd dumped in the park.

A vampire leered at me while he bit a woman, running his hands down her body. I wasn't sure I could control the howl in my head. I was holding Clive. I couldn't hurt him, but my claws poked at my fingertips.

I knew they were vampires. I knew they survived on blood, but bagged blood had been the practice for decades. If these vampires wanted to feed from live donors, there were rules. Clive had explained it all to me long ago. They couldn't take too much and leave the human too weak to carry on. They had to be quick and discreet, mesmerizing the human so they remembered nothing. And they weren't to do anything that could expose the existence of vampires. These bastards had stolen humans from town as party favors.

When the leering vamp squeezed the woman's breast while staring at me, I lost it. I needed to shift and kill everyone in the room. I hadn't been able to eviscerate those two attendants who'd raped Léna. I couldn't go back and kill my own rapist again, but I could fuck up these assholes real good.

I found their blips in my head and a second later, the leering vamp's dust settled on the floor. Another, who was taking off a teen's pants, turned to dust a moment later. Death was too easy for some.

Vampires edged away from the unwilling blood donors, shooting looks at one another, trying to determine who had the power to kill like that.

Cadmael! I shouted in my head. He'd been leaning against a far wall, gazing at the grotesque display, but he turned when I called him. *Clive's been poisoned.* Was I sure Cadmael wasn't the one who had done the poisoning? No, but I needed help. Clive trusted him, so I put aside my own misgivings.

I knew my eyes had lightened to wolf gold. Feeling woozy when Cadmael arrived at my side, I moved Clive's head, so he stopped feeding and I said, "Take care of him for a minute."

I stalked across the room and pulled up the shirt hanging from the first woman's waist and guided her toward the door. I left her beside Cadmael and went for the next. When a vamp stepped in front of me, I walked around him. "No. You will not do this," I snarled, pulling women away from black-eyed vamps with their fangs bloodstained. I think they were so preoccupied by who had just handed two of them their final deaths, they ignored me murmuring to the women and helping them dress. The lights flickered again and I looked up at the chandelier. "Quit it!"

I pulled a man away from a vamp who had had about enough of my shit. He leaned in to attack me, but I slammed him in the stomach with all my strength, making him double over and vomit up the blood he'd ingested.

"I knew I should have brought my sword," I muttered, collecting the humans they'd stolen, helping them put their clothes to rights. Thankfully, vampires were pretty much all out for themselves, so no one jumped me to retaliate for the humiliated vamp who had just let a wolf get the better of him.

"You steal people, feed from them, sexually assault them, and then dump them in alleys as though their lives are meaningless. You might as well shout from the rooftops that vampires are among them!"

A Renfield reached out to grab me, but I broke his arm while throwing him across the room. The crack of bone was loud in the suddenly silent room. Vamps sidestepped the minion, letting him slam into the wall.

My brain felt like it was on fire but I tried to rein it in, not wanting to hurt the already traumatized humans. "So arrogant and careless. The townspeople will realize what's up here in this old asylum. Expect a modern-day mob with pitchforks, otherwise known as drone strikes. Do you honestly think they'll hesitate to level this hellhole on top of you?"

"They are vermin before us," shouted the asshole whose dinner I had taken away from him. "We are greater, more powerful than puny humans. Or bitch dogs who have no place in this Guild."

He got lots of agreeing grunts on that one.

"So powerful," I sneered, helping a man put his t-shirt back on. There were ten humans and I'd been pulling them all toward the door. "And while you're napping during the day, they can break in and stake you."

I heard a click at my ear. For the second time this week, someone had pulled a gun on me. I was too angry to think about consequences. If I hadn't been weakened by feeding Clive, I probably would have crushed as many blips in the room as I could before they took me down.

I was fast, though, especially when I was pissed off. I didn't think. I just reacted, snatching the gun away and slamming it into the Renfield's head. Judging by the looks of shock on the vamps, they hadn't thought me a real threat, more like tonight's entertainment. The expressions of more than a few became pensive as they seemed to assess my threat.

"Sam." Clive was pleading with me to stop. Weakened as he was, he couldn't protect me from all of them and he knew they were about to silence me for good.

"Don't worry. I can take care of myself. I'm getting these people out of here."

I heard a thump behind me. "And if she requires any help," a man in heavily accented English said, "I'd be more than happy to lend a hand."

I turned to find the dark-haired vampire with the large mustache.

"We'll be like Robin Hood and Little John," he said with a smirk, "stealing from the undead and giving to the living."

TWELVE

Where's Fergus When You Need Him?

"Now wait a minute," Sebastian said, striding toward our group by the door. "You can't take them. We have a protocol in place."

I had my arm around a tiny girl who couldn't have hit her teens yet, ushering her with the others. I spun back, eyes bright gold. "Does your protocol include the abduction and molestation of children? Do you kill the ones who prove too difficult? I've heard people wearing misbuttoned clothing are found dead in alleys in this town. Is that part of your protocol?"

He opened his mouth to respond but said nothing, his eyes turning black.

"And does your protocol," I continued, "allow for your victims to remember just enough of what was done to them that they are haunted by nightmares? How many have taken their own lives because they couldn't live with the trauma they'd endured here?"

I took a step forward to separate his smug head from his blood-sucking body, but a hand fell on my shoulder.

"Take the child out with the others, yes?" Vlad said. "I'll deal with this. Wait for me at the door."

He was right. The humans were the priority right now, not my rage. I looked into her blank eyes and felt my own filling with tears. Nope. I needed to hold it together and get these people out.

Cadmael beside him, Clive was walking under his own power, helping to keep the humans moving forward. He paused. *The tunnel door?*

He's not going to want us to compromise the Guild's secrecy, so I assume so.

He kept them all going down the main hall.

How are you feeling? I asked.

Like I've been dead for a thousand years.

I'm sorry.

It serves me right for not being more careful. It's been a few centuries since I was poisoned. I'd forgotten how painful it is.

Is there anything more we can do?

You've already done it. Your blood stopped the cramping. I'll recover.

Vlad met us when we reached the door. He opened it and we all filed in. When it closed, though, he didn't head down the stairs, instead pointing to the right.

Waving his hand in front of what appeared to be an earthen wall, he triggered a mechanism and a panel slid open to a narrow passage. The humans couldn't see in the inky dark, so I turned on the flashlight on my phone and Clive did the same. We both aimed our lights at the ground as Vlad led the way.

"I've seen no listening devices here," he said. "I don't believe the current Guild members even know this passage exists, so we should be safe enough."

"I didn't know," Cadmael said, "and I've been a member almost since the beginning."

"Good," Vlad said.

One of the humans staggered and Cadmael reached out to keep him upright and moving.

"Where does this tunnel let out?" I asked.

"Behind the Bloody Ruin. There is a small youth hostel nearby. Someone is at the front desk around the clock. We'll leave them there."

"Okay, but you have to wake them up. Otherwise, they'll be at the mercy of human predators. And this little one has to have family frantic, trying to find her." We couldn't just leave a group of mesmerized people in front of a hostel and take off. They were our responsibility now.

"We won't, darling," Clive said. "I realize it's foremost in my mind right now, but perhaps poisoning would work for a cover story. They'd all eaten at a kiosk and got sick, feverish. That might explain the lost time."

"I'll call Viktoria. It's the pack's job to protect the people of Budapest. They can escort them to different clinics," I suggested.

"Yes," Vlad agreed. "The wolves can take them to the proper authorities. Wait until we're close to the hostel and then call."

We were silent for the rest of the walk. Finally, Vlad stopped us. He looked at Clive and Cadmael. "Poisoned sausages? Vomiting, diarrhea, fever, too sick to leave the public toilet?"

"Yes," Clive agreed. "Then too disoriented to know where they were and how to get back. Do they have wallets? IDs?"

"No," Vlad said. "That's the first thing they destroy so there's no link to the Guild."

"You two are the most powerful of your kind in the world." I didn't want to use the word *vampire* in front of the humans. "Why didn't you stop this? What's the point of having that power and authority if you're not going to use it to do the right thing?"

Cadmael glared at me. "I haven't been here in at least a decade. I only came to support Clive."

"That's a cop-out, if I've ever heard one," I said as he glared at me.

"Sam, we're on the same side. Cadmael is an ally," Clive said.

"No, she's right," Vlad argued. "I knew what they did, and I chose to absent myself rather than stop it. It's dangerous and plays into the desire some have to openly rule over humans."

"Let's get rid of these humans before we have this discussion," Cadmael said, sounding as though he disapproved of everyone and everything, but especially me.

The vamps got to work, mesmerizing each one of the humans to forget what had happened, laying over a new memory of being sick from food poisoning. When they were done, Clive and I walked them out of the passage—the tunnel door was hidden behind a rusted dumpster—and then over to the hostel. It had a light by the door, glowing on the dark street.

I called Viktoria. It took her a moment to answer.

"Yes?"

"Sorry to call so late, but I need your help. What happened to that teenager was happening again tonight."

"What?" Her anger was palpable through the phone. There were multiple growls in the background. Good. Hopefully that meant the pack was together.

"We got them out, but they need protection until the effects wear off and they're feeling more themselves." The little one beside me started to shiver, so I wrapped an arm around her shoulder. "One of them is a child, so there's probably a search party looking for her."

I had to pull the phone from my ear when an anguished howl pierced my eardrum.

"Where are they?" she demanded.

"We're outside the youth hostel on the street behind the Bloody Ruin where I met László and his friend. I'll wait with them. I don't want anything to happen before you get here."

Angry voices shouted over one another but I didn't understand the language, which in this case was probably for the best. The phone went dead and I pocketed it.

You should go. They're very angry. I said to Clive.

So I heard. Darling, they're not happy with you either. I don't want to leave you here alone.

I thought about it a moment. *Stay nearby. I'll need you to get back in the Guild anyway, but your presence here will only make them angrier.*

As I agree, I'll go, but know I'm close if they decide to take out their anger on you.

There was a bench, so I sat a few of them on it while we waited.

A couple began rubbing their stomachs. One put his hand over his mouth. They were coming out of it. The wolves arrived as two shot up and vomited into nearby bushes.

Viktoria came straight to me. "What did you do to them?"

"I got them out, with the help of three vampires who had nothing to do with any of it. They were disgusted by what the others were doing."

She scoffed at that, drawing the child away from me. She spoke to her in Hungarian.

As quietly as possible, I said, "They were given the memory of eating tainted meat from a street vendor and then being violently ill in a public restroom. They're coming out of it now and their stomachs are cramping."

"Still, you cover for them. They attack children and you shield the monsters," she sneered. "You're as bad as they are. I should have known only garbage associates with leeches."

László snarled something in my direction. Viktoria gave me a look of disgust, waving me away, while she took the child from my side, ushering her to the larger group.

I walked down the road and turned toward the river, away from the asylum. Clive would find me. Right now, I just wanted to breathe clean air and walk. I understood I was the only one they could curse for what had been done to those poor people. I got it, but I still felt like crap.

Eventually, I made my way to the Chain Bridge. Leaning on the rail, I looked over the edge as the Danube rushed beneath. Lights from the bank danced on the water. If Fergus were here—and my leg was strong enough—we could go for a run and I could shake off this melancholy. Alas, my sweet boy was half a world away.

Needing to focus on anything other than tonight, I stared at the water, wondering about the cruel prince, his glass castle and mermaid daughters. I needed a happy ending. I hoped she'd escaped with her fisherman.

Clive leaned on the rail beside me. "You know what they said was aimed at my kind, not you, right?"

"Yeah." I shrugged. "The people are getting taken care of, which is all that matters." I turned my head to study him. "I don't think there's any coming back from what I did in there." Thunking my head against his shoulder, I added, "I'm sorry. I wanted that Counselor job for you so badly."

He wrapped his arms around me. "Don't be silly. If you hadn't done it, I would have. Unfortunately, I was indisposed at the time."

Standing straight, I tried to check his color in the light of the bridge. "How are you feeling?"

"Less like writhing in pain for a few hours, thanks to you." He kissed me and I was finally able to relax. He was going to be okay.

"As far as the rest of them are concerned," he continued, "you entertained some profoundly bored vampires and gave them something to talk about."

"I guess there's that. Do they know I'm the one who—"

He kissed me again. *Never mention that. As far as they're concerned, it could have been me, Vlad, or Cadmael. No one thinks a werewolf could destroy a vampire like that, and we don't want to do or say anything that makes them suspect, all right?*

Okay. I broke the kiss and then gave him another quick one before resting my head on his chest. *If I didn't screw up your chances, shouldn't you be in one of those meetings?*

I would imagine it's chaos right now. Two are dead. I wasn't watching, so I have no idea if they were Guild members or underlings. Either way, there'll be upheaval.

I've been thinking about the timing of the poisoned goblet. Do you think they took advantage of the creepy, Kubrick-esque spectacle to try to kill you, or was the spectacle created in order to kill you?

A chicken or egg situation.

I squeezed him around the middle. *I mean is it one person trying to eliminate you or did the Guild invite you here to kill you?*

We've been causing trouble in the vampire world of late. He kissed the top of my head. *So I've been wondering the same thing. I was under the impression Sebastian was an ally, but he's been acting strangely.*

Could that Ava chick be messing with his head? She seemed pretty sketchy to me.

Possibly, but I wouldn't have thought her strong enough.

Maybe she's only pretending to be weak. Or maybe *she's actually ancient and just escaped from a prison created eons ago to hold her. She had to dig her way out, as the prison was part of a hidden city far beneath the earth. No one knows her because she's been chained up longer than any of you have been alive. She's biding her time, learning about this new world, and about the vamps who will soon be her servants.*

Hmm, less possible. You need to listen in on one of our meetings and then tell me how she's an all-powerful mastermind.

Done and done. Let's head back so I can eavesdrop.

THIRTEEN

Don't Make Me Have Him Hurt You

We made our way back up the hills, along empty streets. A block from The Bloody Ruin, Clive paused and listened. *Dogwalker, I believe.*

A moment later, a woman walking her German Shepherd appeared around the corner. The dog growled at us, not that I blamed him. I'm sure we deserved it. The woman gave us a nervous nod. Clive said something to her in Hungarian and she smiled, the tension easing in her shoulders.

We turned up the next road and ducked behind The Bloody Ruin. Clive waved his hand, now wearing a thick gold ring with a large ruby in the center. The passage opened and we stepped in before the door slid shut again.

"Cool ring," I said, turning on my phone's flashlight.

"Vlad let me borrow it so I could get you back inside more easily. He wants you to keep it while we're here." He took it off his finger and handed it to me.

The ring was weighty, the dark ruby huge. "Really?" I shined the light on it. "This looks like a family heirloom that I do not want to lose. Maybe you should hold on to it." I tried to pass it back, but he wouldn't take it.

"Sorry, love. I was given very specific instructions. Consider it a compliment. He wants to make sure you can get in and out whenever you need."

"What about him? Doesn't he need this?" I asked.

Clive put the ring on my thumb and then held my hand. "He says he has other ways."

We walked quietly for a while, having to move single file because of the narrowness of the tunnel. Clive changed the hand he reached back to grab mine with, so I had to switch hands with my phone.

It hit me why he might not want to hold that hand. "Does it bother you that I'm wearing Vlad's ring?"

"Very much, but it would bother me more if you couldn't move freely in this mausoleum of vampires. Your safety is more important than territorial jealousy."

We walked on in silence.

"You know," I said, "it's actually a pretty ugly ring, if you really look at it."

He turned and gave me a big kiss. "It is, isn't it? Brutish. Lacking in subtlety and beauty."

"My thoughts exactly," I said.

"I do so love you. Now bring that hideous hunk of junk over here and get us out." He stepped back to make room for me.

I waved my hand as I'd seen Vlad do it and the panel slid open. Cadmael and Vlad were leaning against opposite walls, silently waiting.

"That took longer than I'd thought," Vlad said.

I felt my cheeks pink. "Sorry! That was my fault. I didn't realize anyone was waiting for me, so I went for a walk."

"She needed a moment," Clive said. "The wolves took out their anger on her."

"Always anger with wolves," Cadmael said.

"Standing right here," I grumbled.

White teeth shone in the dim light as Vlad grinned at me.

"Besides," I said, "they had reason to be upset."

"True." Vlad pushed off the wall, the humor leaving his face as he addressed Clive. "Have you been approached by anyone grumbling about the Guild being too soft, too content to hide our kind?"

Clive looked between the two men. "Why do you ask?"

I stuffed my hands in my pockets with a sigh. "Always so cagey. Conversations take forever with you guys. How about if you all accept that you respect and trust one another and then just say what you want to say?"

Clive shook his head, but Vlad laughed.

"And this is what you get," Vlad said, "when you take a wolf to mate."

"Yes," Cadmael said disapprovingly.

"No, no," Vlad began, pointing a finger at Cadmael. "I meant no insult. I appreciate the frankness of wolves like this one. She didn't stop to weigh the consequences of shouting at vampires or taking away their food. She did what she felt was right and was ready to deal with the consequences. Because of that—even though I don't know her—I trust her more than either of you."

Speaking to Cadmael, he added, "but you said *yes* as though you were agreeing with my disparagement of her. Why is that?"

"Cadmael thinks I'm a vicious dog who isn't terribly bright, a gold-digger, and far beneath Clive," I answered for him.

"No," Clive said. "My *friend* would never think, let alone say, anything so cruel to the woman I love more than anything in this world." He may have been answering me, but his focus was on Cadmael. "My *friend* would never do anything to make my wife think she was unwelcome in his presence."

Cadmael looked every inch the Mayan warrior, eyes fierce, jaw clenched as he stared past Clive at me.

"People are allowed to dislike me, Clive," I interrupted. "You two have been friends for a very long time." I pulled Clive away from the stare down. "It's fine. I already pissed off a room full of vampires out there." I gestured toward the heavy metal door. "Don't make me the reason you lose a close friend and ally."

"I don't think those things," Cadmael finally said, his voice deep in the charged silence. "I worry. In the last year he has fought wolves, countless fae assassins, demons, and scores of our own kind." He shook his head. "As Vlad said, you jump in to do what you believe is right, but who is left fighting to keep you alive?"

Clive started to speak, but I squeezed his hand. Cadmael had the right to say what he needed to say.

"You *are* my friend," Cadmael continued, looking at Clive, "someone I value a great deal, and there are precious few of those." Turning to me, he said, "I don't hate you. I worry that his loving you will mean his final death."

I let out a harsh breath, feeling that prediction like a punch in the gut.

"I'm already mostly dead," Clive said.

I looked up and found him watching me, his eyes crinkling. He'd used my old joke to take the sting out of Cadmael's words. The cramping in my stomach relaxed.

You and I know better, he told me.

I kissed him and then turned back to Cadmael. "This last year has been nuts. I'll give you that, but most of it has had nothing to do with me. Leticia had been causing trouble in the nocturne long before Clive and I got together."

"Because he'd killed Leticia's mate for not protecting you," Cadmael countered.

"Oh, someone's been listening to gossip. Clive killed Étienne because he made a habit of ignoring Clive's orders. What would you do if one of your vampires consistently rolled his eyes at your wishes and did whatever he wanted?"

Cadmael didn't respond, but we all knew the answer.

"Étienne was killed after he blew off guard duty and I was almost killed by a kelpie. That part's true. But is it why he was killed, Clive?" I asked.

"I gave him his final death because a girl—a seventeen-year-old who'd been brutalized and dumped in a city where she knew no one—was under my protection. I'd informed the nocturne of her status and he ignored my orders to guard her, as he had done before, because he believed a scarred little wolf wasn't worth his time."

"That wasn't his decision," Cadmael said.

"No," Clive agreed. "It was not. The only reason she survived was because I heard her scream when the kelpie crushed her and began taking bites out of her. Leticia, Lafitte, Aldith, Garyn can all be traced back to me killing the Atwood men for what they'd done to my sister a thousand years ago. I will point out the one who's stood by my side through every battle this past year, fighting enemies much older and stronger, is this one right here. As Sam says, you don't have to like her, but I won't have her disrespected."

Cadmael was silent, studying me. I felt him push on my mind, trying to read it, but I smacked him away and slammed down the mental barriers, my candy-coating keeping him out.

The anger disappeared from his face, but I didn't believe it. I still felt a strange tangle of emotions radiating from him. "My apologies," he said.

"Accepted," I shot back. "Good. That's done." I turned to Vlad. "What were you saying?"

Shaking his head, he crossed his arms over his chest. "So glad that's been settled. I asked Clive if he'd been approached by anyone wanting the Guild to loosen our restrictions."

"I have," Clive said, wrapping an arm around me. "In subtle and not so subtle ways. I've had people refer to the recent battles in San Francisco, wondering if the Guild had responded, if I thought the Guild had the right to censure us. It was done in a way that could have been mere gossip, but the gleam in their eyes told a different story. I believe they wanted to know how far they in turn could go before the Guild would step in."

"One said it was nice for Clive and Russell that Eli was such an absent Counselor, as neither had to deal with any Guild reprisals," I volunteered.

Clive nodded. "As though we had been the aggressors, bringing in a legion of vampires and starting brawls in the streets.

We did what we could to mitigate the spectacle, altering the memories of those who saw us."

"If anyone deserved to be punished, it was that whack job Garyn," I added.

"I believe we took care of that for the Guild," Clive said.

"Yeah, we did." I put up my hand and he high-fived me.

Cadmael looked pained by our exchange.

I leaned into Clive. "Sorry. I think I'm losing you your street cred with the other vamps."

"I'll survive," he replied.

"Will you?" Cadmael asked. "Someone poisoned you tonight."

"Yes," Clive said. "We discussed that on our walk tonight. Was it the Guild, as far as either of you know?"

"The Guild?" Cadmael asked, his brow furrowed.

"We wondered," I said, "if Clive was getting slapped down by the Guild for, well, the stuff we've just been talking about."

Vlad scoffed. "Have you any idea how many dead can be put to my name?" He shook his head. "Garyn should have known who she was going up against, the alliances you've forged. Stupid vampires deserve final death."

"A faction within the Guild?" Clive asked.

Vlad and Cadmael shared a look.

"If so," Cadmael said, "they're being very quiet about it. Of course, they know I consider you an ally. Vlad, though, could best be described as your belligerent acquaintance. Has anyone approached you about Clive?" he asked Vlad.

Vlad shook his head. "No. And until a couple of days ago, they would have found me an interested audience."

Clive tilted his head. "What changed?"

Vlad grinned under his heavy mustache. "I'd always thought you a pretty playboy. Powerful, sure, but no one serious. I've been paying attention to you lately and I've realized you cultivate that"—he gestured to all of Clive—"that act so opponents underestimate you. It's easier for you to strike when they aren't expecting aggression."

"Nope," I said. "That's not him."

Clive kissed my temple. "It's alright, darling. I've never liked him either."

Vlad laughed at that. "And that's what changed. I'd heard you'd taken a mate and assumed it was another one of your perfect women, but then I saw this one."

"Hey," I interrupted. Looking at Clive, I grumbled, "You're right. I don't like him either."

Clive smiled and hugged me. "Not so fast, love. I believe a compliment is coming. If not, I'll kill him for you."

"Make it hurt," I whispered. We both turned to Vlad, and I gave him my suspicious squinty look.

"You're beautiful, yes, but not like his other lovers—"

"Okay. That's it. Go kick his ass!" I stepped back so Clive could get him.

Clive studied Vlad a moment. "You're remarkably bad at this. I feel certain a compliment is coming for my wife and yet you're doing it in a way that is incredibly rude." He turned back to me. "I honestly believe he's merely awkward, rather than intentionally insulting. Let's give him a moment to take his foot out of his mouth. If he doesn't, I'll deliver his death in whatever manner you see fit."

"Deal," I said, and we returned our attention to the Impaler.

He looked down at the ground, muttering something in another language. "I miss that." When he looked back up, he focused on me. "My third wife, my heart, was a werewolf. You remind me of her. When I watch you two together, I see it, what I had with her. I recognize what it's like to constantly be in contact, touching, kissing, talking. He boasts of you fighting by his side. His partner. His wife.

"Yes, you're quite beautiful," he continued, "but that's not it. I don't see mere appreciation in his gaze. He loves you completely, as I loved my wife. So, my opinion of him has changed," Vlad said.

I felt suddenly teary, though I kept it in check. Patting Clive's arm, I said, "Stand down. He can live."

FOURTEEN

Let the Undead Smack Down Begin!

"So, who are these anti-Guild people, and are they causing real problems or just taking the edge off their boredom by complaining?" I asked.

"There is a contingent of my kind," Clive began, "that misses feasting on entire villages."

"Good times," I deadpanned. "Wasn't that also when vampire hunting was a valid career choice?"

"Indeed," he said. "They want the Guild to loosen up their restrictions."

"It's not just feeding," Cadmael said. "They want a place in politics so that laws can be changed and created to benefit us."

"There aren't already vampires in politics?" I asked. "That's surprising."

Clive led me over to a stone outcropping. "Sit down. Rest your leg. And, no. Do you know of any politicians who only campaign at night? Be a bit suspicious."

Laughing, I sat. "Good point."

"We work behind the scenes, influencing those in power," Cadmael continued.

"Okay," I said, "but those are usually the ones with the real power. And they don't have to shake hands at a county fair at midday in June."

"Which is why they're still grumbling and not acting," Clive said.

"They've progressed past complaining," Cadmael informed him. Glancing at Vlad, he added, "We understand why you had to kill Garyn and her people. The problem is that it's created a vacuum in our power structure. For all her faults, Garyn firmly believed we had to remain hidden from the human world. Given how she kept all her children in line, they agreed with her."

"Most of the vampires you handed their final death," Vlad said, "were Masters. We have positions in the Guild to fill, but more important are all the City Master positions that are vacant. Into that vacuum, there are a flood of vampires who are sick of hiding in the shadows. It's not just politics. They want humans to know and fear them."

Clive and I were silent for a moment and then I blurted out, "Are they undead idiots? Have they seen how humans deal with the things they fear? Jeez, if you want the military in every country around the world working together, just announce that vampires are real and they want to be in charge."

"I must admit," Clive said, "that shocks me, much like what we just witnessed in the meeting room shocked me. Is this contingent behind the abduction and murder of humans for entertainment? This isn't the Dark Ages. There are eight billion humans on this planet and the vast majority have smart phones that link them with the internet and social media. In that heightened hysteria over the existence of vampires, how long would it take for a video to be posted of a dark streak across the asylum property with a door opening and slamming before hunters, armed with the latest weapons, break in, kill us during the day, and then blow up the building in case they missed anyone?"

"There's going to be an app within an hour of the announcement," I said, "to share nocturne locations and advice on killing you guys. Video tutorials will turn everyone into weekend vampire hunters. They can't be that arrogant, that shortsighted."

"They can and are," Cadmael replied.

"You guys kill each other for being crazy and possibly breaking the secrecy rule," I said. "Can't you do the same for stupidity?"

"Again, can and do," Vlad said. "The problem with whisper campaigns is knowing whether people are just talking or if they're actually trying to recruit others. We need our people to respect and abide by the Guild's dictates, so we can't exterminate without reason, not unless we want to drive more to their cause."

The vampires considered the problem silently. I let them. I was more concerned about the attempt on Clive's life. "Sorry, but back to the poisoning. Are we thinking one of these disgruntled, I-miss-raping-and-pillaging vamps had his Renfield give Clive the poison? Because if so, I have a candidate to suggest."

"Vamp, Renfield? Why does she talk like this?" Cadmael asked.

"She's right here," I said, "and Vamp-ire. That one's pretty obvious."

"And Renfield was that hideous, scurrying human in that book about me," Vlad said.

"You didn't come off well in that book, did you?" Clive smirked.

"Don't make me make your beautiful wife a widow," Vlad replied. "In answer to your question, though, it's possible. It's also possible that one of the candidates competing for the Counselor position decided to take out the strongest opponent."

I elbowed Clive. "He thinks you're the best one," I whispered.

Grinning, Clive fished his buzzing phone from his pocket and checked the screen. "Gentlemen, it seems I'm being paged." He looked between Vlad and Cadmael. "Thank you for sharing this information with us. I will listen more carefully and prod where I can. If I learn anything, I'll let you know."

"Wait," Vlad said to me. "You didn't say. Who do you think poisoned your mate?"

I glanced at Clive, who didn't seem concerned with my sharing info. "Thomas. The first night we arrived, he went straight for Clive with murder in his eyes. When Sebastian appeared, Thomas disappeared. I saw him again tonight. I pulled a woman from his grip, and he looked as though his mind was racing with all the different ways he wanted to hurt me."

"Interesting," Cadmael said. "Thomas was the one who approached me, concerned about rumblings he's been hearing."

"What happened tonight, that had to be okayed high up, right?" I asked "I mean, this is apparently a pattern, as Sebastian talked about protocols. How long have they been telling all the rest of the vamps that secrecy is paramount and then stealing humans for snacks whenever they feel like it?"

Vlad and Cadmael shared a look. Vlad said, "Neither of us come here often. He came for Clive and I came to see you." He shook his head. "I have no idea when this became a practice. I will say, though, that Sebastian is not acting like himself."

Cadmael nodded. "We should have changed Guild Masters by now. When I asked about it, others seemed to want Sebastian to stay. As I didn't want the job, I let it go. Clearly, I shouldn't have. There's something going on here beyond reenacting gatherings from the Middle Ages."

Maybe it was because memories of Garyn were still fresh in my head, but I asked, "Is there anyone here—besides maybe Cadmael—who has the ability to possess, for want of a better word, another vampire?"

The men were quiet, thinking.

"You all say Sebastian has changed. Do they want him in charge because someone is controlling him and therefore getting what they want while staying in the shadows?"

The silence felt heavy.

"My head hurts," I said. "I feel like we're in *Clue*. It was Professor Bitey, in the lounge, with the poisoned cup. And possibly the Jedi mind tricks."

"Again," Cadmael grumbled, "what is she talking about?"

Grinning, Clive pulled me toward the door, ignoring Cadmael.

"Isn't it super suspicious if we all walk out of this tunnel together?" I asked.

"Do you know how I can move so fast you can't see me?" Clive asked.

"Sure."

"They can too," he said.

Clive opened the huge, screeching metal door. We walked out, closed it, and continued down the hall.

Did they get out? I asked.

If they didn't, it's their own fault. Will you be okay if I meet Sebastian? Sure. Go play with your friends. I'm going to try to sleep.

We stopped at the turn leading to our bedroom.

Sweet dreams, darling. He kissed me and all thought dribbled out my ears. There was only Clive. When we finally broke apart, his eyes were vamp black and he was walking me backward to our room. *He can wait.*

"No, no. You have a meeting." *If the Guild is still standing when we're done here, I want you to be a part of it. They need you. Besides, I've already caused enough of a scandal tonight.*

He paused, his eyes lightening to their usual stormy gray. *You're right. We've probably pushed it enough for one night. Fine. Sleep well, love.* He gave me one more kiss and then headed back toward reception while I went to our room.

After I closed and locked the door, I put my bag on the coffee table. "Listen up," I whispered to the ghosts I knew were lurking. "I need sleep, so you guys need to leave me alone. Megy! Okay?"

I received no response, which I took as hopeful. I went to bathroom, took down my hair, brushed my teeth, and considered whether pajamas were a good idea. I had to get changed regardless, so I decided to chance it.

Bed or couch? Why did the bed make me feel more vulnerable? I turned on the fire, turned off the lights, and lay down on the couch. Clive had said it was okay to listen in on his meeting, so that's what I decided to do.

Closing my eyes, I searched my mind for the cold green blips that meant vampires. They were harder to see than normal. The haze of ghosts obscured them. *Megy!* The blips came into focus and I searched for Clive. Finding him, I squeezed into his blip.

Hello again, love. You chose a good time to visit. They're testing our fighting skills.

Looking out through his eyes, I saw a training room with mat floors. The other two men, Oliver and Frank, were only wearing trousers. *Do me a favor and look down.* He did and I saw that he too was barefoot and shirtless. *Nice!*

Don't make me laugh, please. They'll think me quite mad.

The women had changed out of their dresses and were wearing tank tops and yoga pants.

Do you fight each other? Because that seems like a really good way to get rid of the competition.

No. Points are taken off for killing our opponents. We'll be fighting a few of my kind who are known for their superior skills.

Is it a free-for-all, or do you get to watch and assess the others?

One at a time, so we, along with Guild members, can judge. He glanced around the room. Sebastian stood by a far door. Cadmael, Vlad, two men, and a woman waited along the opposite wall, not talking to each other or the applicants.

Who are the others?

The woman is Chaaya. She's one of the Asian Counselors. The smaller man with the long dark hair is Dakila, also an Asian Counselor. The last one, the tall one with sandy-colored hair, is Henry. He's the other Australian Counselor, along with Thomas. Those three, Vlad, and Cadmael are the judges.

But no pressure, I said. *And what's with the timing of this? They poison you and then make you fight? This is all a plot.*

I'll be fine. I'm quite extraordinary, remember?

I snorted as Sebastian opened the door beside him. A Black vampire, dressed only in dark trousers, walked in. He surveyed the five applicants and then nodded at Clive.

Noab was an Ethiopian warrior in life. He's an excellent strategist and rarely ever loses a fight.

Does he choose who he wants to fight?

No. I'm sure that's Sebastian's decision. Noab and I have fought on the same side in many a battle over the years. If the choice is left to him, he won't go against me.

"Oliver?" Sebastian said. "This is Noab. He is your opponent today. Please step onto the mat."

Oliver did, as did Noab. Everyone else moved against walls, away from the fight.

"Begin," Sebastian said.

Noab moved so fast, I couldn't track him. Suddenly he was in the center of the mat and Oliver was crumpled at the base of the far wall. To his credit, Oliver stood, shaking it off, and then moved back into position.

When Noab lashed out, Oliver blocked and delivered a rib punch. Unfortunately, that triumph was short-lived. He was flipped and went facedown on the mat with Noab on his back, his hands around Oliver's neck.

"Stop," Sebastian said.

Noab stood and held out his hand to Oliver, who took it, shaking out his sore arm.

"That was embarrassingly fast," Oliver said. "Thank you for not taking my head."

Noab nodded and then moved to the wall where the judges were standing.

Frank had a smirk on his face. It was brief, but I saw it.

Sebastian opened the door again and this time a tiny Asian woman walked out.

Oh, no, Clive said. *I don't envy whoever is going up against Wei. She's deadly and vicious with it. She's not going to want to pull her punches.*

I found myself chanting, *not Clive not Clive,* over and over in my head.

Don't worry, darling. We've never been allies, but I know how she fights.

"Delores, you will be sparring with Wei. Please come to the center of the mat," Sebastian said.

Like the other women, Wei wore a black tank top and yoga pants. She wore her hair in a very short pixie cut, insuring no one could get a grip on it. Her eyes were a magnetic amber brown, and her lips were hitched up in a sneer.

Delores glared at Wei and moved forward.

I like this pairing. They're both dirty fighters. Nothing is off-limits to either of them.

Delores charged before Wei moved, but that was clearly Wei's plan. She stepped into Delores at the last moment, slamming an arm into Delores' stomach, using her momentum to spin out of Delores' reach. Doubled over, Delores shot out a well-placed fist, breaking Wei's knee. Wei went down, tumbling toward Delores and pinning her with her good knee. She grabbed Delores' right arm and with a grunt, ripped it off Delores' body.

"Now, now," Sebastian said, rushing forward. "That's enough." He leaned over Delores as she stared at her right arm, the one she'd just picked up off the mat.

"You bitch!" she screamed. "Do you know how long it takes to regrow an arm?"

"Oh, no." Wei made a mocking sad face, slowing getting to her feet, all her weight on her right side. "You broke my knee. You're lucky I let you live." She limped to the side wall to stand beside Noab.

Ava looks green.

I noticed, Clive said. *I believe it's safe to say that hand-to-hand combat is not her forte.*

Ava had reared so far back from the mat, she looked as though she was trying to break through the wall to get out of the room.

FIFTEEN

How Is That Fair?

S ebastian went back to the door and let in a tall man with a dark olive complexion. He had short black hair and big brown eyes.

"Frank, this is Amir. Please come to the mat."

I've seen Amir fight. He's graceful and very fast. It's almost like a dance with him.

Frank was slow to move, that smirk of his gone. When he finally made it to the center of the mat, Amir nodded and waited. Frank, too, waited. No one moved, but the longer it went on, the more pronounced was Frank's attitude of defeat and Amir's of victory. It was similar to a chess master playing an entire game in their head, knowing twenty moves ahead who will win. That same knowledge seemed to be hitting Frank.

"Go," Sebastian said, clearly done with the stalling.

Frank barreled forward, straight at Amir, who slid out of the way, spinning and hitting Frank in the back of the head with a bladed hand. Frank went down and was out.

Amir turned to Sebastian. "He'll wake soon. There should be no permanent damage." He then went to the judges' side of the room and stood beside Wei.

With a look of annoyance, Sebastian went to Frank, grabbed a leg, and dragged him back to the wall opposite the judges. "Ava, please move to the center of the mat," he said, walking back to the door. When he opened it, a man with light brown skin and long black hair, tied in a braid down his back, walked in.

"Ava, this is Salvador."

Strange. I don't know this one. Everyone else has been a renowned fighter, Clive said.

Delores gets her arm ripped off and Ava gets a newbie? Bullshit, that's what this is. Clear favoritism. I swear, Clive, if some robo-vamp walks out to fight you, I'm taking him out myself.

No, you're not. If you do, I'll have to assume you think me too weak to defend myself. Is that what you believe, Sam?

Damn it, Clive! I don't want you to get hurt.

I know. And I'll do my best not to, all right?

I didn't respond.

Sam?

Shh, it's starting.

He growled in my head but I ignored him.

Salvador took a step forward but then stopped. Gaze focused on Ava, he lifted his foot again to move forward but dropped it back on the mat. Closing his eyes, he shook his head and shot forward. She turned to run but didn't get far before he'd snatched her up and threw her at the far wall.

Somehow, Sebastian got there first and caught her. "Remember, we're not doing permanent damage." He put Ava down and then went back to the door.

Delores muttered insults—I assumed—in Spanish while she glared daggers at Sebastian.

Salvador looked over his shoulder to grin at whatever Delores had said, as he made his way to the wall beside Amir.

Interesting. Ava must need eye contact to influence others. Smart of Salvador to realize that.

"Clive, please come to the center of the mat."

I mean it, I said. *Don't you dare get hurt!*

Have faith.

Clive stepped up and turned to the door. Sebastian, though, walked over to the judges' area.

"Clive, as you yourself are known for your fighting skills, we had to adjust the test."

How is that fair?

Shh.

"The judges and I discussed it, and we thought you should have to spar with two of our fighters.

Shit!

He's not done yet…

"But then we realized that you'd be at an advantage, having seen them fight—such as it was—so it was decided it should be three."

"Of your choice," Cadmael added.

When no one said anything else, Clive nodded. "I see." He looked over the four fighters and said, "I mean this as no disrespect to your superior skills, Wei, but as it will take time for your knee to heal, I'll not ask you to spar with me."

She looked pissed off—at her knee, not Clive—and nodded her acceptance.

"Fine," Sebastian said. "Noab, Amir, and Salvador, please take the mat. And go."

Salvador hit the ground immediately, writhing in pain. Unlike Ava, Clive didn't need eye contact to control others or deliver excruciating pain.

The other two fanned out, smiling at Clive.

Clive lifted a hand, curling two fingers in a come-here gesture, and I laughed, knowing he'd done it for me.

Noab moved, disappearing from sight, but then he was flying through the air and crashing through a stone wall. It felt like sections of a film I was watching had been cut out. Noab was ten feet away and then half his body was through a wall. They were too damned fast for me to track.

Clive spun and I got dizzy. Amir was already there, his arm around Clive's neck. Clive reached up and broke the bone, but when he tried to heave Amir away, Amir spun around and swept Clive's legs.

The film jumped—and I was going to hurl—and then Clive was behind Amir, his hands around Amir's neck.

I though Sebastian would call it, but then Clive was the one flying through the air and crashing through a wall.

Clive!

I'm fine, he said, waving a hand in front of his face to waft away the cloud of mortar dust engulfing him. *My fault for not realizing Noab was up.*

"I want to play," Wei grumbled.

"Next time," Clive assured her as he rose to his feet and returned to the mat where the other two were waiting.

"How's the arm?" Clive asked.

Amir shrugged one shoulder. "I can fight with one arm."

Clive turned to Sebastian. "Are swords available?"

When Clive turned his head, Amir leapt forward, but Clive had already moved as well. The movie skipped again and Amir was standing where Clive had been. Clive, though, was now leaning against the wall beside Cadmael.

I relaxed. This was clearly playtime for them.

Clive walked back onto the mat. "So, that was a no on the sword question, was it?"

"No," Noab said. "I've seen you with a sword. I like my head where it is."

Chaaya, the South Asian Counselor who was judging, asked, "Are we concerned about that one?" She pointed at Salvador, still writhing on the floor in pain.

Clive shook his head. "I already released him. I believe he's hoping we'll forget about him so he doesn't have to fight me."

Salvador popped up with a grin. "This is so." He walked over and leaned against the judges' wall. "Now I can watch properly."

"Coward," Noab said.

Salvador smiled wider. "No, please, tell us about being embedded in a wall. Was that fun?"

The film jumped and all of a sudden I was looking at the back of Amir's head and Clive's bladed hand slamming into it. Amir tipped over like a falling log. Clive had pulled the same move on Amir that Amir had used on Frank. Clive stepped over him and squared off with Noab.

Noab flexed, his gaze fixed on Clive. "I told them this was a stupid idea."

"Fun, though," Clive said.

Frank was now awake, sullenly standing by himself and watching.

When Noab moved, so did Clive. I got seasick trying to track what was happening. All I got were flickers of punches and blocks, throws and hits on a continual loop.

Eventually, though, someone must win. Clive flipped Noab, landing on Noab's back, Clive's knees drilling into Noab's spine. When he tugged gently on Noab's neck, Noab hit the mat with his hand, accepting Clive's win.

Clive hopped off and extended his hand to his friend, pulling him to his feet.

Amir, Sandoval, Wei clapped. Cadmael nodded approvingly. The two Asian Counselors shared a wary look. The Australian Counselor laughed, though the humor didn't reach his eyes.

"As there's nothing for the judges to discuss," Vlad said, "perhaps we can call it a night." He checked his watch and then glanced over at Sebastian, who was watching Clive with a thoughtful look on his face.

"Yes. That's it for this evening," Sebastian said, crossing the room to walk Ava out the door.

"When did you arrive?" Clive asked Noab.

"Earlier this evening. We got here as those other guests were being escorted out. It looked as though we missed something, but no one has seen fit to share with us what it was."

"Ask me again someday and I'll tell you." Clive gave him a significant look and then turned to Amir. "It's been a long time. I see deadly grace remains your gift."

Oliver stayed to chat with Clive and the fighters. The judges and other applicants, though, left quickly. The conversation was interesting, but I was exhausted. As I didn't know anyone they were referring to, their voices became white noise. I pulled out of Clive's mind and fell asleep.

———

A DOOR SLAMS, WAKING ME. MY EYES POP OPEN TO SEE A COCKROACH scuttling toward my face. Flying up, I realize I've been sleeping on the floor of one of the rooms in the asylum. I rub at the grit on my cheek, unable to stop the full-body cringe from having anything in this place touch my skin.

A woman in a long gray dress pulls a bedpan out from under the narrow rusty bedframe, pours the contents into a bucket, and drops the pan on the floor, kicking it with her foot back under the bed.

The crash of the pan makes me jump but doesn't seem to wake the woman on the bed. I look more closely and realize her eyes are open, wildly roving around the room. Her head, though, is strapped to the bed, unable to move.

The attendant in gray says something in Hungarian to the woman in the bed, whose eyes fill with tears. The attendant shakes her head as the woman in the bed keeps opening her mouth, though nothing comes out.

A dark stain blooms on the thin, moth-eaten blanket that covers the patient. She's wet herself. The attendant shouts and stamps out of the room, leaving the poor woman strapped down and sobbing silently.

If she'd unstrapped the poor woman, this probably wouldn't have happened, but rather than the attendant taking responsibility, she blames the patient. It feels like I'm watching a Hungarian version of the Stanford prison experiment. These attendants have complete control of the patients and are cruel with it.

I know there's nothing I can do about something that happened decades before I was born, but I desperately want to. I lay my hand on the lump her feet make.

"I'm so sorry." I feel a whisper of the scratchy cloth under my finger-

tips as I squeeze, trying to comfort the memory of a woman long gone. Stepping out of the room, I pass the bucket and look up and down the hall.

Other doors are open as bedpans are emptied into other buckets. One woman is being dragged out of her room by two attendants, while another walks quietly beside her attendant. Both groups are walking toward the main hall. They pass and I follow.

They turn left at the main hall, away from reception. A sconce on the wall flickers, casting a thin, sickly yellow light over the graying tile floor and walls. There's a grainy photograph on the wall of Budapest from over a hundred years ago. Another one has two men in white coats standing in front of a wall of books. And yet another features a group of haggard attendants in gray dresses.

I know old timey photography required sitting for an extended period of time to get the exposure, therefore people don't smile, but this group looks particularly grim. Perhaps it's just that I've seen them in action and have yet to find one behaving like a caretaker rather than a jailer.

The women and their attendants go through the door that leads downstairs to the basement rooms and the tub. The whole asylum is creepy, but there's something about the basement. It feels important, so I descend the steps after them.

SIXTEEN

The Bloody Ruin

The first woman ends up sliding down the stairs. I can't see if she's fallen or was pushed, but the attendants mutter as they pick her up and march her down the hall to the right. The quiet woman and the Gray Dress lag behind. Neither seems eager to follow the group of three ahead.

A distinctive stench has me looking over the railing. A rat scurries beneath the stairs, a cockroach in its mouth. My uneasiness grows as I reach the bottom of the steps. The walls and floor are again a dingy white. It feels makeshift down here, as though this area was an afterthought. No one is in the hall and the doors on either side are closed.

Someone screams behind the door beside me and I jump out of my skin. It cuts off with a gurgle, which is somehow even more upsetting. Coughing comes from behind another door, quiet sobbing from the next.

At the end of the hall, there's an open area blocked by a battered wooden table. At the table sits a Gray Dress with papers she's filling out. Behind her are doors to other rooms. One, the tub room, has a partially open door where the woman who's been dragged downstairs is now being forced into the water that, based on her shrieking, is freezing cold.

The Gray Dress at the table pushes up on a heavy sigh, goes to the tub room door and pulls it shut, cutting off much of the noise.

Behind me, an older patient is escorted to the rickety wooden table. The attendants confer, notes are added to the papers at the desk, and then the old woman is taken to a room on the left with a metal exam table. The door is thankfully closed before I have to witness what happens to her.

What draws my attention instead is a short, dark hall off to the right side. It doesn't appear as though anyone uses it and yet I'm picking up a familiar scent. I walk around the table and go down the hall, hearing a faint growl from behind a heavy door. I can't open it and no one's here to do it for me, so I put my ear to it and listen closely. I might be completely off base, but it sounds like the click of claws on metal, of an animal pacing.

Straining to hear voices, I catch an unmistakable growl. I scented wolf. It's what sent me to this door in the first place, but why would an asylum have a wolf in their basement? If they're holding a werewolf in there, why hasn't she broken out? How is there not a huge scandal about the existence of werewolves?

Something slams into the door I'm leaning against and I rear back.

In bed. In the dark. Beside Clive.

It took a few moments to reorient myself. I was in the now, not the then. I checked the nightstand. Clive had once again plugged in my phone. All the quiet ways he strove to care for me squeezed my heart at the oddest moments. Perhaps it was watching women experience remarkable cruelty and then waking up safe in bed with my loving mate that had me off balance.

I needed to explore the basement, to see if I could find anything left in that room that would tell me if they'd been holding a werewolf prisoner. First, though, I wanted food. I showered, dressed in jeans, a tee, an axe, a jacket, and running shoes. The ring was on my nightstand beside my phone. I grabbed both, gave Clive a kiss, and set out for the town and a meal.

I found another fabulous restaurant and gorged myself before heading back. I had sleuthing to do. I passed a bookshop on the Pest side of the river and stopped. There was a book in the window—well, two versions of the same book. One was in

Hungarian, I assumed, and the other was in English. The one I could read was entitled *Mysterious Budapest*.

I turned around, went into the bookstore, and bought the book. Next door was a chocolatier. What kind of a psycho passes a chocolate shop without stopping? Not a Sam kind, that's for sure. The woman behind the display case spoke very little English, but she understood I wanted her to choose an assortment for me. As I couldn't read the little cards and many of the truffles and cakes looked completely new to me, I waited to see what I would get.

She gave me one to try and it was incredible, a rich dark chocolate covering a currant, maybe, with a hazelnut liqueur. Seeing my smile and nod, she relaxed and continued to fill a large pastry box for me. Honestly, this was probably the most excited I'd been in Budapest so far. I wasn't sure what that said about me, but it probably wasn't flattering.

After paying a large amount of money, I left with a veritable treasure trove of desserts and looked for someplace to sit, snack, and read that would be less distracting than a haunted vampire hotel. I remembered The Bloody Ruin Asylum & Taproom and headed back across the bridge and up the hill.

The Bloody Ruin was quiet at this time of day, with maybe fifteen or twenty patrons, most of whom were sitting at the mismatched café tables outside, in the shade of oversized umbrellas. I went in and stopped at the bar to order a soda, but the bartender recommended a fröccs.

I figured when in Budapest and all. Fröccs was apparently a blend of wine and soda water. One of the variations also had raspberry syrup, so I went with that one. And a water, of course, in case fröccs were not for me. I then took my book, box of chocolates, and two drinks into the dim back of the bar, away from the hubbub, to sit alone and do a little reading.

I skipped over the story of a faithful maiden waiting on her balcony for her love to return from war, a princess who dreamed of a special bird and then gave birth to a leader of the Hungarian people, and a different version of the Danube Mermaid story to skip to the werewolf chapter. I'd read the others later. Right now, I was hoping for a little insight into our local pack.

The chapter started with conflicting theories about werewolves originating in Ancient Greece, while another story said we began in Slavic countries. What I'd read in a special archive in San Francisco was that the Quinns, the original line of werewolves, came from Europe. I supposed many wanted to believe their country birthed the first supernatural beings—or monsters, depending on whichever tale you read.

In one story, werewolves only changed three nights a year. In another, it was believed a bite was not needed to pass on lycanthropy, but it was rather child abuse that created werewolves. I kind of loved that story. I wanted those children to gain the teeth and claws necessary to fight off the adults preying on them.

One story said werewolves went to Hell to fight wicches and demons in order to win back the grain that had been stolen from their people. While I didn't believe they visited Hell, protecting the people of Budapest against other supernaturals seemed in line with the tenets of the local pack.

Speaking of werewolves, I scented one approaching. I looked up and watched Viktoria walk down the center of the bar, into the shadowy corner to find me.

"You're still here," she said, sounding displeased.

"Well spotted," I replied, channeling my husband. Opening the top of my pastry box, I added, "Would you like one?"

She reached in and picked one with a glossy fruit shell that sandwiched something inside. "These are the best," she said.

I looked in, found another just like it, and popped it in my mouth. "Apricot and...?"

Viktoria swallowed and said, "Roasted pistachios. Delicious."

She was right. It was. "So," I said, "are you just checking on me or do you have a message?"

She started to reach into the box again and then paused, checking to see if it was all right. I nodded and she chose a dark chocolate diamond-shaped one with a cursive G on the top. I took one too. This one had a praline filling.

"I thought you'd want to know about the leeches' latest victims," she said.

Glancing around, I didn't see anyone near enough to hear her, but still. "Maybe lower your voice," I said, whispering, "and yes, I want to know. Did everyone get help? Did you find the child's family?"

She shook her head. "Still protecting them." She grabbed a milk chocolate in the shape of a heart.

This time I didn't follow suit. The topic of last night's victims gave me a stomachache. "I protect all supernaturals from discovery."

When I put the book aside, she looked at the cover and laughed. "Not enough monsters in your life?"

My stomach twisted again. I'd tried for years to hide what I was, not realizing the magical community of San Francisco was well aware of what I shifted into and where I went to run. I was getting more comfortable in my own skin, claiming my own power, but Viktoria was getting to me.

I tapped the book cover. "I was just reading about werewolves."

She scoffed at that, taking another chocolate.

"I hoped there'd be local lore in it, but so far it's all conflicting general myths."

"Local?" she said, eyebrows raised.

"It was just a shot in the dark," I said. "I remember reading somewhere about a young wolf—a female—being found by humans. She was imprisoned and studied."

"What? Who told you that?" she asked, clearly agitated. "What are you talking about?"

I leaned back, wondering about her intensity. Did she know something about the wolf who may or may not have been held at the asylum? "I don't know. I read a lot of random stuff on the internet about Budapest before we came.

I remembered because that would be huge if it was true. Is it?"

"Of course not. You don't think we would have found and freed one of our own?" She acted as though she thought the suggestion stupid, but the tension in her shoulders didn't lie.

"Okay. Just a random urban legend." I took a sip of water. "You haven't said yet," I told her. "How are the people from last night?"

"Anemic. Maybe half had to stay in the hospital overnight. The mother of the little girl was out of her mind with worry. They had to tranquilize her. Hopefully she now knows her daughter is back. The little girl is still jumping at shadows."

I stared at my empty glass, wishing there was something more I could have done. I didn't want her to hide for years, as I had. "I'm sorry." I knew it wasn't enough, but I also didn't know what more I could have done.

"How did you get them out?" she asked me. "Did the blood-suckers see you?"

I nodded. "I yelled at the vamps and pulled the people away from them."

Viktoria made a strange choking sound. I looked between her and the box of treats, wondering if she got a nut stuck in her throat.

"You took a bloodsucker's meal away from it?" she asked.

"Not *it*. They're people. And yes. They weren't happy with me, but I think most were more shocked about something my mate had done to stop them." The wolves didn't need to know I had any power over vampires. "My mate is very scary when he wants to be and there are two fewer vamps in your town today. He and a couple of other vampires helped me get all the people out and deliver them to the pack."

She stared at me a moment. "They punished their own for what was done to humans?" Her look said she didn't believe me. "Won't they kill you in retaliation?"

Probably. "I hope not. They respect power and threat. It was lucky that I had three of the most powerful vamps in the world backing me up."

Viktoria sat back in her chair. "Really? We have that kind of fang power in town right now?"

Shitshitshit. "You really don't want to mess with vampires," I said.

"Not true. We really do," she countered.

SEVENTEEN

Please Don't Eat Me

"Yeah. Okay. I get that, but I don't think you understand how crazy fast and strong they are. I don't want your pack to be wiped out because you showed up to a gunfight with a knife," I said.

Her brow furrowed as she tried to make sense of that analogy.

"Meaning they have you outmatched. This town needs you as guardians. If you get wiped out, who's going to protect them? Right now, it's easy for the vamps to ignore you. If you go after them, they'll destroy you."

"Not if we destroy them first," she said with a sneer. "And we wouldn't be very good guardians if we ignored the biggest threat our home has, would we?"

She had a point there. I held up my hands in surrender. "This isn't my town. I'm not a member of your pack or of the G—group of vampires, so I know I have no say in any of this. It's just if the pack wasn't around, who would I have brought all those humans to last night to watch over? If you hadn't been there, they could have fallen prey to other humans. Instead, you kept them safe. I'd hate for the locals to lose your protection."

Viktoria stood and took another chocolate. "I'll talk with my Alpha. We'll see what he says." She turned and left me wondering if I'd screwed up the delicate balance here by opening my mouth. Damn it.

I went out the back of the Bloody Ruin, into the side street, and quickly ducked behind the dumpster. When I got to the end of the tunnel, I listened at the door and then checked my mind for blips. I didn't want anyone, Renfield or vamp, to see me coming out of the super-secret tunnel. I waved my bag holding the ring in front of the door and it slid open. I stepped out, went to the large, metal screeching door, and opened it just enough to slip out. I hated that the damn door told anyone interested where I was.

The hall was quiet. I couldn't hear heartbeats like the vamps could, but I could hear footsteps, and I didn't hear any of those. Stopping at the door to the basement, I tucked the pastry box and book under my arm and looked for a way in. Nothing. The door was almost impossible to see, but I'd gone through it twice in dreams.

The San Francisco nocturne had release points in the walls beside hidden doors. You had to know where to touch, but when you did, a door popped open. I sniffed around the faint outline of the door, looking for a spot fingers had touched, but couldn't find it. I was standing directly in front of the door, on tiptoe, running my fingertips through the grime above the door when I heard a quiet snick.

Stepping back, I saw that the door was now ajar. How had I done that? Then I remembered Vlad's ring in my crossbody bag. Like the secret tunnel, this, too, must have been keyed to it.

I pulled the door open and stared into pitch-black. Taking my phone out of my bag, I hit the flashlight and found the stairs I'd seen in my dreams. The railing was gone, but the wooden steps remained, though one was missing halfway down.

Stepping over the hole, I tried to keep my focus on the sketchy staircase, but the creepy graffiti on the walls was distracting, as was the stench of rotting things. When I reached the bottom step without falling through rotted boards, I considered it a win.

I wanted to put the box and book down, but there was no way I was putting food down in here. A thin cardboard box wasn't enough protection against a century of filth and disease.

How odd. The smell of vampire was fresh, not like a vampire once came down here. It was more like a vampire regularly visited this place. The vamp smell was getting muddled with dead rats, insects, and an overwhelming stench of mold, though. I didn't see standing water, but it smelled as though the basement had been flooded at some point.

I turned down the hall toward the tub room, book and chocolates still under my arm, trying to ignore the prickling at the back of my neck. Was something down here with me?

What I focused on was the wolf—if they indeed had imprisoned one. She had been hidden down a hall past the tub room.

When I passed the first open door to a cell-like room, I paused to shine my light inside and jumped. A woman was standing beside a bed. Her hair was a snarled mess around her sallow face. The stained shift she wore hung on her emaciated body. She turned, her eyes sunken, her gaze hot. She curled a lip, snarling as she moved toward me.

Megy!

She paused, tilting her head, the sneer turning into a leer as she looked me up and down. She said something, but it didn't sound like Hungarian. Shit! I didn't know how to say *Go!* in any other languages.

Holding up a hand, I pushed with my necromancy. She stumbled back a step and then moved toward me again, her mouth gaping, broken, blackened teeth glistening. I pushed again, but she didn't pause.

Lashing out like a snake, she bit my jaw, her broken teeth digging in. Curling her arms around my neck, she held me close, trying to rip the flesh from my bones. The stink was repugnant. What she was doing stung, but the smell was far worse.

"What are we up to?"

I jumped again and spun, finding Vlad in the light from my phone. "Jeez, dude. A little warning would be nice."

"You're the one lurking outside my door. I heard a heartbeat and came to investigate. The question is, what are you doing down here?"

"Oh. Uh." The ghost was still trying to eat my face. It was horribly distracting. "Nothing much. Just sightseeing."

"I see," he said, moving my hand so the flashlight was aimed at our feet and not his face. "Instead of walking around in the fresh air and sunshine of Budapest, you found a hidden door and went for a tour of a reeking basement filled with vermin. Yes?"

I nodded, which proved awkward with the scary woman hanging off my jaw. "Yep. I like visiting those off-the-beaten-path places."

"I see." He glanced around and then back at me. "And are you enjoying this new experience, having your face gnawed upon?"

My hand dropped, the flashlight mostly illuminating the side of my leg now. "You can see her?"

He nodded. "That one belongs here. Cannibalism seems to be her thing."

"Do you know what language she speaks?"

"Romanian. Why?" he asked.

"I need to get her off my face, but I don't speak Romanian. How do I say *go away*?"

"*Pleaca de aici* should do it," he said.

I had him repeat it a few times and then I gathered my magic, unspooling it and wrapping it around my hands. I pushed, shouting *PLEACA DE AICI* in my head.

The ghost zoomed back into her room and disappeared.

"Thanks. That worked," I said. "Wait. How do you see them? I thought vampires couldn't see ghosts."

His mustache twitched. "Haven't you read the stories about me? I am extraordinary."

I gave him my squinty look. "That's not it."

His expression darkened, his eyes turning black, but I wasn't buying it.

"Cut it out. You're not really angry."

SEANA KELLY

His hands went to his hips as he glared. "What makes you think I won't take your head for gainsaying me?"

I couldn't very well tell him that my necromancy allowed me to pick up on his emotions, so I just shrugged. "I know things. Do you carry wicche blood?"

His expression turned thunderous.

I had a moment to worry I'd read him completely wrong before it fell away.

"I do. On my mother's side. Not much, though. Just enough to see ghosts." He studied me a moment. "Has Léna visited you yet?"

"Léna? You've seen her too?" Relief washed over me. I wasn't alone in this haunted madhouse.

He tipped his head down the hall to the left of the stairs, a direction I'd never gone in a dream. A door stood open and he waved me in, closing it behind us.

Oh. This was Vlad's room. The walls were papered in a dark pattern. Wood floors had been put in. A large bed stood to the side, but Vlad walked to the far wall, tapped a button, and the fire roared to life. Beside the hearth was one chair and one sofa, with a coffee table in between. Bookshelves lined a wall. Around the fireplace were mounted swords, axes, assorted daggers, and a mace.

"Kind of a fun warlord chic vibe you've got going here," I said, plopping down on the couch.

Vlad took the chair and put his feet up on the coffee table. "So happy you approve," he grumbled.

"Why are you down here, away from all the other vamps?" The fire felt nice after the chill of a ghost plastered to me.

"You answered your own question." He shook his head. "I hate this place. I told them not to buy it, that we could find any number of abandoned castles to turn into Guild headquarters. Unfortunately, as I'm the only one who sees ghosts—not that I've told them that—I was outvoted. They wanted to be closer to a city and an airport."

I sniffed the couch but didn't pick up a rodent scent. "How do

132

you keep the rats out?" I kept glancing into shadowy corners for tiny black eyes.

He raised an eyebrow. "You read Stoker. Don't you remember? I control rats."

I rolled my eyes at that.

"Fine," he said. "My kind repels living things—except you, apparently."

"Wrong again. Our dog Fergus loves Clive." Maybe Vlad repelled things, but Clive didn't. Then again, Clive had said he missed riding horses, that they didn't tolerate vampires.

"And what kind of dog is Fergus?" he asked, relaxing into the conversation.

"Irish Wolfhound. We brought him back from Wales, along with his dragon friend Fyr." That wasn't a secret, was it? There was something about Vlad that made me spill more than I should have.

I put down the box and book on the coffee table and pulled up photos on my phone, showing him Fergus. He was on the beach, at the end of one of our runs, the ocean behind him.

Vlad leaned forward to see the image and nodded, "A very handsome beast." He was quiet for a moment. "Why *again*?"

"Hmm?"

"You said I was wrong again. When was I wrong the first time?"

"Oh," I said, mirroring him and putting my feet up on the coffee table. "You said you thought Clive was just a pretty boy, using his face to curry favor. That's not him at all."

"No?"

I knew I should shut up, but I liked Vlad. Granted, being as powerful as he was, he could have been manipulating me, but I didn't think so. I'd kept my candy-coating in place. The man had laid waste to legions, but I trusted him, and I didn't like him not thinking well of Clive.

"Is he handsome? Of course," I said. "I'm not blind. That's the least of his gifts, though. He's brave and not just in the I'll-take-on-the-monster way. He'll do what's even harder. He'll stand down and let me fight my own monsters. I know how much he wants to do it for me, but—"

"He knows, for your own piece of mind, your own confidence, that you have to do it yourself," he finished.

"Yes," I breathed. "That's it exactly."

EIGHTEEN

Why Do Ghosts Have To Be So Creepy?

"I t was the same with my Ilona. I wanted to slay any who caused her the slightest unease. She wanted me to train her instead, to show her how to use my weapons."

My heart clutched. "Clive taught me to fight with swords and my axe," I said, tapping the handle behind my head.

"I saw that in the alley." He leaned forward. "May I see it now?"

I pushed my jacket back and pulled out the axe. It shone, almost glowing in the firelight.

Vlad made a sound of deep appreciation and reached for it. "Fae?"

"Yes. Don't touch it, though. Clive says fae metal burns vamp skin. This one has been spelled to protect me from the king's assassins. I don't believe it'll be instant death for vampires, but it seems best not to test that theory."

He stood, opened a drawer, pulled on a leather glove, and then took the axe from me, weighing it in his palm before swinging. As he moved through a series of fast slashes, I had a moment to worry my head was about to be separated from my body. Instead, he flipped the axe in the air, caught it, and handed it back.

"Magnificent." He was so fast, I wondered if he'd switched

axes on me. Mine was, after all, quite valuable. When I tilted the blade to the firelight, I caught the faint fingerprint of Algar, the queen's captain of her guard. Satisfied, I sheathed the axe and sat back.

"He trained me in hand-to-hand, as well," I said, "but if I told him I didn't want to fight, he'd breathe a sigh of relief and love me just as much. He's fair and open-minded. I know lots of older supernaturals can become stuck in their thinking. That's not Clive. His mind is fluid, always taking in new information and altering beliefs based on it.

"And he's secretly kind. As you loaned me your ring, I think you'll understand. He makes choices based on the safety and comfort of those he considers his, not just his own needs. I was a traumatized, scarred teenager dumped in his city. He could have let an underling deal with me and forget about it. He didn't. I'm no one special, but I was one of the supernaturals in his charge, so he kept me guarded and checked on me regularly to make sure I was healing."

I felt a kiss on the top of my head and flinched.

"Nonsense. You've always been special," Clive said. He walked around the couch, taking in the room, and then sat beside me. "Now what brings you to what I assume is Vlad's room in a hidden basement?"

Vlad smirked. "She described it as warlord chic."

Clive gaze went to the wall of weapons. "I see her point."

"I went exploring," I said. "I didn't know Vlad lived down here."

Clive nodded slowly, pulling my hand into his. "But why the basement? I thought you'd be out touring parliament or eating a five-star meal. Instead, I find you here."

"Léna is quite persuasive," Vlad said.

Clive looked between Vlad and me. "Léna?"

Vlad must have noticed the panic in my eyes because he said, "I misspoke."

Defeated, I sighed and leaned into Clive. "No. He didn't. This place is lousy with really fricking disturbing ghosts, one of whom is Léna. She was pregnant and hidden away here. On the first night, she was raped by two male attendants from the men's side of the asylum."

Clive wrapped his arm around me.

"I forgot," Vlad said. "You don't speak Hungarian and therefore wouldn't have understood the whole story. It was her father who had been molesting her, who had impregnated her in the first place. He didn't want the scandal or the questions, so he committed her here with a large sum of money to make sure his problem went away. She had a younger sister at home. That was what she was crying about as they took her away. She was pleading with him to leave Lara alone."

Clive pulled me in closer. "And she's been haunting you?"

"All of them have. They mess with me when I'm awake and haunt my dreams when I sleep," I said. Poor Léna. "I hate her father even more now. I didn't think that was possible."

"I knew I should have moved us to a hotel," Clive murmured. "And this is why I keep finding you asleep on the couch. Are they doing something to the bed?"

"More vulnerable," Vlad said.

"Yes. Exactly. I can sleep on the couch, and it feels more secure for some reason," I said.

"It's an illusion, of course," Vlad explained, "but the back of the couch makes it seem as though they have to come at you from one direction."

I thought about that. "I think you're right."

He nodded. "They don't bother me as much as they used to, but I was watching you at the gatherings—"

"Where?" Clive interrupted. "I never saw you."

"There are medallions in the molding that are peepholes. I had no desire to talk with any of them, but I'd heard you were bringing your mate and I wanted to see her," he said. "We all heard her heart beat faster, but I think I was the only one watching to know she'd been looking at the portrait when it happened. I've seen that madman lean out of the frame, the blood dripping from his hands as well. When I saw her reaction, I knew the ghosts had found a new audience." He paused. "That was also why I gave her the ring, so she could get out whenever she needed to."

"*She's* right here," I said, annoyed to be talked about rather than to.

"Apologies," Vlad said, "but I was replying to your husband, who is not yet sure if I can be trusted near you."

You should have told me, Clive said in my head.

"I didn't want to screw up your chances with this job." I answered him aloud to let him know I thought Vlad could be trusted.

"Darling." Clive shook his head. "The decision had been made before we boarded the plane. Why they brought all of us here to go through these ridiculous meetings and tests is beyond me, though there *is* a reason." He turned to Vlad. "Do you know?"

Vlad shook his head. "We'd already agreed to offer you the position. I have no idea why Sebastian called us in, or even if it was him. The email was from him, but I can't say whether he's being influenced. I will say that I've noticed Sebastian staring at that portrait over the fireplace for no apparent reason. He's never so much as blinked at the other ghosts when they pop up, but that portrait seems to have him fixated. He's never mentioned noticing movement in the frame, but I don't suppose he would, as it would make him appear mentally unstable. Which, of course, is why I tell no one about seeing ghosts."

"If not ghosts, we know Ava has some mental abilities. Maybe she's the one influencing him," I suggested.

Clive shook his head and Vlad said, "Not enough. She has to maintain eye contact."

"Okay, well, what do they get from having you all here in Budapest?" I asked.

"We've left our homes possibly open to invasion," Clive said.

"They already tried that. It didn't work out so well," I joked. "Besides, Russell's holding down the city."

"So why this group? Here? Now?" asked Vlad.

"Maybe it has nothing to do with you guys," I said. "Maybe someone is using the North American Counselor position as an excuse to get Frank here or Delores or whomever to execute," I said.

"Except no one's done that," Clive said. "They were here days before we arrived. To be honest, the rest of us didn't need to be called. Invite whoever you want dead, tell them others are coming, then when they get off the plane, kill them. This is too elaborate for that."

"It could be you," Vlad said, staring at me. "There's no scenario that puts Sam in Budapest right now if she weren't here with you." He turned his attention to Clive. "Did you decide to have her join you or was she invited?"

Clive thought about it a moment. "It was an offhand comment as we were about to hang up. Sebastian said that Budapest was beautiful in the summer and that perhaps my wife would like to see it." He swore under his breath and stood, pulling me to my feet. "I'm taking you home."

"Not yet," I said.

"Whyever not? This place isn't safe for you."

"Clive." I patted his chest. "It's a haunted mental asylum filled with vampires. It was never safe. Meanwhile, as long as we're being honest and upfront, I had a dream about someone being held here who may or may not have been a werewolf. I came down here to check out the room."

Vlad stood. "By all means, let's investigate." He went to the door and held it open for us.

I went first, but then shoved Clive in front of me. "There's a ghost coming up on your right that likes to bite off faces."

"So kind of you to think of me," Clive said.

"Don't even." I held on to the back of his jacket, my face pressed against his spine. "She won't bother you."

I turned my head away as we passed by the door. Unfortunately, that meant I was looking in the direction of the open door across the hall where a skeletal woman lay, her eyes open and glazed over, staring straight at me. Her jaw dropped open and the rattling sound of her pleading echoed in my head.

"Is it her?" Clive asked, no doubt because my heart had begun to gallop.

I shook my head against his back. "Keep going to the open area at the end of the hall, please."

When he stopped, I looked back down the hall we'd just walked through. The top of the face biter's head was visible as she peeked around the corner of her door at me. Hopefully, that meant she'd stay in her room. I studied the doorways. Most were open, the doors long gone. Not all, though. The tub room had a closed door.

"Doesn't it freak you out to have closed doors down here? Anything could be behind them," I said to Vlad.

"Generally speaking, I'm the most dangerous thing around, so no," he replied.

"Good point." I looked at Clive. "This is the tub room. They took Léna here her first night, put her in a cold bath in her shift. The water plastered the thin fabric to her body, making the pregnancy obvious."

I opened the door on its screeching hinge. The scent of rusty water and mold overpowered me as I shined my flashlight. Tiles were broken or missing. A large metal tub caked in filth still sat in the middle of the smallish room. The ceiling was black with mold, the part that was still up. Pieces had begun to fall in the corner.

"Why is it hotter in here than out there?" I asked.

"Perhaps it's the heat generated by the hyphal growth of the mold colonies," Clive responded.

I elbowed him. "Look at you, breaking out your science facts. You're kind of hot too," I said.

"Not here, darling. I'd rather we limited your exposure to black mold," Clive responded, wrapping an arm around me, trying to guide me toward the door.

"Wait," I said. "Do you hear that?" It sounded like the sloshing of water against a hard surface. As my bookstore and bar was situated beneath the water line of the San Francisco Bay, I was quite familiar with that sound.

"The maddeningly slow heartbeat? Yes, but I have no idea what it is," Clive said.

"Heartbeat?" I looked at both vampires. "You hear a heartbeat? I meant the water sound."

Vlad nodded. "I've been hearing a slow heartbeat since we first looked at the building, almost a hundred years ago. Sometimes it's stronger, sometimes weaker. This is the loudest I've ever heard it."

"I know of no animal with a heartbeat that slow," Clive said. "Perhaps a blue whale, but I doubt they've been holding a blue whale in the basement for over a hundred years."

"Like I said," Vlad responded, "it's never been this loud. It's usually so faint, it's easy to ignore."

"Well, now I want to rip out the walls and floor to see what they've imprisoned," I said, looking for hidden doors or hatches.

"Is this where you saw the wolf?" Clive asked.

Reluctantly, I went back to the hall. "No. There's just something about that room. It's important. I feel it." I turned to where the shadowy hall should have been and found a wall. "That wasn't in my dream," I said, pointing.

NINETEEN

Storytime

V lad walked over and tapped on it. "I hear an echo. It's open behind this wall." He glanced back at me and then spoke to Clive. "Take her around the corner while I knock it down."

Clive picked me up and moved me.

"What the heck?" I demanded.

"We don't want you inhaling whatever's released when he breaks through the wall," Clive said.

There was a cracking sound, but it wasn't nearly as loud as I'd been expecting.

"Just a cheap board," Vlad said. "Leaning on it would have brought it down."

We came back around the corner to see Vlad holding a thin piece of wood in front of him to break through a century of cobwebs.

"Thank you for doing that," Clive said. "Sam hates spiders."

I wanted to refute it, but my badassery couldn't stand up to spiders. I'd never particularly liked them, though I appreciated their place in the natural world. After that incident in Meg's church when a demon sent a swarm of spiders at me, I was far more jumpy around them.

I angled the flashlight up, so I could make sure they weren't up there waiting to drop on me. It looked like I was safe enough for the time being.

Clive went to the door and tried the handle. It was locked. Making a fist, he gave the door a short jab right above the knob. It popped open. He stepped in and looked around, Vlad on his heels. Their night vision was better than my own.

I stepped over the threshold and then Clive was there, blocking me. His expression said it all. It was bad. He wrapped his arms around me and squeezed.

When Vlad cursed, I steeled myself and stepped back from Clive, shining my light around the room. It was large, more of an exam room than a bedroom. A metal table stood in the center, covered in dried blood, fur, and the grime of more than a hundred years.

To the right was a table and chair. On the wall, papers were tacked up, charts and reports I couldn't read. What was crystal clear, though, were the diagrams of a girl and a wolf with lines indicating where she had been cut open and examined in both forms.

Stomach clenching, white noise filled my mind. I knew my voice was too loud, but I had to hear myself over the turbines in my head. "Am I reading this right? She was ten years old?" I pointed at the diagram.

Clive rubbed a hand up and down my back. "Yes."

Her name, Aliz Csonka, was at the top of the page. I opened the camera on my phone and began taking pictures of every sheet of paper tacked to the wall.

"What are you doing?" Clive asked.

"I want it translated. I want to know what they did to her."

I hadn't realized I was crying until Clive wiped my face and laid a kiss on my forehead.

"We will."

I moved the flashlight, looking for a bed of some kind and instead found a cage. I couldn't stop my feet until I touched the bars. Crouching, I studied the child-sized skeleton. Around her neck bones, there was a heavy band that was chained to the wall. The cage was made of sturdy metal, the chain barely long enough for her to lie down.

There were no fibers under her. "They didn't give her a blanket or clothes," I said.

"The better to study her from that little table and fill out their charts," Vlad spat.

Cold metal. They'd chained up a naked child, caged her, and did experiments. I couldn't keep the growl from my throat.

"I suppose we should be thankful it was a quick death," Vlad sneered. "I worried that slow heartbeat I'd been hearing and ignoring was from a starving wolf walled into the basement of an asylum."

I looked up at him. "How do you know it was quick?"

He pointed at the girl's skull.

I stood and moved to his side of the cage. There I could see the hole in what would have been her forehead. "It was like putting down a cow for them, wasn't it?" I knew it was too late, but I would have given anything to tear them all apart. Slowly.

"We can't leave her here," I said. "She needs a proper burial."

Vlad yanked open a cabinet, studied its contents, and threw it across the room. Metal implements spilled out and I turned away.

"There are grave markers near the woods in the back of the Guild," Vlad said.

Shaking my head, I swallowed, my throat tightened. "No. Not here. Not on these grounds. She needs a real cemetery, not a dump site where they discarded all the others who didn't survive this place."

"We'll take care of her," Clive promised.

"No. I will. I want to look up her name, see if there are relatives in a cemetery around here. We can't take her home, but we can at least do that."

"Yes," Clive said. "When it gets dark, we'll go out and find her people."

Nodding, I went back to the cage, grabbed the door, and tore it off its hinges, throwing it as Vlad had. Taking off my jacket, I knelt beside her and gently laid it over her, my tears splashing on the fabric.

"Come on, love," Clive said, helping me up. "Let's go upstairs. We'll get you another jacket and then we'll go out and look for the Csonkas."

I took his hand and squeezed, following him out of that hellish room. "Don't you have to attend one of those gatherings?"

Scoffing, Clive said, "If they wanted me to attend, they shouldn't have poisoned me."

Vlad waited for us at the stairs, my pastry box and book in his hands. He handed them to me, and I waved him up with us.

"Come to our room. How much time do we have before you guys can go out?" I asked.

"Roughly thirty minutes," Vlad said.

Clive paused at the door, listening. After a moment, he opened it and stepped out. "Can we assume no cameras are pointed in this direction?" Clive's voice was so low, I barely caught the words, but Vlad nodded.

The door snicked closed as we made our way down the main hall before turning right, into the hall of bedrooms. At our door, Clive pulled out his key and glanced back at Vlad, who gave him a barely discernable shrug of one shoulder.

We all went in and Clive closed the door. Keeping my voice low, I said, "Why are you guys acting so weird?"

Clive went to the closet and pulled out the jacket I'd worn yesterday. "Our kind rarely ever visit each other's rooms. And certainly not to chat."

I looked between the guys. "So, if anyone sees us walking out together..." I left the rest of that sentence unspoken, my cheeks flaming as I turned to Vlad. "Sorry. If you want to go, we can meet up later."

Vlad walked over to the couch and sat down, stretching his legs out. "Given what they normally say about me, this will be a nice change. Keep them wondering."

145

"We were all together in Vlad's room—" I realized why things were a little tense when Clive found me there, why Vlad was explaining to Clive how I'd ended up in his room.

I turned to Clive. "Sorry. I didn't mean to worry you."

He gave me a soft kiss. "Your loyalty was never in question. My only thought was how to explain a pile of dust in Vlad's room if he'd tried anything with you." He helped me on with the jacket and we sat in the two chairs opposite the couch.

Pulling out my phone, I looked up Aliz Csonka while Clive and Vlad discussed the best way to move her. "Oh, Csonka—or however you pronounce it—is a pretty common name. There's a museum, and a statue, and a machine shop, a glass blower, a lawyer, a high school, a bus stop… This is dumb. One of you needs to do the search. I can't read Hungarian, so I don't know what it's telling me."

Clive reached over for my phone and started tapping.

Vlad's brow was furrowed, his expression dark.

"Is something wrong?" I asked.

Clive glanced up at Vlad and then resumed searching.

Shaking his head, Vlad said, "No. Just thinking."

He misses his wife, love, Clive told me.

"You mentioned your wife Ilona when we were downstairs," I said. "Can I ask how you met? Given how vampires respond to me, I doubt it was a typical meet cute."

He tilted his head and finally said, "I don't know what that means, but we met in the woods." He paused again. "I should go back. I saw her for the first time in the palace. She was a cousin of the Hungarian King, Mathias Corvinus.

"Between campaigns, I was often summoned to the palace to report." He shook his head. "How many times am I supposed to say *we killed them all*? They wanted to hear every grisly detail while painting me as a madman. My first two wives were daughters of nobles, the marriages arranged to create alliances. They both hated me." He shrugged. "I wasn't the kindest of men. They were probably right to turn to other, gentler men while I was away at war.

"My second wife had died the previous year in childbirth." He paused again, the silence growing. "I wasn't looking for another wife. I'd planned to report to the king and leave. Ilona was in the throne room, standing with other ladies of noble birth." His mustache twitched.

"Beautiful, she was. Long dark hair and big brown eyes, she was taller than the other women, taller than me. And bored. She looked especially bored. Instead of leaving, I stayed for the evening meal and watched her—"

"But not in a creepy way, right?" I interrupted. "You didn't scare her, did you?"

Clive's shoe tapped my sneaker.

"What?" I said to Clive. "I like him and all, but that doesn't mean it's okay for him to be creeping on some poor teenager."

Vlad closed his eyes a moment, his expression relaxing almost into a smile. "No. I did not bother her, merely watched as her father negotiated a marriage for her with an old man, a wealthy one with a rattling cough and large boils on his neck.

"She clearly wasn't interested, so her father yanked her away from the others to hiss in her ear, his meaty fingers digging into her arm. I wanted to beat him for that alone, but it wasn't my place to intervene. Had the father pushed it, I was contemplating asking the king to step in. He owed me."

"That was nice of you," I said.

He tipped his head to me. "Ah, yes. I'm famed the world over for my niceness." With a little headshake, he continued, "Ilona was even more strong-willed than she was beautiful. He sent her away from the excitement and glamour of the palace to punish her while continuing negotiations."

"Probably also to control her," I said. "To keep her away from other men while he got the best price for her."

Nodding, Vlad continued, "Yes. His goal had been to hide her away in the country home until it was time for the wedding. She traveled by carriage with servants. A little after sunset, they were overtaken by thieves."

"Oh, no." I'd read stories. Usually they just robbed, but often they were more violent.

"The carriage driver carried a dagger, which he pulled, so he was the first to die. Ilona's family was wealthy. The horses alone were worth quite a lot. The thieves killed everyone and drove the carriage with all her belongings away."

At my confused look, Vlad continued, "Ilona was injured and left for dead. Had she not been so stubborn, she probably would have bled out with the others by the side of the road. Instead, she ripped her chemise and staunched the wound in her chest."

He tapped the space between his heart and shoulder. "Lucky shot. She knew enough about hunting to not try to yank the arrow out. She broke off the shaft and began the long walk home.

"The stench of blood and death drew predators. She was exhausted and blood loss was taking away what little strength she had. She wanted to rest but heard the howl of a wolf and kept going."

I drew my legs up and wrapped my arms around them.

"The wolf tracked her and attacked. She fought as best she could, but he was far stronger. He didn't eat her, as he had some of the others in her party. Probably too full by then. When he left her, she was bleeding from multiple injuries, her body hidden in the brush.

"She said she heard riders pass on the road but didn't have the energy or voice to call out. Angry, cursing her father for sending her to her death, she finally slept, assuming death had come for her. Instead, she eventually felt the warmth of the sun and blinked her eyes open to a new day."

His fingers twitched. "She got herself up, her dress torn and covered in blood, and walked. It was after nightfall when she made it home. The servants panicked, wanting to call for help, but Ilona assured them she was fine. Never felt better, in fact."

TWENTY

Werewolves Bite First and Ask Questions Later

"At the palace," Vlad continued, "I threatened the boil-ridden man to say no to her father. He was quite upset, but I assured him he'd be at the end of a long, sharp pike if he pursued the marriage."

"Nice," I said, grinning.

"He means it," Clive murmured, and I remembered *the Impaler* part of Vlad's name.

"Oh, yeah," I muttered.

Vlad smiled, and it was terrifying. "No one had yet heard about the attack on the road. Ilona hadn't sent word to her father, no doubt because she hated him and didn't want to be called back for a wedding."

"I realize it may pale in comparison to escaping death—twice—but I'm sure she appreciated being saved from the boil-ridden man," I said.

He nodded. "I went in search of her, to tell her I'd stopped the alliance, and to offer myself instead. I took a room at a lodge an hour's ride away and returned each day to court her. At first, I'd been struck by her beauty, but as we talked, I found—as you said about your husband—her beauty was the least interesting thing about her."

149

He stared into the fire. "She was smart, witty—I wasn't used to that—and strong. She loved challenging me, wanting to hear the stories of war and then arguing how I'd done it all wrong and what she would have done in my place."

Clive looked up with a smile, reached over and squeezed my hand, and then went back to researching.

"I fell in love with her, and I think she softened to me. Weeks later, at the full moon—not that that meant anything at the time—she got sick. There were only two servants in the house with her, but both were doing their best to take care of her. She was feverish and sick to her stomach. She didn't want me to see her, but I kept close in case I needed to visit an apothecary."

Staring into the flames, he seemed lost in the memory. "I heard a shout and a scream. I ran into the house and saw a huge wolf break through the back door. I ran up the stairs, looking for Ilona, and found her servants dead on the ground, their throats ripped out."

I covered my mouth. I knew what it was to change all alone with no idea what was happening. Thankfully, I hadn't hurt anyone. I didn't know how I'd have lived with myself if I had.

"Her bed was empty, the sheets ripped. I'd thought she'd been taken by the wolf, strange as that would have been, so I ran out into the woods to look for her. For hours, I tracked the wolf, trying to find Ilona.

"Eventually, I found it in a clearing and made to kill it. It was behaving oddly, though. It just sat under a tree, watching me. When I got close, it raised the side of its lip and growled, but it was half-hearted at best. It was the eyes that got me. The color was lighter, but the intelligence was Ilona's."

"Yes," Clive said. "Sam's eyes lighten to gold, but they're her eyes. I still see her in them."

I didn't know that.

"I hadn't believed such things existed, but there she was, staring at me. I said her name and she came to her feet, backing away. She bumped into the tree behind her, yipped, and ran off again."

"It's terrifying," I said. "Changing for the first time with no warning, no understanding of what's happening." I tightened my arms, wrapped around my legs. "I thought I was going crazy. Everything looked and smelled different. I kept tripping because I couldn't get my brain to understand I had four legs."

A shiver went through me. "I thought it was a nightmare I couldn't wake up from. And I hadn't killed anyone, hadn't had the scent and taste of blood on me. The poor thing was probably in shock."

Vlad had turned his attention from the fire while I spoke. He nodded. "That was what I thought too. I'd seen young men in war after they'd killed for the first time. Eyes huge. Body trembling."

"Yes," Clive agreed. "The enormity of taking another's life, of not only cutting off their potential, but that of everyone connected to that person, everyone who might have come after that person. It can drop a man to his knees."

Vlad studied Clive a moment. "I know your reputation. You've killed countless numbers over the centuries, but I would guess that you were the one on your knees after your first kill."

Clive went back to tapping and scrolling. "It was so long ago. Who remembers?"

The corner of Vlad's mustache lifted.

"I went back to the house and waited for her to return. Midmorning, she came out of the woods, dazed and naked. I gave her my coat and took her in to clean and tend to." He shook his head. "There are no manuals."

Clive chuffed out a laugh. "Sam is annoyed by that as well."

"I mean, if you're part of a pack, okay," I said. "There are others who can guide you, but if you're all alone?" I threw my hands up. "It's a life of trial and error."

"Yes," Vlad said, "but we figured it out together. We married—"

"Did you bribe or threaten her dad?" I asked.

He smiled that scary smile again. "Guess. I bought a large parcel of wooded property and had a house built. Once a month, she had a safe area to run in and hunt. I made it far enough away from her family that they rarely visited."

Pausing, he stared into the fire again. "We were happy." He scratched his jaw. "First time in my life I was happy. It lasted a little over a year. I was called back for another battle. I had to leave Ilona. That was the battle where I was mortally wounded.

"As I laid bleeding on the field, I wished only to see Ilona one last time. That was when the vampires came, feeding from those of us on the edge of death. The one who changed me knew who I was, said I was quite the prize."

He looked inward a moment. "I believe he thought he was getting a guard dog."

"Idiot," Clive murmured.

Nodding, Vlad said, "It was his last stupid decision. Clearly, he did *not* know me. I handed him his final death and raced home to Ilona. When I returned, though, Ilona wasn't there. It was the night after the full moon. Our servants were beside themselves with worry. They'd told me Ilona hadn't been in her room that morning. I assumed she'd slept in the woods, but they said they hadn't seen her all day.

"I went out looking. Her trail was easy to follow in this new form of mine. I tracked her to a clearing. There was a lot of blood and the scent of two men. I tracked them to a tavern in the village center, telling stories to all assembled of the huge wolf they'd tracked and killed."

"No," I whispered.

"The short version is I killed everyone in the tavern and found Ilona's wolf dropped on the floor behind the bastards poaching on my land. I brought her home and buried her in the garden beneath our bedroom window."

"I'm so sorry," I said.

He nodded, not looking at me.

In the ensuing silence, Clive said, "I found Aliz's family."

"You did?" I put my feet down and turned to him.

"He found them almost at once," Vlad said. "He was giving me space to remember and talk about my wife."

"Thank you for sharing your memories with us," I said, wiping my face dry.

Brushing off my sympathy, Vlad stood. "Where are we going?"

Clive rose as well. "There's a graveyard beside a small church up in the hills. Darling, meet us just inside the metal door. Vlad and I will go retrieve Aliz and bring her to you."

"Did you learn nothing from my tale?" Vlad said to him. "I'll get the child. You stay with your wife." He left, closing the door quietly behind himself.

Clive opened his arms and I walked into them.

"It's so sad. All of it, Aliz, Ilona, Léna." I hugged him tightly and felt his kiss on my head. "Give me a minute." I went to the bathroom and splashed cold water on my face. Grabbing a washcloth, I dried off and bucked up. We had work to do. Aliz needed to go home.

When I went out, Clive was waiting by the door. He opened it and we walked silently past all the doors on our way to the main hall.

Is anyone watching us? I asked him in my head.

I assume there's always someone watching.

Paranoid much?

Realistic, he responded.

When we reached the door, he pulled a tiny can of mechanical lubricant out of his pocket.

Always thinking, you are, I said. I hated the damn screeching door, letting people know where I was, but I hadn't thought to fix it.

He sprayed the hinges, opened the door a couple of inches, and then sprayed again. We slid through a narrow opening and then he sprayed the hinges from the inside. Placing the can on the earthen ground to the side of the door, he said, *In case you need it again.*

A moment later, Vlad slid through the now quiet door with a

small duffle bag in his hand. He saw me staring at it and said, "There wasn't a better way to transport the child when we'll be running through the streets."

I hated it, but he was right. We went through the tunnel, out past the dumpster, and then Clive swung me up on to his back and we were racing through streets. It wasn't long before we left the town proper and were crossing fields into the hills.

Vlad said something, but it was too low for me to hear.

What did he say? I asked Clive.

He said he scents wolves. As do I. We may be on pack grounds.

Before too long, we came to an abandoned wooden chapel in the woods. Windows were missing, as was some of the roof. Vegetation had overrun the tiny church. Clive put me down and we walked around the side. Headstones, cracked, moss-covered, and leaning, were lined up in drunken rows.

Silently, we walked in different directions, trying to read the worn stones, looking for Csonka. The markers were so different from American ones. These looked like stories, like sentences about the deceased. I had no idea what was written, but it felt more personal than the simple names and dates on ours. Not knowing Hungarian, I had to just scan, looking for the right letters in the right order.

"Here," Vlad whispered.

Clive and I went to him, and we studied all the stones in this section with that name, looking for dates that might coincide with her life, her family.

"Here," Clive murmured. Reading the Hungarian, he said, *Here lies Csonka Lenci, Born in Szentendre, Daughter to Takács László and Klara, Wife to Medárd, Mother to László, Keve, Aliz. Rest in peace.*

Yes. I squeezed his arm. *We need to bury her with her mother.*

Clive knelt and began to dig, with Vlad dropping to help. I should have been paying attention to our surroundings. Instead, I was holding the duffle bag with Aliz's bones, hoping she'd been reunited with her family on the other side long ago. As I'd never seen her ghost at the asylum, I hoped it was so.

An angry shout made me jump. Before I could register the movement, Clive and Vlad stood between me and the angry man. László, the Buda pack Alpha, was standing at the tree line, a look of horror and outrage on his face.

Clive said something, but then László threw his head back and howled.

From the forest, wolves stalked toward us. At least forty of them surrounded us.

Shit.

TWENTY-ONE

Werewolves Aren't Known for Their Trusting Natures

The Alpha snarled something at us and the wolves moved in. "Stop," I shouted.

Clive translated. *He says we have no right to be on pack lands.*

"And we have no desire to trespass in your territory. We're only trying to return a child to her mother." I didn't know how common the name László was, but given his reaction to our touching this grave, I wondered if I was holding the remains of his sister or daughter.

Clive translated. *You have Viktoria's contact. You dumped the bloodsuckers' victims on us. Made us clean up their mess. Made us cover for those demons! Now you defile my family's resting place?*

Growls filled graveyard.

Vlad turned and moved behind me, facing the pack. I was being caged in a vampy sandwich.

"Not defiled. We were trying to reunite your family, to return her to her mother." More growls and some snapping jaws. Knowing they hated the vampires, I switched from *we* to *I*. "I found the remains of a werewolf child. She was in an old, condemned building—"

The Alpha interrupted with a word. Clive translated for me. *Where?*

156

I turned to Clive. *Am I allowed to say?*

No.

"I can't tell you that."

Deeper, more angry snarls answered that.

"But there was a paper with her name on it. We—I looked up where the Csonkas were buried so I could return her to her people."

Clive translated. There was silence and then the Alpha stalked toward us. *If you are lying, I will kill you myself.* He stopped, his eyes on the bag in my hand. *What's her name?*

At this point, I was looking over Clive's shoulder at the Alpha because there was no way Clive was letting any of the wolves touch me.

"Her name is Aliz."

At my words, the Alpha howled and demanded something, his arms outstretched.

He wants you to give her to him.

I lifted the bag. Clive took it from me and held it out to the Alpha, who tore it from Clive's grip. He unzipped it and looked inside, dropping to his knees.

They did that thing again, moving faster than I could track. I was on Clive's back. He and Vlad leapt over the ring of werewolves and raced back toward the Danube.

Sorry, love. I had to get you out. There was no more logic or reason at that point. He was mourning and we were the ones who'd brought him his sister's bones.

Are we sure Aliz is his sister?

Vlad was right, Clive told me. *I'd found this graveyard as soon as I started searching. While he told you about his wife, I texted the San Francisco Historian for any information about this girl, the name, the Alpha, whatever he had. He responded while you were in the bathroom, washing your face. László, the Alpha, was attacked by a rogue werewolf when he was thirteen and his sister was ten.*

They almost lost her. It's honestly a miracle that a child survived the attack. She and her brother shifted that next full moon. Hunters heard the howls and went in search of them. Aliz was young and small. She was no match for them. They wounded her with an arrow and took her, not killing her right away. In her distress, she began to shift back to human.

Oh, no.

The hunters apparently thought her a devil, but when faced with killing the child of a family they knew, they couldn't do it. They took her to the asylum and never spoke of it, thinking it a kindness to the searching, grieving family to shield them from their daughter's dark possession.

László apparently blamed himself. He'd left her, running after a stag. That was how the hunters had found her all alone.

I felt sick to my stomach about all of it.

We were behind the dumpster and in the tunnel before Clive put me down.

"I'm sorry, darling. This puts a damper on you wandering around Budapest on your own. I don't trust the wolves not to hurt you." He took my hand and led the way. "We'll go to the kitchen and find you some food. They didn't know we were coming, so they can't have tampered with it yet."

"Yum," I grumbled. "I love probably-not-poisoned food."

Vlad was about to trigger the tunnel door open when Clive said, "Wait please."

Do you sense anyone on the other side of the door?

I paused, standing behind Clive, out of Vlad's line of view, and tapped into my necromancy, looking for the green blips of vampires. *Yes. Two. Cadmael is right outside this tunnel. Sebastian is waiting in the hall.*

"We can go now," Clive said.

"Why did we stop?" Vlad asked

"Sorry," I said. "That was me." I waved over Clive's shoulder. "All that piggyback riding made my panties ride up. All fixed now."

The look on Vlad's face was priceless and it took all my self-control not to laugh.

We stepped out of the tunnel and found Cadmael leaning

against a carved rock wall. He pushed off, standing straight as the door closed. "Finally."

"Has something happened?" Clive asked.

Cadmael shook his head. "Not yet, but I've been talking with—no. I've been allowing others to talk near me and so have picked up a few things."

"And we're meeting here because?" Vlad asked.

"Do you guys have any folding chairs?" I asked, looking for anywhere to sit down other than the ground. "We could stash some in here for these clandestine meetings."

Cadmael stared at me a moment, much like one would stare at a dog who'd suddenly begun speaking. "Our goal is not to alert the Guild that we're meeting in secret."

"P'fft. Have you met vampires? All you guys do is whisper in secret, foment grudges, and rip off heads." I rolled my eyes. "And if you're that concerned, we can hide them in the side tunnel here. Of course, that means Vlad has to be invited so he can open the door and get them out, but he's cool, so no big deal."

Vlad just stared, but I saw a telltale crinkling around his eyes. He dug me.

Cadmael looked at Clive. "You may find her lack of respect charming, but I do not."

"Rude," I grumbled, moving to a far wall and sitting down. I felt him pushing in my mind again. I didn't know if he was looking for information or trying to mesmerize me into shutting up. Either way, asshole. "And keep out of my head. My thoughts and secrets are none of your business," I snarled, sick of his shit.

A hairsbreadth later, I was dangling off the ground, Cadmael's hand tight around my throat. Clive already had his arm around Cadmael's neck.

"Old friend," Clive ground out, "if you don't release my wife, I'll be handing you your final death."

I felt my eyes lighten and my claws slide out. What I was focusing on, though, was Cadmael's cold green blip in my head. Unspooling the gold thread of magic in my chest, I wrapped it around his blip, fulling encasing him, and pulled while stabbing my claws into his chest.

His eyes bugged out and his cheek twitched. Fangs descending, he hissed, his grip tightening.

"Release her now!" Clive demanded.

I yanked the magic cord, squeezing as hard as I could. Unlike the other vamps I'd killed, Cadmael was too strong to crush completely, but I could make him very unhappy.

"Get your fucking hands off me," I whispered past his grip. Yanking again, I caused him to choke and then drop me as he fell to his knees.

Moving faster than I could track, Clive had me as far away as he could get me in the enclosed area, hidden behind him. I hadn't yet released Cadmael, though.

Darling, while I'm inclined to kill him myself, please don't. I'm afraid we need him.

When I snapped my magic back, Cadmael fell forward and then leapt to his feet. His eyes were on Clive, obviously believing Clive was the one who'd had him in a hold. Interestingly, Vlad was watching me, one eyebrow raised.

"You don't like each other," Clive said carefully, trying to keep his rage in check. "That's fine, but you will stay out of her head and keep your hands off her. Do you understand?"

Cadmael turned away, eyes still black. "She needs to learn her place."

Vlad laughed. "Even I've heard tales of how deadly she is." He glanced at me and then back to Cadmael. "She knows when you're mucking about in her head. How many of us can sense and block you? If there's anyone here who doesn't know her place, it's you."

"They can't be trusted," Cadmael ground out, turning back to us.

"Yeah, yeah," I said, sliding from behind Clive. Almost immediately, his arm snaked out and held me hard against him. "Jeez, did some wolf hurt you once and you've never gotten over it? Try therapy."

You're not helping, Clive said.

I'm not trying to. "I'm sick of your anti-werewolf bullshit. Get over it or get the fuck out."

"This is the Guild," Cadmael said, his voice low and dangerous. "If anyone should be getting out—"

"All right," Vlad said. "Enough. Clive's right. You don't have to like her. Hell, I hate everyone, but I still know how to tolerate allies, especially useful ones."

"What use can she possibly have," he sneered, "besides the obvious one."

Clive moved, but it was Vlad who got there first, slapping Cadmael with such force, he staggered to the side a step.

When dealing with beings who can kill easily, a slap is particularly humiliating.

"Do you have so many trusted allies in your life that you can throw one away, one the age and strength of Clive?" Shaking his head, Vlad paced away. "I don't know what your issue is with Sam. I don't think any of us do, but indulging in this childish antipathy you have for her will lose us one of our strongest weapons against this faction in the Guild trying to destroy us."

Cadmael took a moment to get his facial expression, if not his emotions, under control. "That was why I was waiting here for you, to discuss this, before she interrupted to demand a chair," Cadmael said.

"I believe," Vlad said, "if you'll recall correctly, I'm the one who interrupted, asking why we were meeting in one of the least hospitable locations in the Guild. Sam was merely coming up with a way to make this tunnel entrance more comfortable. You're the one who blew up for no reason." He crossed his arms over his chest. "Now that that is settled, what do you have to tell us?"

Cadmael closed his eyes briefly and then said, "Like Thomas, Henry"—he glanced at me—"the other Australian Counselor, has been seeking me out for no discernible reason this past week, dropping comments about how he thinks the Guild may be overstepping in some respects.

"After I walked the townspeople out with you, he came back with Thomas, wondering why I didn't see feeding from humans to be our right. They launched into age-old arguments about not denying our nature or hiding our power."

Giving his head a quick shake, he added, "I've heard the same points countless times over the millennia and the answer is always the same. Humans outnumber us and we are powerless during the day."

"The ones who are pushing for the dissolution of the Guild," Vlad said, "are too young to have experienced what it was like when Hunters ruled."

"We live quite comfortably in the shadows," Clive said. "Making ourselves known to the world will not only inspire a new generation of Hunters but will cause governments and banks to seize our assets." He finally released the arm around me. "They've obviously never had to feed from livestock in the fields or hide in sewers to escape the sun."

"It's not just the Australian Counselors," Cadmael said. "At least one of the Asian Counselors—Dakila—seems to be spending a great deal of time with them."

"Perhaps instead of these interminable meetings, we should have history lessons," Clive said.

"Maybe you should," I suggested. "The internet is everywhere. Get a channel or site, one you need a password for or an invitation to, and fill it with interviews with older, more experienced vampires. Don't show faces or names, just stories. Teach the youngsters that their desire to be rock stars will lead to your extermination."

They were silent. Whatever. I thought it was a good idea.

"I like that," Clive finally said. "If someone finds it who shouldn't, they're anonymous stories that could just as easily be fiction or the work of a conspiracy theorist in a basement."

Both Vlad and Cadmael looked thoughtful, considering.

"In fact," I added, "we can set it up that way. Make it look like the ravings of a nutjob. Lame graphics. A black background with red font so bright it makes your eyes water. It'll be too embarrassingly bad to be real."

Vlad nodded slowly. "It won't change the minds of the zealots, but it might sway those who are unsure."

"In the meantime," Cadmael said, "we need to keep those three from destroying the Guild."

Is Sebastian still in the hall?

I checked. *Yep.*

Clive rested his palm on the door. "Sebastian is outside. We shouldn't all go out at once."

Vlad gave Clive an appraising look and then said, "Wait here. I'll lead him away." With one more wary glance at Clive, Vlad went through the door.

Nice! Now Vlad isn't sure what other gifts you might have, I said to him.

It doesn't pay to be boring or predictable.

At least not around vamps. Can we eat now? I'm starving.

You tell me, Clive said. *Have they gone?*

I checked. No vamps. "Let's go," I said, grabbing his hand. "Show me where the kitchen is." Clive and I were ignoring Cadmael. He could come or go as he saw fit. I didn't want to spend more time with him than was absolutely necessary.

How's your throat? Clive asked.

Okay. He wasn't trying to kill me. If he had been, I'd be dead. He hates wolves and really wanted me to shut up.

I'm sorry, he said. *I've known Cadmael for centuries. I have no idea why he has such an issue with you.*

I don't want to think about him anymore. I just want to eat.

We slipped around the door and strode down the hall.

The kitchen is in the opposite wing. We were still speaking mind-to-mind. There was no point in letting anyone who might be listening know where we were going.

The men's side? Dang. So far, I'd only dealt with female ghosts— I couldn't believe I'd only now realized that. Men had been in this asylum too. I'd seen the two male attendants. Did they stick to their wing even in death?

As we walked across the white marble of the entry, I slowed. The ghosts I was already dealing with were bad enough. If the men hadn't realized I was here, I didn't want to announce it by walking through their wing. Of course, I did know how to get rid of them, assuming they understood Hungarian, or now Romanian.

Problem? Clive asked.

I sped up. *No, just thinking.* My stomach growled.

We turned down the hall into what used to be the men's wing.

There are offices here for each of the Guild members, including a suite of rooms: sitting room, bedroom, bathroom, et cetera, Clive told me.

Vlad has rooms up here but stays in the basement?

Apparently, Clive responded. *One would assume he finds face-gnawing ghosts and the stench of dead vermin preferable to living beside others of our kind.*

I don't know, I replied. *He's probably not wrong.*

Clive opened the door to a large—and thankfully empty—kitchen. The cabinets were a country white, the appliances a smokey steel. White marble floors continued into this room, the counters a darker, gray-veined marble.

He pointed at a pantry door. "I found the protein bars in there."

I went to the overlarge refrigerator first, looking for real food. There were steaks, but I didn't want to take a Renfield's dinner. I mean, were they dicks to me? Sure, but that didn't mean it was cool for me to steal their food.

Opening one of the drawers, I found sliced lunch meats. "Did you happen to see where the bread was? I can make a sandwich and take it back with me."

Clive opened the door to the pantry, looked in, and came back with a loaf of dark brown bread.

"Perfect." I grabbed condiments, along with a tomato, and got to work. "If you have vampy things to do, go ahead."

He watched me for a moment more. *I'll go find Sebastian. See if I can find out how deep in this he is, how rotten the Guild has become.*

Be careful. Cornered animals lash out.

He gave me a kiss and went in search of answers.

I finished making the sandwich, put things away, and took a large bottle of water and some candy bars from the pantry. As I headed for the door, though, the overhead lights flickered and went out as the ghost of an attendant walked in, his eyes gleaming silver.

Grinning, leering, he sauntered in, forcing me back. He reached out a hand, running a finger down my cheek. It was a whisper against my skin but I felt it, and he knew it. His gaze fired as he tried to force me into the corner.

Hands full, I pushed with my magic. *Megy!*

He staggered back, bared his teeth, and then dove at me. I was slammed into the cabinet behind me, bouncing my head off the corner of the wooden uppers. I had the presence of mind to at least drop the plated sandwich on the counter as I was sliding to the floor, water bottle and candy bars raining down around me.

I'm walking down a tiled hall. A gas lamp sputters sickly yellow light. Something feels off. Passing by a door, a man's face suddenly fills the window as he pounds on the wood, shaking the door in its frame.

A large, meaty fist shoots out, hitting the door beneath the window, and the patient falls back. Angry, sneering words in Hungarian issue from my mouth.

No wonder I feel weird. I'm in a bigger, taller body. I don't want to be in this guy's head. I recognized him in the kitchen. He's one of the men who attacked Léna on her first night.

He stops at the next door, uses his key to let himself in. A sweaty old man with an uneven beard is lying in his bed. The smell is overwhelming. The man has soiled himself. He raises a frail arm, barely lifting it off the mattress. His voice is weak, but he seems to be asking for help.

The attendant lifts the thin blanket, sees the mess, and curses at the old man, shaking his head and walking out. In the hall, he locks the door again. Another attendant comes around the corner, and they talk. The asshole forcing me on this ride-along points back at the door we just exited.

The other attendant shakes his head and begins to move on, but Asshole grabs the other guy's arm and yanks him back, sending him into the wall. Voice deep, he seems to threaten the other one and then walks on.

A door opens to the left and a slight man with dark, thinning hair and a mustache, wearing a white coat, waves in the asshole. A dirty, sweaty man in his forties is strapped to the bed, but one of the straps—on his right wrist—was ripped, or perhaps bitten through.

The patient is waving the freed fist, trying to hit the White Coat. The White Coat moves his little table on wheels away from the bed and says something to the attendant, who pulls a new strap from his pocket.

The angry man's focus changes from White Coat to Asshole, screaming at him instead. His flailing fist catches Asshole on the cheek before Asshole wrestles the patient's arm to the bed frame. Asshole throws his weight on the man as he straps him down again.

With the man unable to move, White Coat takes a large glass and metal syringe from the bowl on his rolling table, moves back to the side of the man's bed, and gives him a shot. The man continues to rail for a minute and then loses steam, his head dropping back, his eyes becoming vacant.

The White Coat is already leaving as the man's mouth hangs open. Asshole circles the bed. He looks out the door, sees White Coat entering the next room, and goes back to the now sedated man. Asshole says something low and guttural before his fist shoots out, punching the man in the jaw. A whimper comes from the patient. Asshole chuckles on his way out.

Around the corner, another White Coat appears. This is the man from the bleeding photo. Even in living color, his skin is pasty and his eyes almost black. He says something to Asshole before moving into one of the patients' rooms.

Asshole grumbles under his breath but continues down the hall, opens a door, and heads into the basement. Muffled shouts erupt as the door closes.

TWENTY-TWO

He Had It Comin'

A sshole descends the stairs and turns down a narrow corridor, walking through a section of the basement I haven't seen. There are no rooms off the corridor, just a weak lantern lighting the way.

When he finally turns a corner and emerges, I see the back of the Gray Dress sitting at the table near the tub room. He's crossed the entire basement and is on the women's side of the asylum now.

No, no, no. I don't want to be in his head, seeing through his eyes. I know what he does to women. My stomach twists. Please. I can't.

He stops at Aliz's door and knocks three times. An attendant opens the door a few inches, one eye looking out. They speak and then the attendant inside opens the door, allowing Asshole to enter. The attendant walks him to the small observation table. He goes through the papers and Asshole nods, waving the other away. He's got it.

When the other attendant leaves, Asshole prowls around the room. He stops at the cabinet and opens the doors. Picking up a long metal rod with spikes at the end, he smacks it into the palm of his other hand and approaches the cage.

Aliz is watching him with wary eyes. She's curled up, making herself as small as possible.

He says something and jabs with the stick, but she rolls away from him, out of reach. He moves to the other side, jabbing and missing her.

She's fast, popping up. Even standing awkwardly, trying to cover her nakedness with her hands, she's faster than he is.

He feints left and then runs right, stabbing through the bars, but Aliz anticipates his move and this time, instead of moving away from the sharp spikes, she moves in and rips the rod from Asshole's hand.

Growling, she spins, sending the spikes back through the bars like a javelin. Her aim is true. The spikes go through his left eye into his brain, dropping him on the spot.

Head pounding, I opened my eyes, still sitting on the floor of the kitchen. "Good job, Aliz," I whispered as I stood shakily and collected my things.

Returning to my room was thankfully uneventful. Two vamps and a Renfield saw me walk by, but they all pretended not to notice me, which was fine and dandy by me.

After eating the sandwich and one of the candy bars, I did the math to figure out what time it was in San Francisco. Knowing Owen should be at work, I called.

The line rang twice and then I heard Owen's voice. "Sam! We were wondering when you were going to check in."

My nerves settled just hearing him. "I should have made this a video call so I could see all of you." Dang it.

"We still can," he said, and the line went dead.

A moment later, my phone rang. When I swiped, Owen was there, standing behind the bar. "That's better," he said. "Where are you? The place looks fancy."

I glanced around our room. "It is, actually. You know how vampires love their antiques, marble, and crystal chandeliers." I rolled my eyes. "How is it there?"

"Good." He turned the phone around and did a sweep of The Slaughtered Lamb, my bookstore and bar. "Everybody wave at Sam," Owen said.

People turned to the phone, smiling and waving. I missed them all so much. This trip was rough. So much of what I was dealing with in the now—and especially in the past—was disturbing, if not downright horrific. It was good to remember there was still light and life in the world, still wonderful friends I loved very much.

I waved back, beaming like a loon. "I miss you guys!"

When Owen's sweep made it to the end of the bar, I saw Fergus standing up, his paws on the edge, with Dave leaning against the wall behind him. Fergus' mouth hung open in a doggy grin before he barked happily.

"How much longer are you going to be?" Dave asked.

Fergus came around the bar and leapt up on Owen, almost knocking him down, in an attempt to get closer to the phone.

"Hi, buddy! I miss you too. I hope you're having fun with Alice and Fyr." I so wished he was here on the couch with me. The asylum ghosts wouldn't be nearly so upsetting if he were sprawled across my lap.

"Alec's the official dogsitter now. They switched off, so he was at our house last night. Since Fergus likes being in the bar—and Alec was visiting his grandmother today—I have him with me."

"I hope he's being a good boy," I said.

Owen laughed. "That tail of his is no joke. He took out a very old vase, but Alec was there to catch it before it smashed on the floor. We've already learned not to leave drinks on coffee tables or he'll sweep them off when he walks by."

My heart swelled. I wanted to be there. "Sounds about right. Sorry, Dave, I didn't answer your question. We should be home in a few days. There's just some final stuff Clive is dealing with."

"Good," I heard him grumble. "There are cookies for you in the freezer."

"Score!" As if I needed another reason to long for home. "Any problems I should know about?"

"Not a problem," Owen said, the camera back on him. "Since it's summer, Meri wanted more hours, and I gave them to her. You need to see the new display she's made." He started toward the bookstore and then stopped. "Never mind. I'll let her show you when you get back."

The camera bounced as he walked into the kitchen. "We got

another order of books." He went into the storage room and flipped the camera around. "Eight boxes. I haven't touched them, as I know you love processing them. I just wanted you to know that they arrived."

I sighed. "I wish I was there with you guys."

Owen's brow furrowed and he moved across the kitchen to stand beside Dave. "Is something going on?" He lowered his voice, so none of the sensitive ears in the bar could hear. "You've got shadows under your eyes. Do you need help?"

"No. It's okay." I glanced around, feeling the ghosts pressing in on me again. *MEGY!* "This place is crawling with the strongest ghosts I've ever encountered."

Dave face was on the screen. "Can they hurt you?"

I thought about the face-gnawing ghost. "Not really. I can feel them and it's uncomfortable, but they can't really hurt me, not physically. I keep getting dragged into horrible memories of the abuses they endured, though, which is no picnic. Of course, it was far worse for them. I've also pissed off the local pack."

I shrugged. "Nothing I can do about it, though. I was just trying to help, but now I'm the public face of the bloodsuckers and they have to hate someone, so... It's fine. We're almost out of here."

"Sam," Dave said, "you know I can be anywhere in the world. If you need me, you call me."

My throat tightened and I nodded. We weren't where we used to be in our friendship, not since I'd learned some hard truths about my mother's death, but I knew he was doing what he could to look after me, whether I wanted him to or not. "I know. Thank you."

He handed the phone back to Owen and resumed cooking. Owen gave me a concerned look but held his tongue, heading back to the bar.

"Okay, talk to Fergus one more time and then I'll let you go," Owen said.

He turned the phone and there was my handsome Irish

Wolfhound, sitting like a good boy, eyes shining as he stared at me and whined.

"I know, little man. Not too much longer. I'll be home soon, and we'll go for a run on the beach."

He jumped up and I recognized my mistake. He tore back and forth, from Owen to the stairs. I'd used the R-word and now he wanted to run.

"Now you've gone and done it," Owen said. "I'll call Alec. His lunch with Benvair should be done by now. He can run here and then run Fergus back with him."

"Sorry and thank you, Owen. For everything," I said.

"No problem. Alec's probably looking for an exit strategy about now anyway. Take care of yourself and let us know if we need to mount a rescue mission." The picture bobbled, as he had to get Fergus under control. The last thing we wanted was Fergus accidentally knocking over one of the elderly wicches in his enthusiasm.

The call ended and I sat staring at the black screen.

I flinched when the bedroom door opened. Beloved stormy gray eyes had me relaxing a moment later. "Did you find Sebastian?"

"I did." He reached for my hand and pulled me up into a hug. "I've missed hearing you laugh."

Head in the crook of his neck, I breathed in his scent. "You heard me?"

"Given my kind's sensitive hearing and desire not to be overheard, we speak in hushed tones, so, yes, I heard you down the hall. It made me happy and wish I hadn't been so selfish to bring you here with me."

Holding me close, he kissed my ear. "You could be home with Fergus and your friends, unpacking new books."

I warmed at the thought. "I do love all those things, but I love you more." I squeezed him hard. "And if I wasn't here, Aliz wouldn't have been found and returned to her family."

"Starting a war with the wolves," he added.

I ignored him. "And you never would have become friends with Vlad."

"I don't believe *friend* is the word you're looking for."

"Sure it is." I leaned back to run my finger down his chiseled jaw. "You like and trust him. Don't pretend you don't."

Tilting his head, he caught my finger between his teeth, licking the tip. Letting it drop, he swooped in to kiss me. Clive's kisses were potent things.

Head spinning, I finally surfaced and found myself on the bed. "How'd I get over here?"

"You really should be more aware of your surroundings, darling," he chided as he pulled my top over my head, my bra being flung after it.

"What are you doing?" I asked.

"I thought that would be obvious," he said, nuzzling my throat.

"No. I mean, I thought you had vampy stuff you had to do tonight?"

His fangs slid into my neck as he drew in my blood, my body throbbing in time with each pull. I supposed it didn't get more vampy than that. I was going up in flames and couldn't think past Clive. Only Clive.

His hand dragged across my stomach and then slid down between my legs. When had I lost my pants? His clever fingers teased and swirled as I squirmed on the sheets.

Clive, now, please.

He took one last swallow as his fingers sent me over the edge and I was floating on waves of pleasure. I was only vaguely aware he was moving and then his mouth was on me everywhere, kissing and suckling, as he moved down my body.

When his tongue replaced his fingers, I was shooting up and over again, exhausted, energized, and blissed out.

He moved up my body, grabbed my hips, lifted, and then plunged into me. I lost my breath again. Straining, I wrapped my legs around him, meeting him stroke for stroke. The pressure built until my mind blanked and my body exploded.

Flying. This time, Clive was right there with me.

Vibrating, skin oversensitized, I ran my hands up and down his back as he slid down my body, resting his head on my breast.

While I was getting my breath back, I told him, *It's amazing how quickly I got used to having you all to myself when we left the nocturne.* I ran my fingers through his hair, scratching his scalp. *Coming here meant losing you to vampy meetings again for most of the night—which is fine. You need to do what interests and fulfills you—but it's awfully nice to have you all to myself, even for a little while.*

He kissed the side of my breast and then rose, resting on his elbows, so he could see my face. *Which makes this harder to ask. Would you mind terribly if we stayed a little longer? You're right. Something rotten is festering in the Guild. We could leave and let someone else deal with it, but who? And how long before we have more coming after us?*

He kissed me again. *There's something wrong with Sebastian. We were never close, but I've met with him on multiple occasions over the centuries. I tried peppering a few comments, a couple of memories, into our conversation, looking for recognition. It wasn't there. If that really is Sebastian, he's been altered in some way.*

Are they connected? I thought of the nightmares, the ghosts, vampires, and Renfields. *This place is filled with the strongest ghosts I've ever encountered. The asylum memories I've relived have been horrendous. The cruelty is unreal, and yet not. I've read about nineteenth century mental asylums and, yes, a lot of what's happened tracks with those accounts, but a hidden werewolf? That slow heartbeat you and Vlad hear? I've been on edge ever since you guys told me that. Is another supernatural creature, like the wolf, imprisoned here?*

Clive rubbed his cheek against my own. *We'll find out.*

Is it this place? Is it the building that's cursed and therefore cursing all who enter? I asked.

I rather hope not, but you're right. Something's going on and we need to figure out what it is.

TWENTY-THREE

A Bloody Mess

I t was late, or I suppose quite early, so Clive and I relaxed under the covers. I turned onto my side and he moved in behind me, wrapping an arm around me.

"Go ahead and sleep, love. It's been a long day and night," he said. "I'll watch over you."

I'd intended to stay awake and talk. Unfortunately, too little sleep did me in and I was out.

I'm walking across the cold white marble of the entry and hear whispering. I stop at the door to the gathering room, where the voice seems to be coming from but find only Sebastian, standing alone in front of the fireplace. Head tilted up, his focus is on the dark-eyed, angry man in the frame. I can't hear what's being said but I see the portrait's lips moving. I take a step toward them and they both turn to glare with murder in their eyes. I flinch and then...

I'm climbing stairs. With each step, the staircase flashes, strobing between clean and bright and old and dingy. Where is this? No one's mentioned the upper floors of this building. I assumed they hadn't been remodeled yet. At the top, I step out into another ward, white—leaning toward gray—tiles beneath my feet. A Gray Dress hurries down the hall, her arms laden with an overflowing basket of dirty linens.

Muffled cries and shouts from locked rooms echo down the hall, but I don't follow the Gray Dress. Instead, I see the back of a woman I think is Léna turn down the far left hall. A dark wood floor shines in the low light. Wait. Where are the white walls and tile?

I look back to the right. Where a moment ago a Gray Dress was, I see more dark wood, carved moldings, a bookcase, and a different portrait of the angry man.

I follow the back of the girl I'd seen earlier. This place looks nothing like the asylum, so I suppose it must not have been Léna. Unless she's guiding me through others' memories now. My head hurts. I wish I knew what was going on.

Crossing to what I think of as the men's side of the asylum, I turn the corner and feel immediately chilled. There's no lamp, so even the weak, yellow light I've accustomed myself to is gone. It's deeply shadowed, the only dim light coming from open doorways along the hall. Where did the woman go?

I stop and look through a doorway, finding only dust and a stripped mattress on a metal frame. The image flickers and it's a plush sitting room. A woman with large, frightened eyes sits in a chair, her hands clutched in her lap, her knuckles white. Flicker. An empty asylum room.

I don't like this. The whole place gives me the creeps, but this hall in particular has a bad feel. Just being here makes me wish for a long, hot shower to wash away the sticky grime of cruelty and abuse.

Looming at the end of the hall is a tall wooden double door. It looks nothing like anything else in the asylum, nothing like the remodeled Guild. Heart racing, I don't want to go anywhere near it. I feel the evil from here, but I can't stop my legs from carrying me closer, can't stop myself from reaching out and pushing open the door.

Flames roar in a huge fireplace. Shadows move. A man—the one from the portrait—in a dark tunic with gold embroidery that glints in the fire-light moves across the large room. His movements are somehow both elegant and menacing. Dark hair tied back, a trim black beard, his lips curl in a sneer.

And then I see the young woman I'd been following. Long dark hair curtains her face. She wears a burgundy gown with flowers embroidered at the waist. Eyes downcast, she seems to have quietly accepted her fate.

SEANA KELLY

He growls something, his words like dagger thrusts.

Cringing away, she almost disappears into the voluminous draperies, mumbling what sounds like Apa. Are they father and daughter?

He shouts and she flinches, pulling in, making herself smaller. When he doesn't receive the response he seems to want, he takes her by the shoulders and shakes her, holding her a foot off the floor. She struggles, but at one look from him, she subsides.

He brings her face close to his own and snarls something. Eyes closed, she droops. He spits in her face and then throws her farther than a human could. She hits the far wall and crumples as he stalks out of the room.

I go to the young woman, but there's nothing I can do to help. Ages separate us. I can only stand witness to her pain.

Pushing herself into a seated position, she wipes her face and leans against the wall. She pulls her knees up, curling in on her pain. Here, close to her, I can see her eyes. The man's were a fiery black, but hers are a shimmering lilac, a color no human has ever had. Are they fae?

Wiping the crystal tears from her golden skin, she firms her petal pink lips as she stands, bracing herself against the wall with one arm until she can stand on her own. She walks to the door, water lilies blooming in her footsteps before they wither and disappear in her wake.

I follow her out of the room. Where did she go? Even the flowers on the floor are gone. I travel down the hall, but it's far longer than I remembered. None of this looks familiar.

The lights flicker and the walls change. I'm somewhere else entirely. This is the exam room I'd seen in the basement. The man in the white coat from the bleeding photograph is here, as is Léna. He has her strapped down to the table, a Gray Dress assisting him. Léna looks terrified but is talking in a calm voice, repeating something. The White Coat slaps a hand over her mouth while he says something to the Gray Dress.

The Gray Dress looks between the two, clearly uncomfortable, but he barks at her and she goes out to the hall.

The White Coat's tone changes. Now his words are quiet and soft as he runs his hand over Léna's cheek and down to her shoulder.

No. Not again. I whip out a hand, claws extended, but they slide right *through the White Coat. Léna, though, turns her head away from him, blinking back tears, and meets my gaze.*

With a jolt, I was in the dark and instantly alert. Quiet footsteps were rounding the bed. Clive was beside me, his arm still wrapped around me. I didn't move, didn't change my deep breaths, but I pulled in his scent. Renfield, and one I recognized. This was the one who'd handed Clive the poison, who'd followed me into town.

I almost sat up and asked what the hell he was doing in here when I caught the scent of metal and oil that said gun. I needed him a little closer. Clive had a tendency to hold on tight when we slept, but I needed room to move. The Renfield had come around the bed, which told me I was the target, not Clive.

Daring to barely lift my eyelids, I saw a sharp, thin beam of light aimed at the floor but moving to the head of the bed. This was it.

With Clive pinning me in place, I swiveled my legs out from under the covers and kicked the Renfield into the wall, giving me a moment to get out from under Clive's arm. Leaping, I took our intruder to the ground, slamming his head against the wooden floor.

"Sam?" Voice groggy, I heard Clive move in bed.

"I got it," I said. "Go back to sleep."

While the Renfield was knocked out, I slipped on a robe. Beating people up while naked was super uncomfortable. I flicked on the nightstand lamp. Where had the gun gone?

Eyes on the wannabe killer, I considered what to do with him. He'd tried to kill me. Was I supposed to send him back to the vampires with a pat on the head, saying, *Better luck next time*?

Kneeling, I looked under the bed for the gun and felt movement behind me. I spun, seeing the gun pointed at my head, and swatted his hand down just as he pulled the trigger.

The bang was deafening, especially this close. Eyes wide, he stared, uncomprehending. The bullet had torn a hole in his lower abdomen. Blood had begun to pool beneath him as he spat a stream of angry Hungarian words at me. Clive was suddenly standing in front of me, pushing me back.

Handing me the gun, he gestured to the other side of the room. "Darling, move away, please, and while you're over there, perhaps you can tell me what's going on."

Standing in the doorway to the bathroom, I said, "I woke up to someone in the room. He had a penlight and a gun. He was about to shoot me when I kicked him into the wall. I thought he was out cold, but I forgot what you said about black-shirted Renfields being stronger. Anyway, he came to much faster than I'd thought, and he had the gun again aimed at my head. I smacked it down and he ended up shooting himself. Is that smell normal?"

"Yes," Clive said, dragging on his trousers. "He ripped holes in his intestines. It's a painful death he has in front of him."

"You could take away his pain," I suggested.

Clive looked at me as though I'd grown a second head. "As he tried to kill you—twice—I don't think I will." He punched the Renfield, putting him out for real this time and stopping all the Hungarian cursing. Lifting the man's feet, Clive dragged the creep across the room to the bedroom door. He swung it open and revealed Vlad standing in the hall.

"Was that a—" Vlad looked down at the bloody Renfield. "Ah, I see it *was* a gunshot." He glanced through the bedroom door, his brows furrowed.

I waved. "I'm good."

Clive looked back at me. "Sunset isn't too far off. I'm going to move him before all the others awake."

"We may be cutting it close," Vlad said. "I've noticed a few others rise before the sun goes down."

Vlad went with Clive, no doubt to get the story. I, on the other hand, showered off the blood spatter and got dressed, ready to deal with the fallout. There was no way the vamps were just going to accept a dead Renfield, especially a black-shirted one, if I was involved.

When I came out of the bathroom, Clive was dressed and our

bags were packed. "Gather your things, love. I'm getting you out of here."

I grabbed my toiletry bag, stuffed it in my suitcase, and put on my running shoes. After strapping on my axe, Clive helped me into a short jacket and we headed to the door, only to find Sebastian, a very angry Thomas, a one-armed Delores—who gave me an appraising look—an expressionless Cadmael, and Vlad. Who winked.

"Clive," Sebastian said, "we can't let you go. Thomas is rightfully angered by his assistant's death."

"Whereas, I," Clive began, moving in front of me, "am angered by Thomas sending his assistant to murder my wife in her sleep."

Sebastian raised a hand. "Now, now, we can't know exactly what happened. Before Thomas' man succumbed to his injury, he told us your wife shot him."

I stepped to the side of Clive to better see the vamps in the hall. "He brought the gun into our bedroom. He walked around the bed to me and aimed it at my head. His intent seemed pretty clear. I defended myself. And he ended up shooting himself. I never touched the gun."

"No one cares what a dog—"

Clive had Thomas by the throat against the hall wall. "Apologize or I take your head."

"Tempers are high," Sebastian said, "but that doesn't mean—"

Clive slammed Thomas against the wall again. "Now."

Thomas was not without skills himself. He struck out at Clive, knocking him back. Sebastian and Vlad stepped between them.

Pointing at me, Thomas said, "She must pay for the life of my assistant. It is my right."

By this time, other vamps had left their rooms to watch this play out.

I had to pay him? How much did assistants go for, and could Clive loan me the money?

"I will stand in her stead," Clive said.

Thomas shook his head. "She stole from me. It is my right to challenge her."

Oh, shit. He didn't want cash. He wanted to fight me.

Sebastian looked at Clive. "I'm afraid he's correct. It is his right to challenge her. We can't let you leave until this is decided."

"Watch us," Clive growled.

This was about to get ugly fast. Sebastian was a weak paper pusher and Thomas was clearly an asshole, but Clive could be doing a lot of good for the North American Masters, assuming the Guild survived our visit.

I patted Clive's shoulder. "It's okay." I turned to Thomas. "You can smell your guy in our room. Clearly, he was trespassing. How is his death on us if your guy was where he shouldn't have been? With a gun?"

"You probably invited him in," Thomas countered. "We all know about dogs in heat."

Clive tensed under my hand, so I stepped in front of him. "So, your theory is that although I'm married to one of the most intelligent, powerful, and drop-dead gorgeous men in the known world, I chose to invite the human with the weak chin and the crazy eyes into our bedroom, knowing full well that Clive can wake when the sun is up? That's your thinking at this moment?"

Vlad's mustache twitched but Thomas' eyes were more than a little crazy as well.

Tilting my head back, I whispered over my shoulder, knowing everyone in the hall would hear, "Apparently, there are no intelligence tests for Counselors."

Thomas leapt forward but got slammed back by Vlad

Sam, don't. I'll handle this.

Not this time. I've got it.

"Vlad was in your room," Chaaya, one of the Asian Counselors said. "Perhaps three is what you enjoy."

I sighed and glanced at Clive. "I knew that was going to bite us in the butt. Oh, well. If Mr. Angry Pants over here wants to blame me for his own stupid assistant shooting himself, then whatever.

So, what do we do? Arm wrestle? Poker? Foot race? No word puzzles, though, okay? I'm surprisingly bad at those."

Sam…

It has to be done. I'll be fine.

He's very strong and an excellent fighter, Clive told me.

Are you saying I'm not? I'll kick his ass.

If you die, I'll be quite put out.

TWENTY-FOUR

Let's Get Ready to Rumble!

"Perhaps we should move to the sparring room," Sebastian said, "and we can settle this." He glanced down the hall at all the vampires and Renfields watching. "That seems the best way to put this incident to rest."

As much as I don't like it, Clive told me, *he's right. We need to deal with this before we leave or it will follow us.* He took my hand and we moved down the hall.

A lot of angry vamp eyes were directed at me. *It's fine,* I responded. *I mean, what's the point of being trapped in a haunted asylum with a herd of vampires if you don't get into a melee and start tearing off heads?*

My thoughts exactly and I don't believe herd *is the proper collective noun for my kind.*

A pride? That seems pretty fitting. A flamboyance of vampires? I suggested.

We mostly wear black, Clive said mind-to-mind. *We're not terribly flamboyant.*

How about a flock? You guys turn into bats, right?

I believe the collective for bats is a colony, he told me, *which doesn't sound terribly intimidating.*

Well, I'm sticking with my old favorite, a gaggle of vampires.

Fair enough. He kissed my hand. *Did that settle your nerves?*

Mostly. How large do you think the group is that wants us dead? I wondered.

I think we're about to find out, he said.

Do they hate me because I'm a werewolf or do they actually think I seduced and killed that putz?

My question as well. I was led to believe I'd be meeting with a few members to discuss what being a Counselor entailed and if it was a good fit for me. I was encouraged to bring you and now I'm wondering if it has all been a setup to get rid of both of us in a way that my friends— Cadmael for one—wouldn't take issue with.

And Sebastian's part of the setup? I asked.

It's seeming more and more likely, yes.

I really do think Vlad's on our side, I told him. *Cadmael might hate me, but he cares about you. If those fighters are still here, Noab, Wei, Amir, and Salvador seemed to like you too. If it becomes an all-out war, they might fight on our side.*

Darling, no one is going to risk their own lives. They may secretly root for Thomas, but they won't lift a finger to help him. We're selfish creatures, clinging to our undeath.

We filed into the sparring room, where even more onlookers were waiting. I supposed we were tonight's entertainment.

The crowd ringed the large room, staying back against the walls. Sebastian moved out onto the thin mat. "Thomas has challenged Samantha over the unlawful death of his assistant. Can the two combatants come forward."

"Just a sec," I said. Clive helped me off with my axe sheath and jacket together, so people wouldn't see the axe. I patted his hand, asking him to hold them for me. "Love you." I gave him a quick kiss and moved out onto the mat.

Clive stepped out after me. "As Samantha's mate, it is my right to fight beside her."

"Aww, that's sweet, but I've got this." I lowered my voice,

again knowing everyone could hear me. "We already know he's not too bright. I don't think this'll be hard."

"Thomas," Sebastian said, "Clive has demanded his right as the mate of the challenged. You therefore may have a second fighter as well."

Thomas surveyed the room, his gaze resting on Dakila, one of the Asian Counselors, the one Cadmael had said he'd thought was part of the we-want-the-world-to-know-about-vampires contingent.

Dakila stepped out onto the mat and inclined his head, saying, "I offer my services."

"Accepted," Thomas said triumphantly, smirking at Clive. Thomas and Dakila seemed quite confident in their ability to overpower us.

I didn't understand it. They'd seen Clive fight the previous night. Had someone been feeding them lies? Perhaps the strategy was to take me out quickly, knowing Clive would be too distracted to fight them off effectively.

Thomas had broad shoulders and a scar on his neck, which was odd. Vampires healed quickly. Was it new? Legs braced and arms relaxed, Thomas stared daggers at me, which honestly made no sense. I wasn't anyone to this guy. Beside him stood Dakila, shorter with long dark hair and deep brown eyes. The arrogance written all over his face made me want to punch him.

I grabbed the jacket-wrapped axe from Clive and looked for Vlad. If there was anyone in this room who could be trusted to look after weapons, it was Vlad. I carried the bundle to him, knowing he'd know what the jacket hid.

"Can you watch this for me?" I asked.

"All my life I've dreamed of becoming a valet," he grumbled.

I took that for a yes and handed it over.

"Sebastian," I began, "can I ask a quick question before we start?"

"Yes." He was visibly annoyed I was delaying the fight.

"Just real quick," I assured him. "Thomas, you seem to really hate my guts. I don't know you at all and let's not pretend that you actually care about your minion's death. So why are you actually pissed at me?"

"A vampire mated to an animal is an abomination," he sneered.

Confused, I looked at Clive. "Is he channeling my aunt?" Turning back to Thomas, I waved. "Abigail, is that you? How's Hell treating you?"

"She's insane," Dakila muttered. "Let's get this over with. I've got better things to do with my time."

I gave them both my middle fingers—a double bird, if you will —and then unsheathed just those two razor-sharp claws. With a smile, of course. I was a lady.

Darling, time to tap into that part of your brain that Thoth taught you. We need you in god-mode now.

On it. Probably. Who the hell knew? Thoth said I worked harder when I was protecting someone else. Okay, brain, I need to save Clive. Let's do this.

I located the two vamps' green blips in my head and began to squeeze. Their eyes went black and their fangs descended. Both also glared at Clive, assuming he was the one fucking with them.

Sebastian said, "Go," and Dakila was on me.

I was still registering the word *go* when he was reaching for my neck. I raked my claws down his face, scraping his skull and popping one of his eyes. Ducking under his outstretched arms, I pivoted behind him and rather than the more elegant, bladed hand that Amir had used to the back of Frank's head, I bulked up my arm, made a fist, and with all my werewolf strength punched him in the back of the head.

His skull cracked, the sound loud in the quiet room. You can say this for vampires. They're silent fighters. Dakila staggered forward but shook it off and turned to me again. If vamps could get concussions, he'd have one. One eye was black, but the other was his normal brown.

His movements were off, not as fluid as they had been. Even an injured vampire was deadly, though. I desperately wanted to check on Clive but didn't. I needed to focus on my opponent, not distract Clive from his.

Dakila shook his head again and then moved forward. He took two unsteady steps and his legs bunched. He was going to jump, and I was ready. God-mode engaged.

There were no skips in time, no movie jumps. I was moving as fast or faster. Dakila flew at me like a torpedo but I stepped to the side, running my claws down his body and hooking onto a rib.

Like an Olympian throwing the hammer, I spun with my claws in his chest until I had the momentum to send him sailing across the room and head first into the stone wall. His blip in my head was losing color. I almost had him.

Voices began to register in the room, but I wasn't listening. It sounded like so much white noise, a gnat circling my ear.

I went to the wall, yanked Dakila out. His eyes fluttered. His arms flexed, trying to move. I fisted my hand in his long hair, holding him up off the mat. I didn't stop to think. It had to be done if Clive and I were walking out alive.

I raked my claws through his neck, his body dropping in dust and his head disintegrating in my grip.

Striding back to the center of the mat, I looked for Thomas and found only Clive watching me, eyes vamp black, a vicious smile on his face.

I do so love to watch you fight. His expression hardened. *Down!*

I hit the mat as he leaped over the top of me. Rolling over, I looked behind me and saw Clive ripping someone's head off, effectively stopping the asshole trying to get the drop on me. It was Clive's signature move for a reason.

"And that's what you get, you big cheater." Jeez. What happened to two against two? And what did the now headless guy have to do with Thomas and a dead Renfield?

I checked all the blips in my head, and three standing beside Chaaya had taken a step onto the edge of the mat. They weren't as old or as strong as Dakila or Thomas or, for that matter, whoever Clive had just handed his final death to.

Turning to the side, I studied the three who didn't seem completely sold on this idea. They wore matching expression of disgust and fear. I liked the fear.

"Yes?" I said. "Did you have a question for the class?"

Feeling Clive step up beside me, I squished one of the blips in my head and he dropped to the mat, his body a desiccated husk. The other two looked far less sure about taking us on.

Then I felt a power step out behind us.

Behind you! I've got these two.

The two glanced at their dead comrade and then at me alone, Clive busy fighting whoever was back there.

"So, I guess honor is just out the window at this point. I fought my accuser. What the hell gripe do you two have with me?"

"You gave Dakila his final death," the one on the right said.

"Duh." I shook my head. "They challenged us. We killed them. That's how this works."

Apparently, they were done justifying the attack because they streaked across the mat. I grabbed one of the blips and squeezed, popping it, as I leapt straight up, flipping forward and landing behind the one still enjoying his sort-of life for the moment. Side-stepping his buddy's pile of dust, I slashed my claws at his neck but he ducked, so I only got the top of his head. His scalp was in ribbons, but he was still alive.

He landed a punch and I went flying. It was hard to breathe, but I stood and moved back. Squeezing his blip with all I had, I glanced at Clive's fight in time to watch a head roll. My breathing was shallow. I had at least one broken rib. The guy hadn't noticed Clive yet, but Clive had noticed me.

I'm okay, I told him.

You're more than okay, he said, grabbing the last vamp's head and crushing it between his hands. *You're magnificent.* When the vamp was dead, Clive ripped off his head, seemingly as an afterthought.

We met in the middle of the mat, and he gave me a hard kiss. We were both still standing.

The rest of the vamps and minions watched us with varying degrees of mistrust, loathing, and fear. But there was one with a smile on his face. Vlad enjoyed a good ass kicking.

"Anyone else?" I asked.

TWENTY-FIVE

The Shit Is Hitting the Fan

C live addressed Sebastian before looking at all the other vamps assembled, "And this is what comes of being weak. The Guild has now lost four more Counselors. For what purpose? My mate and I do nothing to threaten my kind. I've made San Francisco my home for two centuries, but it's only been the last year that we seem to be fighting wave after wave of aggression. Why is that? What's changed?"

Expression hard, Clive scanned the room. "And don't you dare say my wife. She has nothing to do with Garyn's obsession—"

"She does, though," Cadmael said. "Your mate is not just a werewolf. We all witnessed that today. Before we saw her in action, we felt it. Do you think there's any here—besides the humans—who didn't feel her approaching the Guild when you first arrived? Who doesn't feel the power, the magic radiating from her?"

He moved forward, onto the mat, and gestured to me. "I've been tracking her since she was born."

Clive looked between Cadmael and me. "What are you talking about? Why would you have any knowledge of Sam?"

Cadmael held up a finger. "The origin line of werewolves. The only female born wolf." He held up a second finger. "The daughter of the strongest wicche line in existence. Daughter of a wicche who would have ruled the Corey Council had her sorcerer sister not killed her." He held up a third finger. "A woman who the queen of the fae counts as one of her own."

How the fuck does he know that? I demanded of Clive.

It seems we have a spy very close to us.

"And by giving this little speech," Vlad said, walking toward us. "You've ensured that everyone in this room will share that information around the globe. That these two will never have a moment of rest from the never-ending attempts to kill them. My question is why she bothers you so much?"

Vlad glanced at me and then back at Cadmael. "Sam is no threat. A two-minute conversation would tell you that. She's a child."

"Hey." I may not be six hundred years old, but twenty-five was hardly a child.

Ignoring me, Vlad went on. "You, a being thousands of years old, have been tracking her since birth? Garyn might have been obsessed with Clive, but you're the one obsessed with Sam. Why?"

"I don't answer to you," Cadmael thundered, sending everyone but Vlad, Clive, and me to their knees.

"No," Clive said. He was expressionless but I felt the deep betrayal he was experiencing. "But you can answer me. We've been friends for hundreds of years. I trusted you, as I trust very few. Why would you do this?"

Cadmael stood silent and then finally said, "This doesn't concern you."

"I beg to differ." Clive's tone was neutral, but his eyes were vamp black.

"Sam," Vlad said, holding up my jacket, "may I borrow this?"

I nodded, pretty sure he didn't mean the jacket.

"Clive?" he said.

"Yes," Clive responded to whatever Vlad had asked.

Mayhem. Not a moment later, dust piles dropped all around the mat. Sebastian tried to run for the door, but my axe flew through the air and pinned his head to the wall. Beside him, Ava's headless body dropped and then Chaaya's.

No more than a minute later, less, blood spattered the walls and pooled on the floor. Dust hung heavy in the air. They'd killed everyone. To protect me, Vlad and Clive had killed everyone who'd heard what Cadmael had said about me.

Stomach turning, I had trouble breathing. They were all dead because of me.

Cadmael grabbed his head, his eyes screwed shut as he grunted in pain. "Get out of my head!" he shouted and then snatched my arm with a force this side of breaking bone and hauled me close to him. "You and I are going to have a talk." He dragged me from the room while Clive and Vlad stood blood-covered and motionless.

I'd only traveled to the second floor in a dream. I didn't even know how to get there, but Cadmael did. He hauled me down the hall, through a hidden door, and up stairs. It was pitch-black. The windows had been boarded up long ago.

I tripped on broken tile and smashed my knee against the floor, but Cadmael kept a tight grip on me and kept moving. When we took a turn, I felt it again: the sick, sticky evil from that room at the end of the hall.

I dug in my heels, trying to rip out of his grip, slashing his arm with my free hand. He backhanded me. My head remained on my neck, barely, but my cheek exploded. Dark spots obscured my vision. He tugged my free hand, pulling my wrists together and tightening his fist around them both. Short of chewing off my own arm, there was nothing I could do.

He pushed open the tall wooden double doors, throwing me in. I hit the side of a settee, jarring my broken rib, and a fire roared to life in the stone fireplace. The room looked almost exactly as I'd seen it in my dream. Dustier, perhaps, but the furniture, the artwork, even the candles on the mantle were all the same.

Cadmael shoved me onto the settee and then took the chair by the fire. "Why are you here?"

I didn't understand the question. "You brought me here."

"No. Here. In this house. How did you get in?" Cadmael had taken an instant dislike to me when I'd met him almost a year ago, or I supposed his hatred had been growing my whole life. I couldn't think about that right now, though. The point was I was familiar with his usual look of disdain. This wasn't that.

He radiated anger. His normally stoic expression had changed to barely contained rage and his eyes were all wrong.

"Clive brought me," I said.

He blew out a breath and sat back in the chair. "And who is that? Another fisherman? One of the servants? Did he let you in to visit Cordelia or one of her sisters?"

Okay, I was pretty sure Cadmael wasn't here anymore. Given where we were, I thought Scary-Angry Man from the dream might have had his hooks in Cadmael, now that Sebastian was no more.

"I don't know who Cordelia is," I said.

He scoffed. "Lies. Always lies. Thieves who come sniffing around what's mine." Pushing up from the chair, he paced in a strange arc in front of the fire. "I've been cursed with disobedient girls, but none so great as Cordelia."

He picked up a mermaid figurine, looked like he was going to throw it, and then reluctantly put it back. "We'll just see. Caine!" he shouted.

The door opened and a man in a black tunic and hose appeared, bowing to Angry-Man-Wearing-a-Cadmael-Suit. "Yes, sire."

"Bring me Cordelia."

The man looked uncomfortable before tipping his head deferentially. "Sire, she is still being punished."

The angry man smiled sharply at me, his hands fisted at his sides. "And that is what happens to all who go against me." Turning back to the man at the door, he said, "Dry her off and bring her up."

The servant left and I said, "Sir, can you tell me your name." All these silly hyphenates were getting to be a bit much.

Pausing, he glanced back, his brows furrowed. "What an odd

question. You sneak into the prince's palace to steal his property and you ask who I am."

With a shake of his head, he walked to the window, brushed aside the drapery, and gazed out. "You're all vermin, sneaking in under doors, hiding in the grain, sniffing around my possessions. Worthless and thoughtless as they are, the girls are mine. Even when they sneak out to dance with common trash like you."

It felt more like he was talking to himself, voicing an oft-repeated complaint.

Was I me in this whole scenario? It didn't seem like it. Who was I filling in for, though? He'd said another fisherman. Did that mean I was a fisherman or that another fisherman had tried to see his daughter earlier? Was I a dude? What did the prince see when he looked at me?

It didn't take long until the young woman I'd seen in the dream was pushed through the door, the servant closing it quietly but firmly behind her.

Her face was swollen and bruised. The gown she wore covered her from the neck down, but she was holding herself like she was hurting. "My lord, you sent for me?"

"I did," he said. His eyes had a glint that was more than a little crazy. He pointed at me and said, "Who is this?"

Cordelia glanced at me and then back at her father. There was something communicated in the brief look, but I didn't understand it, not knowing her or the situation currently being played out.

"I know not," she said.

He grabbed her arm hard, causing her to gasp, her eyes to well up. Given the state of her face, her whole body had probably been battered. The prince dragged her to me. "Been whoring yourself out to so many you don't even remember, is that it?"

"No, my lord. I don't know this man. I haven't left the palace. You have guards watching me. You know I haven't gone anywhere." She blinked back tears, never shedding a single one.

"One of your sisters then," he growled, shoving her aside.

When the prince turned his back to us, walking to the fire

again, he stepped over something directly in front of the fire. Whatever it was must have been why he was pacing in an arc around it.

Cordelia turned and sent me a frantic look before giving me her back and saying, "Surely not. My sisters would never go against your wishes." Her gown was soaking wet, her hair dripping on the thick carpet.

Caine, the servant, had said that she needed to be dried off before being brought to him. How in the world was she being punished?

He scoffed. "Your sisters? They glide around the palace, beauty fading, playacting devotion, but their lies are a poison in my ear."

He spat into the fire. "Lies and manipulation." He turned to Cordelia. "And you're just like them. They're whores too."

I flinched at the word, at the unhinged rage behind it, and I wondered if he *punished* her sisters as well. This guy was a psychopath, and a strong one. He'd taken control of Cadmael, one of the oldest and most powerful vampires in the world. And I had no idea how to escape.

When the prince spun away again, returning to the window, Cordelia turned to me and mouthed *megy!* Only it wasn't Cordelia's face. It was Léna's.

She ran to him and threw herself at his feet, holding on to his legs while she cried, begging for his forgiveness.

I rose silently and moved to the door. I didn't want to do anything to attract attention. The problem was that even though the prince was engaged with Cordelia, Cadmael had a vampire's acute hearing and awareness of nearby warm, blood-filled bodies.

Reaching for the doorknob, I heard a yelp. Prince Cadmael had picked up Cordelia-Léna and thrown her at the fireplace before barreling across the room at me. Cordelia-Léna's gown caught fire and she howled in pain, but I was already tearing open the door and flying down the hall.

Vampires were silent, but I knew he was right behind me. I raced through the pitch-black, digging my mental claws into his blip in my head, trying to slow him down or throw him off. I knew I wasn't strong enough to kill him, but I tried.

I couldn't see, but I felt the air change. I wasn't in the hall. Sliding, I turned to the left and ran for stairs I'd never find. Screaming, *Clive!* in my head, I hoped for a rescue.

Instead, a large hand palmed the back of my skull and spiked it into the tile floor.

TWENTY-SIX

A Portrait in Pain

A soft woman's voice whispered urgently in my ear. I had no idea what she was saying, but I got it. I had to go now. Lifting my head, I felt the world swim and I retched, causing even more pain to roll through me.

The whispering was louder and sped up. Okay, okay. I got it. I lurched to my hands and knees and then tipped over, falling onto my side. My stomach tensed, but there was nothing left to come out.

I'd had enough concussions to know what a bad one felt like. The pain had tears running down my face, but I tried again. Cadmael was too powerful to be wandering around this joint with a homicidal maniac in charge. Clive and Vlad were down there and last I'd seen, they'd been frozen.

Blowing out a breath, I got to my hands and knees again, listing hard to the right. Fighting through it, I pushed to my feet and felt a cold hand steadying me. When I seemed to be standing on my own, she took my hand and led me through the dark to the stairs. Yes, I had good night vision, but that wasn't too helpful in absolute darkness.

She stopped me and then put my hand on a railing. Using that, I made my way slowly and painfully down the stairs. I leaned on the wall as I went, scraping off filth and spiderwebs, but I couldn't let myself care. Showers existed. I'd be clean eventually. For now, I needed to stay alive and make sure Clive remained only partially deadish.

"Hey," I whispered, "did I tell you I'm pretty sure I met your daughter?"

The hand on my arm went ice cold. Wait. Did she understand me?

"You have the same eyes. Same color. Same shape. Hair's the same too, though hers is short. Her name's Viktoria. She's a were-wolf and a total badass. You'd like her. We can talk later. Kinda busy now."

When I finally hit the bottom, my knees gave out but I caught myself and leaned against the wall before trudging toward the slice of light that meant door. Unsheathing a claw, I slipped it into the narrow gap and popped the door open.

Light after absolute darkness was like adding heavy metal spikes to my already pounding head. I heard crashing somewhere in the Guild. It wasn't here though, so, squinting, I held onto the wall and made my way back to the sparring room.

It was even worse than I'd remembered. Dust and blood had mixed to form a thick red sludge on the mats. Gore sprayed across the white walls. In the middle stood Clive and Vlad, seemingly frozen.

Clive?

No response.

Shoving off, I took one unsteady step and then two. Trying to tip my body to the left to compensate for my leaning so hard to the right. I was moving faster—panic will do that to you—but it still seemed to take forever to get to them.

Vlad was facing away from me, my axe still hanging from his bloody, gloved hand. Clive, though, was facing my direction. His eyes were blank and that alone had me moving faster.

Clive! I screamed in our heads.

Nothing. His eyes were still vamp black, his fangs glistening on his lips, but he wasn't here with me anymore. What had Cadmael done to them?

There were more crashes, and they sounded closer. The sparring room was a few doors down from the gathering room. The crashing seemed to be coming from the Guild offices, but my sense of direction was screwed up, so I couldn't be sure.

Gripping Clive's shoulder, I lifted up and kissed him, hoping true love's kiss would break the spell. It didn't. Stupid fairy tales.

Looking around the room for inspiration, I thought again of fairy tales. The fae. I turned my head, still holding on to Clive so I didn't fall, and stared at the axe in Vlad's gloved hand. Fae blade. Vampires couldn't touch the metal. It blistered and burned their skin. The blade had been spelled to kill any fae who attacked me without provocation. I was pretty sure the queen would agree that everything happening here was provocation enough.

Fuck. I knew what I had to do.

Leaning against Vlad, I yanked on the axe handle until I got it out of his grip. Moving it to my left hand to counter the list to the right, I made my way back to the door and listened hard. It wasn't easy with the pounding in my head, but I tried to keep track of the sounds of destruction. They were closer. I was pretty sure they were closer and louder.

Hanging on to the door, I leaned out into the hall. Nothing. I counted doorways. It looked like I had to get past two rooms before I made it to the gathering room, which was where I needed to be, assuming I was correct in how to fix this mess.

I padded out, as quietly as possible, switching the axe to my right hand so I could hold the wall with my left. My brain felt like it was too big for my skull. I focused on that third doorway. I just needed to get there and hope like hell this worked. Then I could lie down and enjoy a nice long coma.

One doorway down. A crash behind me made me jump. I looked over my shoulder. Wait. Which direction had that come from? I couldn't see anything, but I knew he was getting closer. Risking a fall, I moved faster.

Almost tipping over, I caught myself and gritted my teeth through the pain. Second doorway. Dark spots filled my vision, the white noise getting louder. I grabbed the doorknob, bracing myself upright, but the door hadn't been closed completely and it gave way, taking me with it.

What was that hissing? I blinked my eyes open. Shit. I was on the floor again. The whispered hissing became more urgent, and I heard something hit the wall of the room next door. The gathering room. Cadmael was already there.

Shitshitshitshit. Could I still make this work? I rolled to my stomach so I could push up to my hands and knees again, coming close to passing out. I knew I was in a time crunch, so I was panicking while trying to breathe through the pain. First thing's first. Stand up. It took a few attempts, but using the axe handle and the wall, I got myself upright. I was in a strange twilight space, between consciousness and unconsciousness. I knew it wouldn't take much to put me down, so I had to get this done.

Moving faster, racing against an unwilling nap, I made it to the gathering room and looked in. The room had been trashed, holes punched in walls, furniture smashed into shards. Cadmael stood in front of the fireplace, staring at the portrait of the prince.

Hopefully that'd keep him occupied while I moved as quietly as I could behind him. *Pleasepleaseplease.*

I was a couple of feet away, using the axe as a cane, when he flinched, stood straight, and spun. Eyes vamp black and more than a little crazy, he stalked toward me, his hands fisted. I'd never survive a punch. It was now or never.

I lifted the axe, but his hand was already around my throat, squeezing. I was about to die. This sucked.

"Why is it always you?" he growled.

Twisting my arm, I brought the axe over my shoulder. He squeezed harder and my head exploded in pain all over again. As my vision went dark, I threw the axe, hoping against hope it hit its mark.

TWENTY-SEVEN

More Questions Than Answers

"Sam? Sam!"

The sound came to me from down a long tunnel, far away and fuzzy around the edges.

"Sam, darling, can you hear me?"

I heard the *darling*. Clive was okay then. That was good.

Later—I think later—I woke in a softer place. I hadn't tried to open my eyes yet, but it smelled better too. Clive. It smelled like Clive and not mouse droppings, thank goodness. He must have bathed me.

Blinking, I brought our room into focus. The fire cast flickers of light across the ceiling in the cool dark.

My head still hurt, but nothing like I thought it would if I lived through whatever in the hell all of that had been. And I definitely hadn't been sure I would. I didn't know how I had, unless my theory was correct.

"Clive?"

And then he was there, leaning over me. "Hello, you." He brushed a stray hair off my face with the lightest of touches.

"Are you why my head doesn't hurt as much as I thought it would?" I'd been clenched and panicking ever since I saw him frozen and unresponsive. Seeing him here, impossibly handsome, made my heart beat faster.

"I would imagine so," he said. "It's getting close to sunrise, so I won't be able to keep it up much longer, though."

"You're here and so am I. We're both somehow okay. That's enough." Lifting my hand, I brushed my thumb across his cheek. "I love you, you know."

"I do," he said, leaning in to give me a soft kiss.

I could just lie here forever, quiet and content, but I needed to know. "What did I miss?"

"Well," he said, walking around the bed, "quite a lot." He lay down beside me, propped his head on one hand while his other rested on my stomach. "When you threw your axe into that portrait, it broke whatever spell was holding Vlad and me.

"We followed your heartbeat to the gathering room and found you crumpled on the floor and Cadmael in a daze with the skin burned off his hands. We tried to question him, but he had no idea what was going on. He did finally confess, though, to having been experiencing blank spots in his memory over the last week or so. He was more belligerent to you than normal because he thought you were the one screwing with him, as you're the only one who always knows when he's dipping into your mind and the only one who's ever been able to keep him out."

"Huh. Well, on one hand, yay for breaking the spell. On the other, a vamp of his strength and power having blank spots is concerning," I said.

"We thought so too." He pulled the covers up so they covered my chest.

"He snatched me from the sparring room," I said, "and took me to the prince's study on the second floor."

"He did what?" Clive's arm wrapped possessively around me.

"It wasn't really him. The prince—the one in the portrait over the fireplace—was possessing him, inhabiting him, whatever it was. He was the prince, and I was a fisherman—I think. I'm not entirely sure what role I played other than possible suitor to his

---

daughter Cordelia. The poor thing was already battered. The prince was quite mad, and I believe fae."

I thought about it a moment. "I've never heard of fae ghosts. Is that a thing?"

"You'd know better than I would," he said. "So Cadmael was possessed by the ghost of a fae prince?"

"I believe so. I mean, he's never liked me, but I didn't think he actively wanted me dead before."

Clive's eyes went black. "He cracked your skull and crushed your throat."

I patted his arm. "I think it would be more truthful to say the prince did those things using Cadmael. I hoped the fae blade would break the connection, maybe even kill off what was left of the prince. By the time I made it to the gathering room with it, though, Cadmael was there, staring at the portrait. He had me by the neck when I threw the axe. Now you tell me the rest."

Clive closed his eyes and gently kissed the side of my head. When he opened them again, they were back to stormy gray. "The axe was in the portrait. The skin of Cadmael's hands had been burned off, so we wondered if he was the one who'd thrown the fae blade or if he was trying to free it. Since we scented the blade on your hands, we assumed you'd put it there, so we left it where you put it."

"Good," I said.

"I swear, Sam, we are never again traveling out of San Francisco without a healer." Leaning forward, he rested his lips against the side of my head. "I can take away your pain, but I can't heal you. I called Lilah to see if she knew a healer in Budapest."

I tapped his arm. "But you're not allowed to tell anyone where the Guild is."

"Darling, Vlad and I put paid to that when we killed everyone in that room. There are now only a handful of Counselors in the world: Cadmael, Vlad, and the ones who weren't here."

Grimacing, I said, "That doesn't sound good."

"Probably not, but I'd do it again. We'll figure something out. We have before and we will again."

"Wait. And you, right? Aren't you a Counselor now? Vlad said they were just going to offer it to you outright and then you won the competition anyway." I remembered who he'd been competing against and what had happened to them. "Oh. I liked Oliver. He seemed like a good guy."

Nodding, Clive somberly replied, "He was."

"I'm sorry."

"Me too," he said. "I don't know how long the prince has been working on Council members, but it might explain some strange behaviors I've seen from people I've known for a very long time."

"There's something powerful at play in this building, though. Maybe the prince's power is what makes the ghosts so strong. I don't know why, but I feel like Léna is behind a lot of whatever has been happening here too. Like the ghosts are siphoning the prince's power and using it."

I paused, considering. "She came to me as soon as we arrived and showed me what the asylum was. She showed me the abuses, the cruelty, and she led me to Aliz so we could return her to her family.

"When the prince—Cadmael—whoever—smashed my head, she was the one whispering in my ear to wake me up and get me going. She knew I had to do something to stop the prince and she helped as much as she could."

I started to shrug and realized my shoulder hurt too. Probably from one of the many times I'd hit the ground today. "This used to be the prince's palace. He was insane and horribly cruel with it. He's probably been poisoning this place for hundreds of years. The asylum was wretched. That might have been his influence, an influence that's also been inadvertently super-powering the ghosts."

"This place is cursed," Clive said, looking around the room.

"No argument from me." And then I had a thought. "English!"

Clive tilted his head. "I am, yes."

Smiling, I rolled my eyes. "Not you. One of the biggest issues I've had with all these supercharged spirits is that we can't understand each other. They show me things and I have to figure out what they mean by their actions, facial expressions, tone of voice, but I could be interpreting it all wrong. Like Vlad telling me it was Léna's father who had been raping her. I couldn't get that from just watching him dump her off."

"It's been so frustrating not knowing what any of them are saying. When Cadmael took me to that room and spoke as the prince, he spoke in English. So did the servant and the daughter. Maybe because it was all coming at me through Cadmael..." I looked away from the flickers on the ceiling to Clive. "Did I dream it?"

"Your cracked skull tells me something more violent than a dream happened," he said.

"Yeah. There's that, but..." I shook my head. It was still throbbing, even with Clive's pain relief. Did the prince use Cadmael because he was the most powerful and spoke my language? My brain was too rattled to unweave it all. "How do you know my skull is cracked?"

"I contacted László, the werewolf Alpha, and asked for contact information on a healer," he said.

"And he gave it to you? He hates us." I didn't think I could have brought myself to trust him.

Clive rubbed his hand over my hip. "He still hates me, but he's softened to you. You returned his sister to him. I may have also reminded him that you put yourself at great personal risk to rescue all the humans and deliver them to the pack. It didn't take much prodding to get the healer's contact info."

"And then you had to take me to him?" I guessed.

"No. I told him to come here. He's not as strong as Lilah, but he knit the bones back together." He kissed the side of my head again.

"But now the wolves know where the Guild is?" I didn't understand why he was so comfortable with that info being out there.

"This site needs to be abandoned. As I said, it's cursed. Vlad is going through the offices now, making sure he has access to all the information. Cadmael went with him, but he's still a little unclear on what's happening, which is quite unusual for him."

"What if the pack breaks in while the three of you are napping? I don't think I could fight off an entire pack in my current state," I said.

"This building has redundant security features. They wouldn't be able to enter, even if they wanted to. And we'll be leaving soon anyway." He tucked the pillow under his head and held me tight. "Let's try to sleep before the sun rises and my ability to numb the pain goes away."

My phone buzzed. I looked at it and saw I had missed calls from Arwyn, my psychic cousin on my mom's wicche side of the family. We'd met each other only recently.

I looked up at Clive. "I'm so stupid. I have someone in the family who can help, and I never thought to call her."

"In your defense, darling," Clive said, "I hadn't thought of it either. That side of your family is new to both of us."

I hit the redial button and then asked, "Wait. What time is it in California?"

Clive opened his mouth to respond, but Arwyn had already picked up.

"Sam, are you okay?" The concern in Arwyn's voice warmed my heart. I had family that didn't want me dead.

"Arwyn, it's Clive. She has a cracked skull and a concussion. The healer just left."

There was a pause and then Arwyn said, "Is that right, Sam?"

I smirked at Clive. Arwyn still wasn't happy with him. Long story short, I'd been abducted by Finvarra, the fae king, while Clive and I were honeymooning in Europe. Clive, Russell, and Godfrey broke into Arwyn's house to get information. Clive had been a rage-filled vamp and therefore not on his best behavior. Arwyn rightfully took offense.

"It is," I said.

"I had a nightmare about you. You're not in San Francisco, are you?" Arwyn asked.

"I'm not. We're out of the country on vampire business," I said.

"Interesting. In my nightmare, you were attacked by a dark-haired, dark-eyed man who was insane, and sadistic with it. He felt fae, but I saw fangs at one point. There was a tidal wave of blood washing down the walls of a condemned building." She paused a moment. "And there were women screaming and howling. It scared the hell out of me, which is why I kept calling."

"Thank you," I said. "I really appreciate that." I glanced at Clive. I was pretty sure this was okay to say. "I believe the man you saw is fae. He possessed a vampire to attack me, though."

"Huh," Arwyn said slowly. "Okay. That makes more sense. I feel like the fae guy is still an ongoing threat. Is that accurate?"

"Unfortunately, I think he probably is," I said.

"I see. What do you know about him?" she asked.

"That's the problem." I glanced at Clive again. "We're in a country where I don't speak the language."

"Which one," she said.

Clive shrugged.

"It's top-secret vampy stuff, but we're in Hungary."

She let out a breath. "From what I heard in the dream, I thought you were somewhere in Eastern Europe. I don't speak the language either, but it sounded Eastern European. What else do you know about him?"

"Next to nothing," I said. "I heard about a folktale featuring a cruel fae prince who brutalized his daughters. I'm not sure, but I think that's who we're dealing with."

I could hear Arwyn moving around. "This is stupid," she said. "Let me ask someone who might actually know." The sound of surf became quite loud. "Good evening, Cecil, Poppy! Wilbur, Charlie, Herbert, I hope you're all well."

Her footsteps slapped on the deck.

"My Uncle Bracken is a historian, magical and human. He might know about this guy."

206

TWENTY-EIGHT

Bracken: the Supernatural Search Engine

I heard knocking and eventually a clicking sound.

"What a nice surprise," a man said. "Oh, you know how I love your oatmeal cookies. Thank you. Come in, come in."

"Sam, I'm putting you on speakerphone. Uncle Bracken, do you remember me telling you about Bridget's daughter Sam?"

"Of course," the man said. "Quinn wolf on her father's side and wicche on ours. A necromancer, you told me."

"Exactly," Arwyn said. "She's in Hungary with her husband on hush-hush vampire business and she's dealing with a fae guy known as the prince who possessed a vampire, trying to use him to kill her."

"Fascinating," he said on a sigh. "I've never heard of a vampire being possessed before." He paused. "Are we sure she's not dealing with a demon?"

"Sam?" Arwyn said, basically asking me to take over.

"Hello, Bracken. Thank you very much for helping us," I said.

"Oh, my dear, you've given me a treat. Now, what can you tell me about him?"

"I've met demons before. He doesn't feel like one to me. He feels fae and he has the golden skin some fae have."

"Mm-hm." It sounded like he was scratching a pen or pencil across paper. "What did he say and do?"

"He talked about his disloyal daughters—no, girls. I don't think he ever called them his daughters. The folktale I heard about said daughter, but he said girls. Anyway, the story was that he was a cruel prince with many daughters. It said he had a grand palace at the bottom of a huge river and that the water turned blood red from him beating them."

"The Danube Prince," Bracken said. "Yes, I'm familiar with that tale. That story took place in Vienna, I believe."

"We're in Budapest but the Danube is quite close to us," I told him.

"Just a minute," he said.

There was movement in the background.

"He went to retrieve one of his journals," Arwyn told us.

After a few minutes of a man making *hmm*-ing sounds and turning pages, he said, "Ah, here it is! Researching folktales is a hobby of mine. This journal is from thirty-one years ago. I was just skimming over my notes to refamiliarize myself."

There was a pause. "Sit. Sit. All right. So you understand, when I research a subject, I read through everything I can find, those texts written by humans as well as supernaturals. I also interview anyone who might have pertinent information. For this tale, I read four texts and spoke with a water sprite, a wood nymph, and a dwarf. What I'm going to tell you is a synthesis of all the stories into what I believe is as close to the truth as I could get. All right?"

"Yes, thank you," I replied.

"He sounds like one of our historians," Clive murmured.

"Do vampires have historians too?" Bracken asked. Clive blinked, seemingly surprised that Bracken had heard him through the line. Wicches, in general, don't have the super-hearing wolves and vampires do.

"Of course you do," Bracken continued. "That only makes sense. Might I ask if I could interview you when you have a few moments? I'd be more than happy to drive to San Francisco when you return home."

Eyebrows raised, I wait to see what Clive would say. He gave me a good long look, rolled his eyes on a smile, and finally said, "I'm sure I could find some time to speak with you."

"Splendid! Now let's get back to the prince." He let out a long breath and started again. "I'm not sure if you know, but reproduction is very difficult for the fae. The part of the story that initially caught my interest was this idea of him having many daughters whom he abused horribly. It made no sense. The fae cherish their young.

"The translation in one of the texts seemed suspect to me. The word was daughter, but it struck me that in a Germanic dialect of Middle English—one I've only heard spoken by the fae—the word *daughter* and the word that essentially meant *chattel* or *possession* sounded very similar.

"I could have been wrong, so I interviewed a few members of the fae. I found a water sprite who knew the dialect I'd been looking for and when I asked her about the Danube Prince, she became enraged, the water around her turning turbulent. She told me he was an evil bastard who had abducted other water fae—female only—and kept them imprisoned away from the river. When they tried to escape, to return to the Danube, he'd caught them and beat them bloody to keep them from leaving him."

"I don't understand," I said. "If they knew what he was doing, why didn't Algar or the queen step in to do anything about it?"

"Ah," Bracken said, a smile in his voice, "you know the players. Excellent. The one who calls himself the prince is the younger brother—or relative of some kind—of the fae king—names have power, and we don't want to attract their attention, so I won't use it," he said.

"Yes," I said. "Especially his, as he's regularly sending his assassins after me."

"My dear, I'm so sorry," Bracken said. "He is a horribly petty man who clutches grudges as though they were precious gems.

Anyway, the king protected the prince by exiling him to the human realm. With his captives. The ones the stories refer to as his daughters."

He sighed and then continued. "Some of these poor women had never been in the human realm, had no idea their magic would work differently here. Others were stolen here, water fae from the Danube. One of his prisoners was a mermaid who had been one of the queen's ladies-in-waiting. They were quite close, and though she was water fae, the queen gifted her with flower magic because the young woman so loved the flowers that grew along the banks of the rivers in Faerie."

"I remember," I murmured. "They're gorgeous. We don't have anything like them in this realm. Big blowsy blossoms drooping toward the water, their heads bobbing in the wind."

There was silence for a moment and then Bracken said, "You've been to Faerie? Oh, my dear, I'd love to interview you as well as your husband. My goodness, what a turn this day has taken."

The queen hadn't sworn me to secrecy about Faerie, so I figured it would be okay. I mean, look at this right now. If people hadn't spoken to Bracken thirty-something years ago, we still wouldn't know who we were dealing with. "Sure," I said. "I can tell you some stuff."

"Excellent. Now, where was I? Oh, yes, the queen's beloved friend had been stolen. What I'd been told was that this friend observed the king in yet another of his trysts and had informed the queen. In his rage, he abducted the queen's friend, took her to the human realm, and handed her over to his brother, relative, ally— whoever the prince actually is.

"The queen searched far and wide throughout Faerie. Her guards left no corner of her realm forgotten. The young woman was simply gone. The queen never stopped looking, though, sending her people into other realms to search. She's been mourning the loss of her beloved for a very long time now."

"So, this building we're in right now," I said, "has been a number of things over the centuries, but he referred to it as the prince's palace." A thought occurred to me. "Wait. He's fae. Is it possible he's still alive in here? I'd thought he was a ghost, but do the fae leave ghosts?"

"My dear, if he still there, you must leave immediately. You're dealing with an exiled fae possessing a vampire—something I hadn't considered possible. Their magics are antithetical to one another. If he can do that, who knows what else he can do?"

"Yes," Clive said. "I hadn't thought it possible either. They abhor us. We're death. They're life."

"Perhaps," Bracken said, "that's an indication of how twisted he's become, how removed from the light and power of Faerie. I wish I could be more help. I have no idea how to break a bond that shouldn't exist. I fear only the queen herself could do it."

"Okay," I said. "Thank you so much. We'd never have known any of this without you. When we get home, Clive and I will drive down to Monterey to visit and talk with you."

"Marvelous!" Bracken said. "Did you hear that, Arwyn? We'll have visitors soon."

"Hopefully," Arwyn said. "Unfortunately, right now, Sam's in trouble. In what I saw, he called you a fisherman, but he knows who you are. Or, maybe not who you are, but he senses power and sees a woman and it's pissing him off. Does the vampire have issues with women too?"

I looked at Clive.

"No," Clive said. "I've never witnessed that. He does have an issue with Sam because of her werewolf blood. For whatever reason, he doesn't trust them and therefore doesn't trust her. I thought he'd made his peace with our relationship when we married, but I see now I was wrong."

"Do me a favor," Arwyn said. "Don't be alone with that vampire guy. It feels deeper than just *I don't like werewolves.*"

A chill ran down my spine. "I will."

"And remember," Bracken said, "if the prince knows who you are, then the king will soon know *where* you are."

"I hate that guy," Arwyn said. "Call me if you need anything.

Oh, and that one girl, the teenager. You need to see if you can help her."

"I'm working on it," I replied. I just needed to figure out what Léna wanted.

We said our goodbyes. It was almost daybreak before we finally settled in to sleep.

I woke late in the afternoon. My head still hurt, but it was nothing like the night before. The healer seemed to have done a good job, for which I was grateful. Clive was sleeping beside me, his arm still wrapped around my waist.

Dropping a kiss on his nose, I said, "I have to get up now."

He pulled me in tighter and mumbled, "No."

"Unless you want me to wet the bed, you really need to let me move." I pushed his arm and he relented.

I took a long moment to process my face, the huge black bruising over half of it, my left eye swollen shut. When Cadmael spiked my head into the tile floor, it must have been tilted so I went left-side down. That probably saved me from a broken nose to go with my cracked skull.

I'd trained myself not to look in mirrors for years. I could do it again. Finishing getting ready, I tied my hair up in a braid and considered what I could do before sunset.

I looked in the mirror, tapped into my necromancy, and said, "Léna? I know you can't understand me, but I want to do what I can to help before we leave. Is there something more you need from me?"

I waited a moment, staring into the mirror and seeing only myself—which was not a pretty sight.

"Okay," I said, giving up. I flicked off the light and then saw something appear in the mirror. Stepping closer, I tried to make it out and recognized the fireplace in the prince's study.

Léna's face floated beside the fireplace and she waved me toward her, asking me to go to the prince's room again. My heart sank. Oh, no. Not that. I glanced over my shoulder at Clive in bed before closing the bathroom door and whispering, "I barely survived last time."

Léna waved me to her more urgently and then she and the fireplace disappeared.

Shit. Now what was I going to do? The fae axe seemed to have broken the tie to Cadmael, so I didn't have him to worry about. Hopefully. Vlad—wait. Vlad was up. He could go with me to help if stuff got out of control again.

Feeling better about it, I gave Clive a kiss on the cheek, left the room, and went down the halls to the basement door. *Shoot.* I didn't have the ring to trip the door. Well, hell. I knocked instead.

"Vlad?" I called, and then added, "Can you come out and play?"

"Depends," he said, directly behind me, making me jump, "and shouldn't you be in bed?"

TWENTY-NINE

The Prince's Secret Punishments

I spun and found Vlad smirking. "Sure. Cool. Go ahead and give me a heart attack."

He gestured to my face. "I thought the healer took care of that."

Shrugging, I said, "I'm assuming it was worse. I wasn't awake for it. Clive said the guy knitted my skull back together. My ribs don't hurt, so he must have worked on them too."

"Fragile, aren't you?" he said.

"Dude, are you going to come with me or not?" I was really hoping yes. I didn't want to go back alone.

"Where to this time?" he asked, brushing his fingers over his mustache.

"This way." I waved him with me and headed to reception and the hidden door. "Léna still needs something from me."

"Yes," he said, walking beside me. "She came to me too. Not as strongly as before, though." When we got to reception, he paused at the door of the gathering room, gesturing in. "She showed me the fireplace."

I looked in and saw my axe embedded right between the prince's eyes. Dang. Was I going to have to leave that there? I didn't want to lose my axe.

"Not that one," I said. "We're going to the prince's study upstairs."

Vlad grabbed my arm, stopping me. "Isn't that where all of this happened?" He gestured to my face.

"Technically, no. He caught me in the hall and slammed my head onto the floor there, not in his room." I stopped right inside the hall to the Guild offices and looked at the walls. "Cadmael popped open one of these walls to reveal the stairway up."

"Oh, that's here." Vlad tapped a panel on the left and the panel opened.

I turned on my phone's flashlight and headed up, Vlad right behind me. I shined the beam on the wall. "See that clean line?" Knowing I had leaned against that filthy wall made my stomach flip. "That was my shoulder. And that lighter line above was my head." I wasn't sure how many showers it would take to feel clean again.

"You're talking to the wrong person if you're looking for sympathy. Have you any idea the kind of disgusting conditions I've had to stay in during daylight hours over the centuries? And unlike others of my kind who are at least insensate, I was wide awake for it."

"You win," I said, coming to the top of the stairs. I shined the light left and right. A hall opened up to the right with a large common area directly in front of us, mirroring the reception space below. There were doors to what might have been offices across from us and then another hall on the far left.

Pointing to the left hall, I said, "The prince's room is at the end of that one."

Vlad gestured to a pool of blood and bile on the broken tiles. "Yours, I assume."

"Unless someone else got their ass kicked up here recently, I'll say yes." I started down the hall and felt the sticky evil again. Still. I'd hoped the axe would have killed off the remains of the prince. "Do you feel that?"

"I feel something uncomfortable, something setting off an itch between my shoulder blades. Might that be what you're referring to?" he asked.

"Probably. For me, it feels like a sticky sludge of evil, coating my skin." I shined my light down to the end of the hall, wondering if the tall wooden doors were only in my dreams.

Two eyes shined back at me.

Yelping, I almost dropped the phone.

Vlad steadied me. "It's Léna."

"I guess that means we're in the right place," I said, wishing for nothing more than to be downstairs, safe in bed with Clive.

Vlad gave a grunt of assent and we continued on. When we got to the end, we paused in front of the tall wooden double doors. Vlad and I looked at each other and he pushed one open.

Shining the light around, I saw the room was all wrong. It wasn't a room in the prince's palace anymore. It was an office—or had been anyway. There was a desk to the right, with two chairs in front of it. Mold grew on the wall behind the desk like a giant Rorschach test. Dust and grime covered every surface.

A wall of floor-to-ceiling bookshelves cut the room in half. The few books remaining had been torn and chewed. Nests of paper filled the corners of the room. Huge webs hung like fog, making it hard to see details.

Vlad took it all in. "I see no fireplace."

I pointed straight back. "Behind those shelves. This is only about half the size of the prince's room. There's more back there."

Vlad looked between me and the shelves. "Are we thinking that's where he's been hiding?"

I took an involuntary step back. "I wasn't until now," I whisper-shouted.

We moved slowly into the room and then Vlad had me stand to the side while he went to the center bookshelf. He punched a hole in it, put his hand through the hole, and ripped it down.

There was no wall behind it. The other half of the room was open. The smell, though, hit like a sulfurous punch.

"Demon?" I whispered.

Vlad looked back at me, his brow furrowed, and shook his head. "Thermal spring."

"Oh." Right. I forgot. There were hundreds of thermal springs below Budapest. Why was the smell so strong here, though?

The prince's side was empty of furniture. My running shoes scraped over centuries of accumulated dirt, droppings, and other things I didn't want to think about. Moving closer to the fireplace, I tripped on something. Vlad was there, his hand on my arm to steady me.

Sweeping my flashlight over the floor, I realized I was standing on a board. I stepped off and crouched down. Why was there a half-inch-thick board in front of the fireplace?

Vlad ran his hands along the mantel and then tested stones inside the fireplace. "Sometimes loose stones cover hidden pockets for secreting treasures. I'm not finding anything, though." He stood and brushed off his hands. "Why did Léna show us this?"

"Can you move a second?" I asked. "I want to see what's under here."

He stepped off the board and lifted it before I could. We were hit with an even stronger wave of sulfur and rotting fish.

I slapped my hand over my nose and mouth. "Why?"

Brushing his foot over what looked like a carpet on the hearth, he dislodged built-up dirt and dust, leaving what appeared to be a metal grille in the floor.

I moved forward to look in, but he pushed me back. "Stay there. Clive will kill me if I let you fall in."

"I'm not a moron," I said. Did he think I was just going to toddle into a shaft to Hell? Jeez.

An eyebrow lift was all the response I got to the moron question. Jerk.

He rattled the grille a moment but then stood up and reached under the mantel. "There's a worn spot in the corner. I felt it a moment ago, but the board was on top of the grate."

We both stared down while Vlad touched the smooth spot. The grate clicked and swung into the shaft.

"Oh," Vlad said. "I know what this is." He stepped up to the hole and looked down.

I did the same, shining my light into it. "Damn. That looks deep. Does this go to a dungeon?"

Vlad nodded. "I'd guess the prince had the chute created to dispose of his enemies deep underground, into thermal baths. That's why the smell is so strong in here." He nodded as though he approved of the tactic. "Cruel and effective." Vlad looked up and smiled. "I left my enemies' bodies to rot on display." He looked back down the hole. "I suppose he preferred hiding his."

"Quit being creepy." I knelt, bracing one hand on the edge, and looked down. I heard that sloshing sound again, like I'd heard in the tub room. "Hey," I said, looking back up at Vlad, "is the slow heartbeat louder now?"

He dropped beside me, his brows furrowed. "What did he imprison down there?"

I leaned out farther. "And how is it still alive hundreds of years later?" Two eyes shined back at me in the dark and I about had a heart attack.

"It's Léna again," Vlad said.

"Well, if she thinks I'm just going to jump down the Hell shaft on her say-so, she's lost it." Just leaning over this thing was making me light-headed. I stood and considered the problem.

"Do you know where we can find a rope?" I asked.

"No," Clive growled, making me jump. "You are not lowering yourself into an ancient dungeon with a dying immortal."

"Where did you come from?" I demanded, anger covering my moment of panic, having someone sneak up behind me again. "And I wasn't going to go down." I pointed at Vlad. "I was going to hold the rope so he could go down. I'm sick of you people acting like I'm stupid! I don't get all these injuries because I'm dumb. I'm trying to help."

My eyes filled with tears and then I was pissed off at myself. Blinking, I swallowed and cleared my throat. "Léna is still here, still trapped in this hellhole that killed her because her father wanted his evil hidden from the world. She led me to Aliz, so we could return her to her family. And she wants us to help whoever is down there. Trying to help others doesn't make you stupid!"

Vlad moved away while I shouted, but Clive moved in, wrapping his arms around me.

"I'm sorry," he murmured. "Of course you're not stupid. You almost died yesterday, so I'm on edge. I woke to find you gone. When I followed your scent through a hidden door, I found the pool of blood from your most recent near death, and now here you are, face still blackened, leaning over a sulfurous pit."

"I know," I said, "but someone's down there. Has been for hundreds of years. We need to get her out."

He leaned back and brushed light fingers over my bruised face. "Her?"

"It's a hunch," I said. "Maybe it *is* a blue whale, like you said, but Léna showed me the prince and Cordelia for a reason. And when the servant brought in Cordelia from her punishment, she was wet. Sopping wet."

I ran my hands up and down his sides. "Maybe I'm wrong. Maybe there's nothing down there, but if that poor fae woman has been imprisoned for centuries in pitch-black hot water, we have to help her."

"And we will," Clive said, "but not by following her down a bloody long drop into who knows what."

"I believe that's why she asked about the rope," Vlad said.

Clive nodded. "Point taken. Besides going down there"—he gestured to the hole in the floor—"do we have any other ideas?"

"The tub room," I said at the same time Vlad said, "Basement."

We started to move out and then I caught Clive's arm. "Wait a minute. We need to cover the hole so no one falls in." I leaned over it again. "We're coming!"

Clive picked up one side of the board and slid it back. Before it covered the hole, though, he shouted something as well. After he dropped the board in place and brushed off his hands, he wrapped an arm around me. "I translated for you."

Vlad led the way back down the hall.

"Are there any ghosts here?" Clive asked.

Both Vlad and I shook our heads. "I had that creep attendant who raped Léna corner me in the kitchen," I said, "but I haven't seen any other male ghosts around. I wonder why that is."

"I've noticed that too," Vlad said.

"Given how you said the prince feels about possible suitors around his daughters," Clive said, "he may have run them off, ignoring the women lingering on the other side of the asylum."

When we walked around the blood pool, Clive's arm tightened around me.

"Should we be concerned that Cadmael didn't find us?" I asked. "Is he okay?"

"That would depend," Vlad said, holding open the door at the bottom of the stairs, "on your definition of okay." He turned his head and stared into the reception area. "For instance, would we consider him standing in the gathering room doorway, staring at that infernal portrait, okay?"

Shit. That was all we needed.

The three of us stood together, watching Cadmael stand unmoving.

"Maybe we just sneak by him," I whispered.

Cadmael turned his head and stared straight at me. "You, again," he sneered, turning toward us, my axe in his bloody hand.

Clive and Vlad moved together, standing shoulder to shoulder to block me.

Cover me for a few, okay? I asked Clive. *Let me see if I can push the prince out.*

Hurry, darling. We're no match for him.

THIRTY

Getting to the Bottom of Why Cadmael Hates My Guts

I tapped the wall where Vlad had earlier. When the door slid open, I darted in and closed it behind me. Vowing to take the longest shower known to man later, I sat on a filthy step, closed my eyes, and found the green blips in my head.

Three strong blips. Without all the other vamps around this joint, though, I could now see two more. Shit. They were a pale, sickly, yellowish grass green. Fae. We had company.

I focused on Cadmael's blip and pushed my way in. Normally, I'd never have been able to do that, but with the prince screwing with Cadmael's head, it was easy.

Synapses fired around me, but it was the voice in his head that worried me. Cadmael was staring uncomprehendingly at Clive and Vlad. *Kill them!* the voice kept saying. I felt Cadmael struggling.

I needed to distract the prince, but how? I had no influence over the fae. Then again, he was currently possessing a sort-of dead vampire and I had power over the dead. If he pulled out of Cadmael, yes, we'd be physically safer for the moment, but only until he decided it was more expedient to take control of a scary-powerful ancient vampire again.

I had no idea what I was doing, but I hadn't let that stop me in the past. I brought up an image of Gloriana in all her regal authority and pushed it into Cadmael's mind. The urging to kill Clive and Vlad faltered.

My voice was nothing like Gloriana's, but while pushing her image, I demanded he tell me what he had done with Cordelia.

Like a boxer being pummeled, I was hit with a barrage of memories of girls and young women being snatched, of fury and shouts, of backhands and closed fists. Finally, I saw Cordelia being held aloft by him, his hand around her neck. Tears streaming down her face, her golden skin turning blue, she clawed at his hand before he dropped her through the trap door.

It was too much. These last few days of seemingly unending violence toward women had me screaming in rage. I hadn't been able to do anything to help the women when it was happening, but I could do something about this now.

Dave had once put me in a mental cage to keep me safe from a demon. I didn't know how he'd done it, but sheer will and innate magical ability had me erecting walls around the prince while he lurked in Cadmael's mind. He'd put himself in my domain and I wasn't letting him out.

Locked in tight, the prince's influence over Cadmael disappeared.

Get out! Cadmael roared.

Fuck off, you asshat. An ageless fae prince has been possessing you and I'm the one you yell at? How about, Hey, Sam, thanks so much for keeping me from being a fae puppet and killing my friends? I'll never understand how I'm somehow always the problem.

I didn't think I could maintain the prince's prison if I left Cadmael's mind, but I moved away from his hissy fit and accidentally stepped into a flare of memory.

Cadmael, bare-chested, wearing a hip-cloth, is carrying a baby, holding him up to the others crowded around his hut. Pride gleams in his eyes as he makes a pronouncement in a language I don't understand. The message is clear enough, though.

The memory goes dark and jumps to Cadmael moving silently

through the rainforest, a spear in his hand as he hunts. A small child follows. Cadmael stops, waits for the child to stand beside him, and then crouches, pointing through the trees at a boar snuffling in the leaves.

The child nods, stepping to the side to watch his father. Cadmael changes his hold on the spear, sending it speeding through the air, hitting the boar in the neck. The animal squeals and charges farther through the brush and trees, but Cadmael and his son are in pursuit.

Cadmael leaps, landing on the boar, driving it to the ground. A blade is already in his hand as he finishes off the kill. The child watches intently, his arms moving in imitation of his father's, learning what to do when the time is right.

I feel Cadmael's heart swelling with each new memory, with his son's first successful hunt, with his growth into manhood, until there was nary a difference between father and son, save for a few gray hairs.

I feel Cadmael shying away from the next memory, not wanting to touch it, to revisit the horror. His son and a hunting party of two other men went to bring down a deer that had been spotted from a distance.

Only one hunter makes it back to the village as the sun is setting. People gather around the frantic young man who is bleeding, his eyes wild. Cadmael looks for his son. The hunter's out-of-breath rantings and wild gesticulations become background noise. Grabbing his weapons, Cadmael runs into the rainforest.

He's able to easily track the one who made it back to the village. The ground is disturbed, branches broken. In a panic, the young hunter did nothing to hide his path.

Eventually, Cadmael finds a second hunter. The man is face up, a broken branch dropped on his face. Cadmael studies the scene. The hunter's abdomen has been ripped open, organs torn out and eaten. An animal wouldn't feel shame over a kill, wouldn't hide his meal's face.

Sickened, fearing what he'll find, Cadmael races silently through the forest, following the sounds of yips and growls. When he bursts into a clearing, he sees a deer with his son's spear in its neck. The deer's eyes roll while its legs try weakly to push itself up, to escape. Cadmael barely glances at the deer, though. His attention is focused on a huge wolf, his snout in his son's abdomen, feasting.

Cadmael throws his spear. The wolf senses the change in the clearing and moves, dodging the tip. It stands over its kill, claiming Cadmael's son as his own. Refusing to acknowledge his son's unseeing gaze, Cadmael leaps in with a blade in his hand.

The fight is vicious but short. Cadmael cuts the animal many times, but he's no match for the huge wolf. Bleeding out on the same ground his son has stained red, Cadmael watches as the wolf begins to transform. He assumes in his state he's hallucinating. How could a wolf become a man?

When the transformation is complete, his friend stands over him, eyes wild with excitement. The werewolf, though Cadmael had no word for such a thing, looks between the dead and dying, wiping the blood from his face. He goes to the now dead deer, hefts it over his shoulder, and heads back toward the village.

Cadmael stares up into the canopy of trees, uncomprehending. How could his friend be a wolf? Moreover, how could he kill Cadmael's son? Betrayal courses through him as his blood soaks into the forest floor beneath him.

Later, as he feels himself drifting on to a warrior's welcome in the afterlife, his son waiting for him, a man steps into the clearing. Eyes black, he breathes in the scent of blood and falls on Cadmael, fangs in his neck.

When Cadmael wakes, bursting out from under dirt and branches with a fiery, uncontrollable thirst, he's somewhere else. He experiences a brief moment of worry over his son before he's mindlessly racing through the trees, the forest and all its inhabitants alive to him, their scents and sounds making the hunt laughably easy.

He brings down a boar and feeds, draining the animal, finally cooling the fire in his throat and allowing him to think. He finds a break in the canopy, checks the stars, and slowly, through the night, makes his way back to his village, to the hut of his friend.

Silently, he pads across the packed earthen floor to the sleeping skins and rips out his friend's throat. Eyes bulging, clutching his neck as blood gushes between his fingers, his friend watches as Cadmael kills first the man's mate and then his child. Cadmael does it fast, knowing the former friend has only a moment left of life. Cadmael wants to make sure, *though, that his last moments are filled with a crippling grief that will match his own.*

Get out of my head! Cadmael roared. *My memories are my own.*

I can't. I'm what's keeping the prince contained. You're going to have to put up with me a little longer until we can figure out how to free his prisoner.

"Clive?" I called.

The door must have opened because light fell across my face.

"Hey, listen. I'm holding the prince captive. I have no idea how long I can do this."

"How can I help?" Clive asked.

"Can you take me down to the basement? The tub room?" That room had felt important from the beginning.

Clive swung me up like I was a backpack. "Should we be concerned about Cadmael?" he asked.

"No," Cadmael responded. Looking through his eyes, I saw him look down at his raw hand and drop my axe, letting it clatter onto the marble floor beside him.

"Can you grab that, please?" I asked Clive. "I don't want to lose it."

I felt Clive dip to pick it up and then hand it to me, jogging to the secret door. I kept one arm around Clive's neck and held the axe away from his body, not wanting to accidentally hurt him. As Clive went down the stairs, I heard a high-pitched tone I'd never heard before.

"What's that?" I asked.

"Alarm," Vlad said.

"At a guess," Clive added, "the werewolves are trying to break in."

Awesome. I looked through Cadmael's eyes as he walked back to an office and watched the security monitors.

"The pack is circling the building," I said.

"How do you know?" Vlad asked.

"Cadmael's watching the security monitors," I replied.

"Sam," Clive said sharply.

Patting Clive's shoulder, I said, "He already knows there's something up with me and I trust him."

"Thank you," Vlad said. "And, yes, my guess is you're a necromancer. My mother was a wicche too. You needn't worry. I'm no threat to your mate."

"I'll take that as a promise," Clive said, his voice hard.

"Take it anyway you wish," Vlad said. "It's your wife I like. You, I don't much care about."

I was only sort of listening to them. My focus was on the monitors Cadmael was watching. The wolves looked to be attaching things to the building.

Cadmael relaxed, thinking the time had finally come.

"Uh, guys?" I said. "We appear to have a suicidal ancient vampire and a pack of wolves planting explosives all around this building."

I felt Clive rush back up the stairs and I unleashed my claws, digging them into the wall to slow him down. "Stop. We're not done here. Go back down."

"I'm not risking your life for whatever is down there," he said.

Holding tight to the prince's prison, I opened my eyes and climbed down off his back. "Enough," I said, stomping back down the stairs, turning on the flashlight again. "It's here. I know it is. We have to find the way in."

"Damn it, Sam," Clive growled, following me back to the tub room.

"I'm supposed to do this. I know it." I waved him away. "You guys go check out the other rooms down here. See if you can find a way into the prince's dungeon. I'm searching in here."

Cursing, Clive flew out of the room to check the rest. I didn't see Vlad, so I assumed he was doing the same.

"Léna! How do I get to her." I went to the back wall where I'd heard sloshing sounds and ran my fingers over the moldy, spongy wall. "I swear," I muttered, "if I get sick from mold poisoning because you wouldn't help me, I'm going to be really pissed off."

I remembered that she was easier to see in the dark, so I turned off the flashlight and waited for her to appear. There! In the far right corner, she hovered behind a thick water pipe.

The pipe was only a few inches from the wall and corroded in too many places. Léna pointed to a spot high up on the wall behind the pipe, waving me closer.

Oh, sure. No problem. I gripped the axe hard and then tried to shimmy up a rotting pipe, pulling myself up off the floor, hoping like hell the pipe could carry my weight. I squeezed my running shoes on either side of the pipe and pushed myself farther up.

When my head was close to the high ceiling, I stopped climbing, wedging my feet between the pipe and wall. I had to hold the pipe with my right hand, meaning I had to swing the axe with my nondominant left hand. I was hanging on by a thread and was sure I'd end up hitting myself with the damn axe.

My left leg started to shake. I was not taking it easy on that poor leg. I tried my best to get my torso out of the way and swung the axe. The hit was pitiful and only served to dislodge a section of wet, moldy wall material. My bad leg throbbed but I reached back to hit the spot Léna had indicated again.

"What are you doing?" Clive demanded.

THIRTY-ONE

Ringing Faerie

"Trying to break through this wall. Right here," I gritted out. "Come help me."

Clive grabbed me around the middle and pulled me down. "Let me."

I hated to admit it, but there was no way I was getting through that wall. I'd barely scratched it. I pulled out my phone flashlight again.

Clive leapt up, one foot on the pipe, one on the wall, with his left hand holding himself steady. He pointed to where I'd been pushing. "Here?"

"Yes. That's where Léna showed me."

Nodding, Clive made a fist and punched the wall. A crack appeared. He shook the blood off his knuckles and punched it again. This time, I heard rock scraping against rock.

Vlad ran back in and scrambled up the wall so he was beside Clive. "Together, then. One. Two. Go."

They both punched and the wall crumbled under a tidal wave of steaming water. It rushed in and slammed me against the back wall. Submerged, I panicked and kicked off the floor, surfacing a foot from the ceiling. Oh, jeez. Please don't let me drown on my rescue mission.

As the water spread out through the basement, the level went down a foot or so. Woohoo, imminent death avoided once again. Stuffing the now useless phone in my back pocket, I swam against the rush of water, over the broken wall and into whatever lay beyond.

Blinking my stinging eyes, I searched for Cordelia in the pitch-black. I swam forward with my arms outstretched, wishing I still had a working flashlight. Russell and Godfrey must never learn that I'd trashed another phone. Assuming we made it out before the bombs started, that was.

"Over here," Vlad said.

A light appeared over the surface of the water. Vlad had an actual flashlight in his hand. Where did he find that?

We appeared to be in some kind of submerged cave. Given what we could see, the rocky ceiling was about ten feet above the water at its highest point and perhaps a foot at its lowest.

I glanced back at the hole in the wall and remembered all the water that had just been displaced, meaning much of this ceiling had actually been underwater. Cordelia had only had a small pocket available to her above the water.

Clive was suddenly beside me, pulling my arms around his neck.

Are you all right? he asked me, mind-to-mind.

Yep. I'm fine. I hit the wall, but it was the other side of my head and—shit! I'm not in Cadmael's head anymore. I'm not holding the prince.

We'll deal with it, he said, swimming us over to Vlad, who was hovering beside a rocky outcropping.

When we got closer, I realized the sharp gray rock I'd thought I was looking at was an emaciated, dying mermaid. Oh, no. Poor Cordelia.

Lifting my pinky ring to my lips, I whispered, "We need your help. One of your mermaids has been horribly abused and starved for centuries. Please. She needs help. She's dying." It was Gloriana's ring, but that didn't guarantee she was listening.

Vlad was speaking to Cordelia in another language, but his

eyes were on me as I spoke into the ring. Why did I trust him as I did? No idea. It all had to be done if we were going to help her, so I supposed I just had to hope my trust wasn't misplaced.

Algar, Gloriana's captain of the guard, appeared, crouching on the rocks beside Cordelia. He scanned the water, saw me, and nodded. Resting a hand on the mermaid's head, he appeared to breathe life into her. Skin less gray, scales richer in tone and now adhering to her body, she opened her eyes, gazing adoringly at Algar.

Both Clive and Vlad wore matching blank expressions, which made me want to laugh. Neither wanted to appear surprised by the fae warrior appearing out of thin air and resuscitating Cordelia.

"Algar is the queen's captain of the guard," I whispered.

Gloriana herself appeared, her kaleidoscopic eyes swirling in a very angry black and red. Algar picked up Cordelia and cradled her in his arms. Gloriana laid a hand over Cordelia's heart and the mermaid's skin returned to the gold hue I remembered in that long-ago memory.

Gloriana leaned over and kissed Cordelia's forehead, and then Algar and Cordelia disappeared. The queen turned her furious countenance to me. "Who hurt my cherished one?"

"The prince. He's a cruel man, who imprisoned her in this place centuries ago," I said.

Vlad, treading water beside Clive and me, looked in the same direction I was pointed, clearly trying to understand who I was talking to. The queen was invisible to all but the fae. And me when she felt like it.

"I think he's still in this building. I can—"

"I feel him," she interrupted, looking up into the rock above her head and then she, too, disappeared, along with my headache.

I patted Clive's chest. "Okay. We can go now. The queen's on it."

"Just so I'm clear," Vlad said. "You spoke into a ring and the queen of Faerie and her guard just appeared?"

"It'd be best if you kept that to yourself," Clive warned.

Vlad rolled his eyes at Clive and looked back at me. "If you have a direct line to the queen of the fae, why didn't you call her in a long time ago?"

They swam out of the cave, over the wall into the basement.

"She rules another realm," I said. "She's not at my beck and call." I tried to figure out how to condense the story down. "A little while ago, I had to visit Faerie to deliver a message. The queen liked the engagement ring Clive had given me. As the queen was deciding whether or not she was going to let me live at the time, I offered her the ring."

"Bribery," Vlad said approvingly.

"I guess," I responded. "It didn't feel that way at the time. It was more like I had something she admired and so the polite thing to do was offer it to her. Anyway, when I gave her my ring, she traded it for her own. I really miss my engagement ring. It was gorgeous, but this one has proven to be invaluable."

"It seems so," he said.

"Anyway, I've spoken to her through the ring a couple of times and only when it was an emergency that involved the safety and well-being of her people."

Clive stood at the base of the stairs, the water to his neck. Vlad, shorter, was still treading.

"And that is why the queen listens when you contact her," Clive said. "You fight your own battles, but when one of her people is in grave danger, you let her know." He pulled me off his back and placed me on the second step, so my head remained above the surface.

I started up and then turned to Vlad. "Do you need to grab anything from your room?"

He shook his head. "When you said they were blowing up the building, I went to collect my weapons. They're all I care about here."

"Wait! My axe!" I couldn't believe I'd forgotten it.

"I have it," Vlad said, lifting his gloved hand and my axe above the surface. "Go."

I went through the door first, then held it for Clive and Vlad. As I closed the door to the flooded basement, Clive and Vlad dropped to the floor, writhing in agony.

Shocked, I went to Clive, holding his head so it didn't bang on the floor. Only then did I notice the dark shoes coming to rest beside me. Cadmael. *Shit!*

"You again," he growled, grabbing my braid and yanking me up.

"Ow! What the fuck, you asshole?" I slashed at his hand with my claws, slicing four of his fingers off.

Cadmael stared at his hand a moment, uncomprehending. The prince was back in charge. When he made another grab for me, I cut off his other hand entirely. Vampires could repair injuries like that, but not immediately.

"Release them or your head will end up on the ground beside your hand." I squeezed his blip in my head, causing him to wince. "I'm sick of your shit, old man. You're supposed to be all-powerful, and you let some shitty fae punk who gets off on hurting women possess you? Again? Grow a pair and shove him out," I sneered, figuring one or the other would blow a gasket. It's easier to get the upper hand when your opponent isn't thinking clearly.

Cadmael lunged, but I saw his muscles bunch and so dove forward, rolling by him, my claws out, tearing through his Achilles tendon with a pop. Because there were two people fighting for control of Cadmael's body, he was slower than normal, his movements awkward.

When he spun to go after me again, his balance was off. I had my claws out and slashed at his other ankle, hearing the pop once again. Cadmael grunted in pain but still moved toward me.

Diving at him, my shoulder in his gut, I knocked him over. He tried to punch me in the head, which would have killed me, but he no longer had a fist and so the motion was off. Did it hurt? Hell yeah. Was I dead with a caved-in skull? Nope.

I had vampire blood smeared on my head, though, which was pretty gross. That sort-of punch got my head pounding again. Landing on his chest, I had my claws at his neck. I didn't want to kill him, but I also had no desire to die. It all depended on whether or not the prince could be trusted to properly assess a threat.

Cadmael hissed, his fangs glistening. Springing up from the ground, he dislodged me. My claws pierced his neck. I didn't swipe them through, though. I wasn't sure why in the moment, but his eyes were their normal brown and his scent had changed. The prince was gone. The queen must have found him hidden upstairs and finally killed the bastard.

Cadmael never broke eye contact with me. He wasn't trying to mesmerize me, though. He was pleading with me. "Do it," he whispered.

Clive pulled me away and I was again standing behind him and Vlad.

I tapped Clive's shoulder. "Can you guys wait for us in reception? Cadmael and I need to have a chat."

"No," Vlad said.

"I don't think that's a good idea, Sam," Clive said.

I tried to push them, but vamps don't move if they don't want to. "We're fine. Trust me and go away."

It took another moment, but finally the two of them walked down the hall away from us.

Cadmael looked down at his missing hand and fingers and then at the blood dripping off my claws. I hadn't retracted them yet. I was pretty sure I was okay, but I didn't trust him that far, so the claws stayed out.

"Why did you send them away?" he asked.

"Because," I said, "I figured it out. Why you've been tracking me all my life, keeping tabs on me."

His expression was carved out of stone. He gave nothing away.

Blowing out a breath, I stepped closer and lowered my voice. "I'm very sorry about your son's death—"

"Murder," he growled.

"Yes." I nodded. "As someone who is a werewolf, I can tell you that that man chose your son to kill. Our instincts might be stronger, our drive to hunt more pressing, but never is the human side of my brain gone. He recognized your son and you and chose to kill you both. Why, I don't know, but he was never a friend."

I gestured down the hall. "They don't know what I know. You wanted to die in that rainforest alongside your son. You wanted to enter the afterlife together. Instead, you woke to this eternal undeath, wishing you could end it. Every day for—what—two, three thousand years you've been gaining strength and gifts, but all you've ever wanted was to be done so that you might see your son again.

"You've been tracking me because in me you see your executioner. Finally. And you hate me because it's so close now, you can almost taste it. Your memories of him are all you think about, and you need me to do it already. But I haven't. I've become the one keeping you from your son, and for that I'm despised."

"Do you always talk this much?" he said, finally breaking eye contact.

"Let me say this." I stepped closer. We were almost touching. "If it's really what you want, I'll do it. Know that. Keep it in your pocket. Okay?"

His expression had lost its rigidity, as though he couldn't quite believe what I was offering.

"I've been on the other side. I spent a little time in Hell. Long story. Not the point. Time is different over there. Ten thousand years. A day. It's all the same. When you eventually pass, your son will be there and it'll be just like when you used to take him hunting, when he shadowed you through the forest. The love you feel for him hasn't lessened, has it?"

He shook his head, his eyes glassy.

"It hasn't changed for him either. When you do finally see him again, it'll be just like it was on the morning he left for the hunt. There's a lot you could still do here, though. A lot of good in the world, if you chose to. Vampire society is kind of a mess right now. Do you want to help Vlad and Clive fix it or do you want to go?"

I patted his arm. "No judgment from me whichever you choose. If you decide to stay and work, it'd be cool if you stopped being a dick to me. If it's time and you're ready, I'll tell them the prince had control of you and I had to stop you."

He grunted. "I don't like the idea of people believing a fae man overpowered me."

I nodded solemnly. "I don't blame you. Especially one that was such a sick asshole. It doesn't reflect well on you, if what people remember about you is being a fae puppet."

His eyes went vampy black. "I am no one's puppet!"

I nodded again. "Got it."

He was silent for a good long time, thinking. Finally, he said, "I don't care for you."

"I get that a lot," I responded.

Glaring at me, he added, "I have your promise?"

"You do." I let my claws retract. I was pretty sure their work was done for now.

"I don't have time for this." He turned on his heel and strode off toward reception. "I have things to discuss with Vlad and Clive."

Good.

While they planned, I went back to the bedroom to get our bags. We still needed to get out of here before the pack blew us up. When I opened the door, I found our room empty. Even the chocolates and book I'd left on the coffee table were gone. Hmm.

Do you have our luggage? I asked Clive.

Yes. We need to go, love. Vlad and Cadmael are going to fly back with us so we can talk.

Coming, I told him, jogging down the hall.

The three men were waiting for me in the main hall. "Not that way," Clive said. "There are explosives on the front door. We're going back out the tunnels."

"Cool." I paused, seeing the queen had appeared beside the

men, her eyes back to their more natural—for her—swirling kaleidoscope of gold, blue, green, pink, and purple. She looked petite beside the men, but exuded so much power, it was hard to stand in her presence.

She stepped forward and pressed her delicate hand to my cheek. The pain from fighting Cadmael disappeared. "I am surprisingly pleased with you," she said. "I hadn't anticipated that." She tilted her head, her long silver hair glistening in the low light. "It was good that I saved your life when I did."

"And thanks again for that," I said. "Did you find the prince? Was he still alive?"

Her eyes swirled faster, the colors turning darker. "He was. He's not anymore." Shaking her head, she glanced around at the building. "A spell had been put on this palace by... someone."

She meant the fae king, who was a complete bastard.

"I've been looking for the women he stole for a very, very long time. I never would have found Cordelia or him if you and my ring hadn't been inside the spell. Algar tracked that," she said, pointing to my finger, "and we were able to finally find them."

"What happened?" I asked, desperate to hear about the creep's comeuppance.

"Tick tock, little one," she said, which seemed odd, as I was quite a bit taller than her. In terms of power, though, I was infinitesimal, which was probably what she meant. "The wolves have almost completed their task."

"Oh." Right. I forgot.

"But," she said, "as a thank you for my Cordelia, I'll give you this." She touched my cheek, and a rush of images filled my brain. "Run along now. You can experience my memory later. The bombs will begin in forty-three seconds." And with that, she disappeared.

I ran for the big metal door. "The queen says forty-three seconds."

Clive swung me onto his back again and we were racing through the tunnel. We stepped out behind the Bloody Ruin's dumpster, the dark still thick around us, and I said, "Can you take us to the edge of the asylum property?"

He did, so we had front row seats when the explosions started. I squeezed Clive's shoulder and he let me down. Moving away from the men, I tapped into my necromancy and called to any still trapped in the asylum, asking them to come to me and pass over.

Could I have forced them? Probably, but my Great Aunt Martha had told me never to do that, never to impose my will over the dead. I was taught only to ask. The problem was that many of these spirits weren't in their right minds when they passed. Was it right to let them linger when they didn't have the ability to objectively choose? Did they bring that mental confusion into death, or did it fall away?

I wasn't sure, so I did the only thing I could. Ignoring the booming and the fire, the alarms and the people beginning to gather, I closed my eyes and sent out wave after wave of love and acceptance, calling the spirits to me so that I could serve as a way station to the other side.

Many came, not all, and with each I was gifted with a burst of color, a barrage of memories, as they passed through me.

Out of the corner of my eye, I saw Viktoria step out from behind some trees to watch us. There was no wind, but a breeze seemed to blow just for her, swirling her hair around her face. The last, the one who was shepherding the others, was Léna. She'd stopped to bid her daughter farewell and then her short, pain-filled life ripped through me. I caught a moment of joy when she was reunited with her sister on the other side. Then the door was firmly shut and I was alone again.

Except not really. Clive was there, wiping away my tears and holding me close.

"That last one was Léna, wasn't it?" Vlad asked.

I nodded.

"Good," he said.

The pack is in the trees, Clive told me.

I saw.

László stepped out to stand beside Viktoria. He studied the four of us before his gaze settled on me. He nodded once and then, grabbing her arm, they disappeared back into the trees.

"All right, love. Back up you go. I'm afraid we have no car, so we're running for the airport," Clive said.

Vlad and Cadmael each took a suitcase and then we were racing so fast, I kept my head down on Clive's shoulder to avoid my eyes tearing from the wind. And because it was nice. Clive smelled like love, safety, and home.

"Why are you limping?" Clive said.

"Ask your mate," Cadmael growled back.

Gloriana's memory was pushing at me, so I popped the soap bubble and...

I'm in a dark place. A ball of light shimmers in a delicate hand. It's the queen's hand still wearing my engagement ring. She tosses the light up and a golden glow fills the dark wood corridor. Directly ahead is yet another portrait of the prince. This one is full-length and shows him holding a great sword.

The queen makes a tsking sound and the portrait crashes to the floor. Centuries of dust and dirt cover every surface. As soon as I note it, it's gone. Apparently, Gloriana isn't going to deal with filth.

The dark wood floors and walls gleam. The rugs are thick and lush. She walks like she knows exactly where she's going. She flings open the door at the very end of the hall and steps into a stark room. I would think it was for storage, if not for the remnants of seven pieces of fabric on the cold floor, the withered husks of fae women lying atop three of them.

Gloriana screams and Algar appears beside her. She points. "Look! Look what he has done to my children."

Algar rests a hand on the queen's shoulder in sympathy and solidarity. "Shall I take them home?"

"Yes." She stands a moment more, taking in the scene, and then turns those fiery eyes on Algar. "Find out who spelled this palace to keep me out, to keep my people—even in death—trapped in. I want that person brought to me."

Algar gives Gloriana a deep bow. "Yes, my queen."

Storming out of the room, she trusts Algar to care for her dead and strides down the hall, back to the fallen portrait. She waves a hand at the door, making it disappear, and then throws another ball of light into the dark, fetid room.

The boarded-up windows are suddenly open to the night air. She walks to the moldering bed and looks down on the monstrosity that is the prince.

Skeletal and scarred, he opens the one eye that remains and gazes at Gloriana, disbelieving. His head is dented in on one side and he's missing both his arms and legs. Given the large bloodstain on his rotting tunic, I think it's safe to assume his genitals were removed as well.

He slurs, "What are you doing here?"

She stares down at him with disgust. "Who are you to steal my people?" Her voice is almost a whisper, as though she's trying hard to control her rage. "Who are you to take my children, hide them from me, beat and rape them, kill them, *and still keep them from returning to their home with me? Why would you believe you have that right?"*

He turns his head away from her, casting his one eye toward the large portrait of himself on the wall of his bedchamber. "They deserved pain and death. Look what they did to me. Your precious females banded together to hack me to pieces," he sneers. "And you never found them because you weren't meant to."

It occurs to me that his broken and missing teeth are contributing to his garbled speech.

"No," she says, "you misunderstand." Although the queen never moves, his head twists back fiercely. "I rejoice in your current state. I am proud of my children. I only wish they'd separated your head from your neck. Now, I want to know who helped you hide my people from me."

He scoffs. "Someone you can't touch." He lifts his chin in defiance. "He'll rule while you die slowly in a hidden prison."

Gloriana glances around the room. "Like this one?" She shakes her head. "I'll never understand why those like you and the king cannot comprehend that there is no Faerie without me." She leans in, her eyes swirling with an angry black. "I AM FAERIE!"

She slams her hand down on the prince's chest. What's left of him shrivels up, leaving a twisted branch in his place. "You shall not return home, not even in death. You shall remain forever in this prison of your own making."

She stalks out of the room and the memory goes black.

"Holy shit," I mumbled, blinking my eyes open.

Clive was sitting beside me in one of the big, soft leather chairs in the plane, my hand in his. Vlad and Cadmael were at the two small tables on either side of the cabin. All three turned toward me.

"Are you all right?" Clive asked.

"Does she drop into visions often?" Vlad watched me closely.

"No. She doesn't," I said on an eye roll. I turned in my seat to Clive. "I asked the queen what happened with the prince, but we were pressed for time, so she gifted me with the memory and told me to run. I just watched the memory—lived it? Whatever—while you were all running here."

I told them everything I could remember about what had happened. They sat silently, absorbing it.

"The queen gave you her memory?" Cadmael asked, his suspicion ripe.

"Not all of them," I said. "It's not like we're besties and paint each other's nails. She gave me one memory, I think, as a thank you for breaking the spell surrounding the prince's palace and helping them rescue Cordelia."

"Is she ever going to kill the king?" Clive asked.

Shrugging, I said, "I don't know if she can. I mean, I'm sure she *could*. The question is what else in Faerie gets destroyed if she gets rid of him?"

My jeans were feeling super creepy. I looked down at myself and noticed I was on a towel. Oh! That's what smelled so horrible. Me.

"Okay, I'm off to shower." I glanced at Clive and Vlad. "Why aren't you guys sitting on towels?"

"We've already cleaned up," Clive said. "I wasn't sure if it was safe to wake you, so I decided not to attempt bathing you."

"Fair enough. I'll be back, cleaner and better smelling." I stood, picked up the towel, and went to the back of the plane while they discussed their next vampy steps.

Looking at myself in the mirror, I was more than a little horrified. Things I didn't want to identify clung to my hair and clothes. I'd taken an unplanned dip in a thermal bath that a poor mermaid had been dying in for hundreds of years. I wasn't ready to consider what I'd been swimming in. The night had already been too much without that. On the plus side, though, the queen had healed all my cracks, bumps, and bruises.

Afterward, while they sat in the front of the plane, talking endlessly, I lay down on a couch in the rear of the cabin and promptly fell asleep.

When I woke, Clive was beside me, his arm wrapped around me. I slipped out, hit the restroom, and then went to the front to sit across from Vlad, who was reading.

"You know I own a bookstore, right?" I said.

He looked at me over the top of his book. "Your point?"

I shrugged. "I'm just saying if you're going to buy books anyway, you might as well buy them from me."

"Is that so?" He quirked an eyebrow. "Is Clive experiencing some sort of financial crisis that requires you hawking goods?"

"Clive's money is Clive's. The Slaughtered Lamb is mine. You don't want to visit, don't." I muttered a few insults as I pulled my e-reader out of my bag, reclined my chair, and opened the mystery I was reading. Stupid vampire.

We read silently for a good while and then he finally said, "It was good, what you did."

I looked up and found him staring at Cadmael, who was sleeping a few seats away from me. Not knowing if Cadmael was really out, I kept quiet and continued reading.

And then I remembered. "Hey, where's my axe?"

"You keep forgetting about it. I'm not sure you deserve such a beautiful weapon," Vlad said.

"It's not up to you. Give me my axe."

"I've noticed," he said, getting up and going to a storage closet near the cockpit, "that you haven't been showing me the proper respect." He pulled out an axe and swung it menacingly. "I don't like that."

I put my book aside and stood. "Are you threatening me?"

He held up the axe, admiring the blade's edge and then threw it at my head.

It was so fast, but my hand was up to catch it, to yank it out of the air and use it. My hand, though, was empty.

Cadmael's arm was up, and he was holding the axe handle between his thumb and the one finger that had grown back.

Vlad laughed. "I knew it! You've been faking this whole time, pretending to sleep so you wouldn't have to talk to me." He shook his head and returned to his chair.

"What the hell, dude?" I took the axe from Cadmael. "So if Cadmael had really been asleep, I'd have an axe in my head?"

Vlad rolled his eyes. "If Cadmael didn't catch it, Clive would have."

"Clive is asleep in the back of the plane," I said, twisting the axe head, looking for Algar's fingerprint.

"Clive is standing right behind you. Not that you needed him. You'd have caught it if Cadmael hadn't," Vlad said.

I turned and, sure enough, there was Clive, eyes vamp black, glaring at Vlad.

"What's with all the shit disturbing?" I asked Vlad. "And this isn't my axe."

"It's not? How strange," he murmured, picking up his book. "How can you be so sure?"

I stomped across the cabin to the storage closet. "Mine is made of fae metal and neither you nor Cadmael have blistered hands." I opened the cloth he had wrapped the weapons in. My axe gleamed in the low light. I put his down and picked up my own. Yes, that felt right. Tipping the blade into the light, I saw the pale outline of Algar's fingerprint. "And I know my own weapons, you big jerk. I can't believe I told Clive we should trust you."

I went back to my bag, pulled out the axe sheath and strapped it on, putting the axe back where it belonged, on my back. I glanced up and saw Vlad watching me with a huge grin.

"This little visit to San Francisco should be fun," Vlad said. "We'll be staying with you, won't we?"

Clive snarled a few choice words in response.

Yeah, this should go well.

Acknowledgments

Thank you to my wonderful critique partner C.R. Grissom, who has over the last sixteen years read everything I've ever written (including publishing-related emails). She's a wonderful writer, funny, insightful, and ridiculously supportive. When I was in middle school, I played basketball. Not because I had ANY athletic ability, but because I was the tallest in the class. I pretty much hated every minute of it. The tiny girls who played guard scared the crap out of me. They were vicious and would definitely cut a bitch to steal the ball. Mostly, I let them have it, so they'd leave me alone. C.R. is like one of those girls, but in a good way. She's tiny and will go feral on anyone tries to hurt one of her people. I consider myself quite lucky that she doesn't think I'm an asshole.

Thank you to Peter Senftleben, my extraordinary editor. He has the enviable knack of getting to the heart of the story and then helping me to see my own work through a different lens. Thank you to Susan Helene Gottfried, my exceptional proofreader who always knows exactly where the commas go (unlike myself).

Thank you to the remarkable team at NYLA! You've made every step of publishing a little easier with your wit, compassion, and expertise. Thank you to my incomparable agent Sarah Younger, the fabulous Natanya Wheeler, and the incredible Cheryl Pientka for working together to make my dream of writing and publishing a reality.

Dear Reader,

Thank you for reading *The Bloody Ruin Asylum & Taproom*. If you enjoyed Sam and Clive's seventh adventure together, please consider leaving a review or chatting about it with your book-loving friends. Good word of mouth means everything when you're a writer!

Love,
    Seana

Want more books from Seana?

If you'd like to be the first to learn what's new with Sam and Clive (and Arwyn and Declan and Owen and Dave and Stheno…), please sign up for my newsletter *Tales from the Book Nerd*. It's filled with writing news, deleted scenes, giveaways, book recommendations, first looks at covers, short stories, and my favorite cocktail and book pairings.

Sam's next adventure is **The Mermaid's Bubble Lounge.** It will be arriving in the fall of 2025. Stay tuned for more…

If you're a Sea Wicche fan, **The Wicching Hour** will be out April 1, 2025.

———

What else has Seana written? Well, I'll tell you…

The Slaughtered Lamb Bookstore & Bar
Sam Quinn, Book 1

Welcome to The Slaughtered Lamb Bookstore and Bar. I'm Sam

Quinn, the werewolf book nerd in charge. I run my business by one simple rule: Everyone needs a good book and a stiff drink, be they vampire, wicche, demon, or fae. No wolves, though. Ever. I have my reasons.

I serve the supernatural community of San Francisco. We've been having some problems lately. Okay, I'm the one with the problems. The broken body of a female werewolf washed up on my doorstep. What makes sweat pool at the base of my spine, though, is realizing the scars she bears are identical to the ones I conceal. After hiding for years, I've been found.

A protection I've been relying on is gone. While my wolf traits are strengthening steadily, the loss also left my mind vulnerable to attack. Someone is ensnaring me in horrifying visions intended to kill. Clive, the sexy vampire Master of the City, has figured out how to pull me out, designating himself my personal bodyguard. He's grumpy about it, but that kiss is telling a different story. A change is taking place. It has to. The bookish bartender must become the fledgling badass.

I'm a survivor. I'll fight fang and claw to protect myself and the ones I love. And let's face it, they have it coming.

The Dead Don't Drink at Lafitte's
Sam Quinn, Book 2

I'm Sam Quinn, the werewolf book nerd owner of the Slaughtered Lamb Bookstore and Bar. Things have been busy lately. While the near-constant attempts on my life have ceased, I now have a vampire gentleman caller. I've been living with Clive and the rest of his vampires for a few weeks while the Slaughtered Lamb is being rebuilt. It's going about as well as you'd expect.

My mother was a wicche and long dormant abilities are starting to make themselves known. If I'd had a choice, necromancy wouldn't have been my top pick, but it's coming in handy. A ghost warns me someone is coming to kill Clive. When I rush back to the nocturne, I find vamps from New Orleans readying an attack. One of the benefits of vampires looking down on werewolves is no one expects much of me. They don't expect it right up until I take their heads.

Now, Clive and I are setting out for New Orleans to take the fight back to the source. Vampires are masters of the long game. Revenge plots are often decades, if not centuries, in the making. We came expecting one enemy but quickly learn we have darker forces scheming against us. Good thing I'm the secret weapon they never see coming.

The Wicche Glass Tavern
Sam Quinn, Book 3

I'm Sam Quinn, the werewolf book nerd owner of the Slaughtered Lamb Bookstore and Bar. Clive, my vampire gentleman caller, has asked me to marry him. His nocturne is less than celebratory. Unfortunately, for them and the sexy vamp doing her best to seduce him, his cold, dead heart beats only for me.

As much as my love life feels like a minefield, it has to take a back-seat to a far more pressing problem. The time has come. I need to deal with my aunt, the woman who's been trying to kill me for as long as I can remember. She's learned a new trick. She's figured out how to weaponize my friends against me. To have any hope of surviving, I have to learn to use my necromantic gifts. I need a teacher. We find one hiding among the fae, which is a completely different problem. I need to determine what I'm capable of in a hurry because my aunt doesn't care how many are hurt or killed as long as she gets what she wants. Sadly for me, what she wants is my name on a headstone.

I'm gathering my friends—werewolves, vampires, wicches, gorgons, a Fury, a half-demon, an elf, and a couple of dragon shifters—into a kind of Fellowship of the Sam. It's going to be one hell of a battle. Hopefully, San Francisco will still be standing when the dust clears.

The Hob & Hound Pub
Sam Quinn, Book 4

I'm Sam Quinn, the newly married werewolf book nerd owner of the Slaughtered Lamb Bookstore and Bar. Clive and I are on our honeymoon. Paris is lovely, though the mummy in the Louvre inching toward me is a bit off-putting. Although Clive doesn't sense anything, I can't shake the feeling I'm being watched.

Even after we cross the English Channel to begin our search for Aldith—the woman who's been plotting against Clive since the beginning—the prickling unease persists. Clive and I are separated, rather forcefully, and I'm left to find my way alone in a foreign country, evading not only Aldith's large web of hench-vamps, but vicious fae creatures disloyal to their queen. Gloriana says there's a poison in the human realm that's seeping into Faerie, and I may have found the source.

I knew this was going to be a working vacation, but battling vampires on one front and the fae on another is a lot, especially in a country steeped in magic. As a side note, I need to get word to Benvair. I think I've found the dragon she's looking for.

Gloriana is threatening to set her warriors against the human realm, but I may have a way to placate her. Aldith is a different story. There's no reasoning with rabid vengeance. She'll need to be put out of our misery permanently if Clive and I have any hope of a long, happy life together. Heck, I'd settle for a few quiet weeks.

Biergarten of the Damned
Sam Quinn, Book 5

I'm Sam, the werewolf book nerd owner of The Slaughtered Lamb Bookstore & Bar. I've always thought of Dave, my red-skinned, shark-eyed, half-demon cook, as a kind of foul-mouthed uncle, one occasionally given to bouts of uncontrolled anger.

Something's going on, though. He's acting strangely, hiding things. When I asked what was wrong, he blew me off and told me to quit bugging him. That's normal enough. What's not is his missing work. Ever. Other demons are appearing in the bar, looking for him. I'm getting worried, and his banshee girlfriend Maggie isn't answering my calls.

Demons terrify me. I do NOT want to go into any demon bars looking for Dave, but he's my family, sort of. I need to try to help, whether he wants me to or not. When I finally learn the truth, though… I'm not sure I can ever look at him again, let alone have him work for me. Are there limits to forgiveness? I think there might be.

The Viper's Nest Roadhouse & Café
Sam Quinn, Book 6

I'm Sam, the werewolf book nerd owner of The Slaughtered Lamb Bookstore & Bar. Clive, Fergus, and I are moving into our new home, the business is going well, and our folly is taking shape. The problem? Clive's maker Garyn is coming to San Francisco for a visit, and this reunion has been a thousand years in the making. Back then, Garyn was rather put out when Clive accepted the dark kiss and then took off to avenge his sister's murder. She was looking for a new family. He was looking for lethal skills. And so, Garyn has had plenty of time to align her forces. When her allies begin stepping out of the shadows, Clive's foundation will be shaken.

Stheno and her sisters are adding to their rather impressive portfolio of businesses around the world by acquiring The Viper's Nest Roadhouse & Café. Medusa found the place when she was visiting San Francisco. A dive bar filled with hot tattooed bikers? Yes, please!

Clive and I will need neutral territory for our meeting with Garyn, and a biker bar (& café, Stheno insisted) should fit the bill. I'd assumed my necromancy would give us an advantage. I hadn't anticipated, though, just how powerful Garyn and her allies were. When the fangs descend and the heads start rolling, it's going to take every friend we have and a nocturne full of vamps at our backs to even the playing field. Wish us luck. We're going to need it.

The Bloody Ruin Asylum & Taproom
Sam Quinn, Book 7

I'm Sam, the werewolf book nerd owner of The Slaughtered Lamb Bookstore & Bar. My husband, Master vampire Clive, has been asked to go to Budapest to interview for a position in the Guild, a council of thirteen vampires who advise the world's Masters. The competition for the recently vacated spot is fierce. I worry about Clive, as it quickly becomes apparent that the last person to hold the position didn't leave voluntarily.

Ever the supportive wife, I'm tagging along. I researched Budapest and had a long itinerary of things to do. That is, I did. When we arrive, we find out that the Guild headquarters is in the ruins of an abandoned insane asylum. Awesome. If there's one thing I love, it's being hounded by mentally unstable Hungarian ghosts.

Let's just say this isn't the romantic getaway I'd been hoping for. With Clive in top secret meetings and a bunch of creepy Renfields skulking around corners, nowhere is safe. I want to help Clive because I know he really wants the job, but the other Guild members are ancient and scary powerful. Between you and me, I thought Vlad would be taller.

Wish us luck! We're going to need it.

The Mermaid's Bubble Lounge
Sam Quinn, book 8

The vampire Guild is in shambles. My husband Clive and I might have given more than a few Masters their final deaths—allegedly —so it's fallen on us to fix the problem. Mostly on Clive, that is, as he's the Master vampire. I'm Sam Quinn, werewolf book nerd and owner of The Slaughtered Lamb Bookstore & Bar.

Vlad (yes, that one) and Cadmael are the houseguests no one would want, but we're trying to grin and bear it because the Guild must be rebuilt, and we must make haste as rogue vamps are becoming a big bloody problem.

Finvarra, the fae king who had it out for me even before I helped cause his brother's death, is coming to do what none of his assassins have managed: end me in as painful a manner as possible.

In other news, Stheno and Vlad have been hooking up and we're all a little afraid of those two together.

———

Bewicched: The Sea Wicche Chronicles
Sea Wicche, Book 1

We here at The Sea Wicche cater to your art-collecting, muffin-eating, tea-drinking, and potion-peddling needs. Palmistry and Tarot sessions are available upon request and by appointment. Our store hours vary and rely completely on Arwyn—the owner—getting her butt out of bed.

I'm Arwyn Cassandra Corey, the sea wicche, or the wicche who lives by the sea. It requires a lot more work than I'd anticipated to remodel an abandoned cannery and turn it into an art gallery & tea bar. It's coming along, though, especially with the help of a new werewolf who's joined the construction crew. He does beautiful work. His sexy, growly, bearded presence is very hard to ignore, but I'm trying. I'm not sure how such a laid-back guy got the local Alpha and his pack threatening to hunt him down and tear him apart, but we all have our secrets. And because I don't want to know his—or yours for that matter—I wear these gloves. Clairvoyance makes the simplest things the absolute worst. Trust me. Or don't. Totally up to you.

Did I mention my mother and grandmother are pressuring me to assume my rightful place on the Corey Council? That's a kind of governing triad for our ancient magical family, one that has more than its fair share of black magic practitioners. And yes, before you ask, people have killed to be on the council—one psychotic sorceress aunt stands out—but I have no interest in the power or politics that come with the position. I'd rather stick to my art and, in the words of my favorite sea wicche, help poor unfortunate souls. (Good luck trying to get that song out of your head now)

Wicche Hunt: The Sea Wicche Chronicles
Sea Wicche, Book 2

I'm Arwyn Cassandra Corey, the Sea Wicche of Monterey. Want a psychic reading? Sure. I can do that. In the market for art? I have all your painting, photography, glass blowing, and ceramic needs covered in my newly remodeled art gallery by the sea. Need help solving a grisly cold case? Unfortunately, I can probably help with that too.

After more than a decade of being nagged, guilted, and threatened, I've finally joined the Corey Council and am working with my mother and grandmother to hunt down a twisted sorcerer. We know who she is. Now we need to find and stop her before more are murdered.

The evil the sorcerer and her demon are doing is seeping into the community. Violent crimes have been increasing and as a result Detectives Hernández and Osso have brought me another horrifying case. I'll do what I can, because of course I will. What are a few more nightmares to a woman who barely sleeps?

Declan Quinn, the wicked hot werewolf rebuilding my deck, is preparing for a dominance battle with the local Alpha. A couple of wolves have already left their pack to follow Declan, recognizing him as the true Alpha. Declan needs to watch his back as the full moon approaches. The current Alpha will do whatever it takes to hold on to power, including breaking pack law and enlisting the help of a local vampire.

And if Wilbur, my selkie friend is right, I might just be meeting my dad soon. Perhaps he'll have some advice for this wicche hunt. I'm going to need all the help I can get.

Wicching Hour: The Sea Wicche Chronicles
Sea Wicche, Book 3

I'm Arwyn Cassandra Corey, the Sea Wicche of Monterey. My new art gallery is finally open, my boyfriend is the new Alpha of the Big Sur pack, and my sorcerer cousin is still on the loose. It's been a lot. I'm just sayin'.

Detectives Hernández and Osso are asking for my help again. Bodies have been found torn up in the woods in a manner that has those in the know thinking werewolf. Declan, as Alpha, will need to investigate his pack and help hunt the killer.

We're narrowing in on Calliope and her demon. She can't hide forever, and my uncle might just have the map to where she's been holed up. If it's the last thing I do, I'll make her pay for her treachery.

Did I mention there's a new podcast, hosted by a human, who is coming dangerously close to telling the kind of secrets the supernatural community kills to keep quiet? His latest season is about a certain artistic wicche.

Oh, and I finally met my dad. Like I said, it's been a lot.

About Seana Kelly

Seana Kelly lives in the San Francisco Bay Area with her husband, two daughters, two dogs, and one fish. She recently retired from her career as a high school teacher-librarian to pursue her lifelong dream of writing full-time. She's an avid reader and re-reader who misses her favorite characters when it's been too long between visits.

She's a *USA Today* bestselling author and a two-time Golden Heart® Award finalist. She is represented by the delightful and effervescent Sarah E. Younger of the Nancy Yost Literary Agency.

You can follow Seana on Twitter/X for tweets about books and dogs or on Instagram for beautiful pictures of books and dogs (kidding). She also loves collecting photos of characters and settings for the books she writes. As she's a huge reader of young adult and adult books, expect lots of recommendations as well.

Website: www.seanakelly.com

Newsletter: https://geni.us/t0Y5cBA

𝕏 x.com/SeanaKellyRW
📷 instagram.com/seanakellyrw
📘 facebook.com/Seana-Kelly-1553527948245885
BB bookbub.com/authors/seana-kelly
📌 pinterest.com/seanakelly326

Printed in the USA
CPSIA information can be obtained
at www.ICGtesting.com
LVHW061451141024
793784LV00039B/655